adena halpern

A TOUCHSTONE BOOK
Published by Simon & Schuster
New York   London   Toronto   Sydney

Touchstone
A Division of Simon & Schuster, Inc.
1230 Avenue of the Americas
New York, NY 10020

First Touchstone trade paperback edition June 2010

TOUCHSTONE and colophon are registered trademarks of Simon & Schuster, Inc.

For information about special discounts for bulk purchases, please contact Simon & Schuster
Special Sales at 1-866-506-1949 or business@simonandschuster.com.

The Simon & Schuster Speakers Bureau can bring authors to your live event. For more
information or to book an event contact the Simon & Schuster Speakers Bureau at
1-866-248-3049 or visit our website at www.simonspeakers.com.

Designed by Renata Di Biase

Manufactured in the United States of America

10   9   8   7   6   5   4   3   2   1

Library of Congress Cataloging-in-Publication Data

Halpern, Adena.
    29/by Adena Halpern
       p.   cm.
  "A Touchstone Book."
     1. Mothers and daughters—Fiction. 2. Grandmothers—Fiction. 3. Magic—Fiction.
  I. Title. II. Title: Twenty-nine.
    PS3608.A5487A615   2010
    813'.6—dc22
                                                                2009034570

ISBN 978-1-4391-7112-7
ISBN 978-1-4391-7113-4 (ebook)

This book is lovingly dedicated to my mother,
Arlene Rudney Halpern

contents

I 'm jealous of my granddaughter.

I would never, ever tell anyone that.

Everyone says the older you get, the wiser you get. I don't feel wise at all.

I'm supposed to feel so blessed to be seventy-five years old. Hell, I tell people that myself, but that's mostly to make myself feel better. I tell people that the best part of being older is the wisdom that comes with it. Truthfully, that's bullshit. What else can you say, though, unless you want to completely depress people? Let them find out for themselves when they get here. If someone had told me how much I would truly hate being seventy-five, I would have been out of here a long time ago. Not killed myself. Oh, no, God forbid. I just would have moved to a deserted island and spent the rest of my days away from the harsh reality of a mirror.

So at seventy-five, if I've got all this wisdom, why can't I cure cancer? If I'm so smart, why don't people trust me to swoop in and save the world from utter destruction? Let my seventy-five-year-old girlfriends and me attend United Nations sessions so we can let them know how to make this world a better place. Since we're so smart, let us give our opinions. No one ever asks. You know why? No one else really believes we're so wise. If they did, maybe they'd listen to us more.

I hate being seventy-five. I really do. And I did not want this birthday party tonight, but my daughter, Barbara, insisted on it. Barbara can be a royal pain in the ass sometimes.

After reading what I've said so far you probably think that I'm one of those mean, cranky old ladies who complains about drafts that aren't there, or returns one peach to the supermarket if it's a little bruised, or steals Sweet'N Low packets from coffee shops. I'm not. I don't even like Sweet'N Low. My granddaughter always says, "My grandmother is cool." I think I *am* cool. I keep up-to-date on things—what's happening in the news, reality shows (though I hate them)—and I always try to dress fashionably.

Seventy-five.

I am so goddamned old.

(And by the way, I rarely curse. That's just the best way I can find to express myself right now.)

My girlfriends and I keep telling one another that age is just a number.

"I don't feel seventy-five," my lifelong dearest friend, Frida, says.

"I don't, either," I lie, knowing she's lying, too. Frida looks and acts more like she's eighty-five, but far be it from me to ever say that.

"My mother is a young seventy-five," my daughter tells people in front of me. I hate when she does that. Why does she have to do that?

"I do it because you look so good, and I want to brag," Barbara says. Let me say, it's fine if *I* admit my age, but not when my daughter does. It's no one's business.

"My daughter is fifty-five," I tell them, smiling.

"What did you do that for?" Barbara will ask when we're out of hearing range of the person we've just inundated with unasked-for age information.

"What?" I ask defensively. "You look good, too!" I tell her, trying to act stupid. My daughter would never accuse me of throwing it back in her face. She doesn't think I'm smart enough to do that.

Truthfully, the thing that's pissing me off right now is that if I really stop and reflect, I've still got about twenty years max to stew about all the things I really should have done with my life. That makes me sad. Angry and sad.

First things first: I would never have sat in the sun for all those years. In those days, though, no one knew the damage it could do. I guess that's the wisdom I've gained from getting older. Thanks. When I think of the years I sat by the pool bathed in oil without any protection . . . We didn't have sunblock then. We were *supposed* to sit in the sun back then; it was *good for us*. We let our children play in the sun all day because they told us we should. If they burned, we put cold washcloths on them. They didn't have skin cancer back then; at least I never heard of anyone getting it. Now it's one of the main topics I discuss with my girlfriends. One of us sees a dark spot on our arm and it's an all-day episode of *House* until the doctor tells us it's nothing. Sadly, it wasn't *nothing* for poor Harriet Langarten. That's why we're all so scared. I've become that old lady on the street who walks around with an umbrella on a sunny day. Through the years I've tried every cream on the market to get rid of sunspots and wrinkles. I've had chemical peels and let doctors scrape my face in the hope of undoing the damage I did trying to look tanned and sexy for a cocktail party in 1972.

Second, I wish I had exercised more. We didn't work out when we were younger. We played tennis or golf, but mostly we played bridge at the country club while our husbands golfed. And since most of them are dead, they obviously didn't get enough exercise, either. I joined a gym with Frida a couple of years ago, but we were the oldest people there by thirty years so I gave it up and bought a treadmill. I walked so many miles on that thing I could have walked to China and back by now. Even though I tell people I feel so much better since I started exercising, it's a lie. My feet hurt, my joints hurt, my boobs hurt. They say that beauty must suffer. I feel I've suffered enough, so I rarely get on that thing anymore.

So I went the plastic-surgery route. I've used Botox and Restylane, had one face-lift (talk about PAIN) and a brow lift (waste of money *and* pain), and electrolysis to make me look younger. I can't say that I look all bad, but I definitely don't look fifty, like the doctor told me I would. Quack.

Aside from taking care of my looks more, if I could go back and do it all again, there are a couple of major things I would have done differently.

First, I would have gotten a better education.

In my day, the 1950s to be exact, it wasn't important for a woman to get an education. I know that sounds crazy, but it couldn't be more true. Your parents (at least my parents, and all my girlfriends' parents) discouraged higher education. "You need a good husband," my mother said to me when I told her I wanted to be an English literature major at the University of Pennsylvania. She handed me the application to secretarial school and drove me there on my first day with a sack lunch consisting of two hard-boiled eggs, some crackers, and a nickel for the milk machine. So I learned how to type. I figured I'd read the classics on my own, plotting as if it was devious and underhanded to sneak James Joyce and Dylan Thomas into my home to read when no one was around. Sadly, though, I never did. Who had the time?

Instead, I met my husband.

That's the second thing I would have done differently. I never would have married my husband.

Again, please don't tell anyone I ever said that.

It's not that I didn't love my husband; I did love him. I loved him very much. He was a fine man. If I really had to be honest, though, really, really honest, I'd have to say I do not think he was the man for me.

Howard Jerome was a prominent Philadelphia lawyer. I met him when he was a young attorney just starting out and I was one of the secretaries at the firm. He wasn't the most handsome attorney at the law office, but he was the one who wanted me. Howard was short, bald, and fat, even back then. I was actually smitten with another lawyer there, Burt Elliot, but he had eyes for a different secretary and married her.

"You'll marry Howard," my mother said after our second date. "He's safe."

So I did.

"Thank God," my mother said. "I was afraid you were becoming an old maid."

I was nineteen years old. Nineteen!

Howard was ten years older than I was. We met in September and married in June. That was what we did back then. It was time to get married, so we did. I moved from my parents' house to my husband's house, and I never knew what it was like to live on my own. Once—*once*—before Barbara was born, Howard went on a business trip for two days. That was the extent of my living on my own when I was younger. I smoked a half a pack of cigarettes—the last time I ever smoked—and went to a movie by myself. (And I hope you don't smoke, by the way; it's bad for you. I lost a lot of friends along the way because of it.) That was the craziest I ever got. How I would love to get really crazy, just once.

Barbara also followed my route. She married young—her husband, Larry, is a dentist—and had Lucy. I told her to get a job and wait. But did she listen to me? No. I should have insisted she get an occupation as stubbornly as my mother insisted I shouldn't. I regret I didn't show her that working was important, not just for money's sake, but to do something for yourself. I loved having my daughter, don't get me wrong, but I wish I had done other things first. By the time I was twenty-five, I had a child and a house in the Main Line suburbs of Philadelphia.

Two years ago, Howard dropped dead while eating a corned-beef sandwich at the Nate n' Al deli in Los Angeles. It was completely out of the blue. He'd had some heart issues—a bypass here, a bypass there—but no one thought this would ever happen. Heart surgery is so common among my age group that you start to treat it like it's just another thing you have to do. ("How about dinner Saturday night?" I'd ask a friend. "Oh, Alan is having a bypass on Friday. How about the following Saturday?" she'd reply. Same thing with the prostate operations.)

Anyway, it was the most horrible thing that's ever happened to me. We were in Los Angeles for my friend Thelma Punchick's daughter's second wedding, to an architect. One second we were sitting there having a conversation about whether to go to the Getty Museum or the LACMA, and the next he's keeled over in his coleslaw. I said: "Howard?"

He didn't answer, so I said it louder: "Howard?"

Again, he said nothing.

I knew he was dead, with his face on the table like that, but I was so shaken-up that I thought for a second that maybe he really liked the coleslaw. It was very good coleslaw. I don't know where my mind was. The third time I screamed really loudly: "HOWARD!"

That's when the whole restaurant went silent and I jumped up out of my seat. Two nice-looking men in their thirties were sitting at the next table. I had noticed them earlier, how handsome they were in their T-shirts and khaki pants, and I wondered if they were in the movies. It was lovely how quickly they reacted. One of the men propped Howard up and laid him down in the booth (thank goodness Howard insisted on a booth or he would have been on the filthy dirty floor at this point) and the other gentleman called the paramedics. The waitress held on to me like she was my sister, and I buried my face in her chest. I should have written her a thank-you note, or at least given her a good tip. Anyway, by the time the paramedics came, poor Howard was already gone, and I had to make plans to get him back to

Philadelphia. I don't even want to tell you what goes into trans-ferring a body. Howard was in a casket down in the cargo hold, and I had my purse on the seat where he should have been sit-ting. I sort of wondered if maybe I shouldn't have put my purse there, you know, as kind of a memorial for Howard, but I kept crying and needed my bag handy for my tissues.

The reason I was crying, aside from the fact that my husband had just died and I did love him even though I probably never should have married him, was that Howard always handled everything. I allowed Howard to handle everything, like my mother taught me I should. I was a woman of leisure, while he worried about all the behind-the-scenes stuff. How was I going to get along without him? That was the first time I really started to regret the way I'd lived my life, and every time I thought about it the tears kept coming. Thank God for Barbara. Thank God Barbara knew to call a funeral home to get the body transferred back to Philadelphia. Even though I'd never tell her (Barbara is the type of person who would take a compliment like that and use it as a weapon later), thank God Barbara is there when I need her.

I do miss Howard a lot, more than I thought I would (again, mum's the word). We were married for more than fifty years. I married a man whom I had nothing in common with, but in those days you had to find someone and start a life. And we *did* build a life. It wasn't perfect, but what is? Was he the love of my life? No. Who was the love of my life? Sadly, it's too late for me to ever find out. Barbara thinks I should date, but who am I going to date? Hershel Neal has had a thing for me since I moved into this building. He's always asking me to come up to his place to listen to his Chopin records, but I just shoo him away. I should find some other old man with health problems and let him drop dead in front of me again? No, thanks.

Howard worked hard. He played hard, too, though he didn't think I knew it. Howard had affairs through the years. Did he think I was too stupid not to smell the perfume on his shirt? Did he really think I believed him when he told me he had to work late on Friday nights?

I thought about leaving him when Barbara was little. I thought about just packing up one night and taking Barbara someplace where no one would know us. I fantasized about that a lot when Barbara was young and Howard was having his affairs. It just wasn't something you did back then—leave your husband.

You know what you did? You kept your mouth shut.

Believe it or not, it was almost accepted for a man to have an affair, but oh, no, never a woman. I remember saying to my mother: "He's got a girl on the side."

She shrugged her shoulders and said, "He works hard and he provides for you. Subject closed." And it was. In those days, you listened to your mother and respected her opinion. Not like now—yes, I'm talking to you, Barbara.

After all, was my life so horrible? No, it was not. Howard never put me on a budget, never once. I had all the money I could ever hope to spend. My child was well provided for. We took trips, wonderful trips, all over the world. I've seen every-thing from the Eiffel Tower to the Great Wall of China. With all the jewelry Howard bought me over the years I could cover myself in diamonds from head to toe. Barbara never wanted for anything. She went to the best schools, and in summer she went to camp and then to the Jersey Shore. In those respects, Howard was a wonderful husband and father. If I had left him, what would have been the alternative? That would have been the stupidest thing I ever did. It wasn't the time to do that. Today, it's different; a woman can make a lot of money and be on her own. In those days, do you know that you couldn't even get a credit card unless your husband opened the account for you? It's true! Your husband was the one who had to fill out the credit card application, and even then, when you got the card, it never said your first name. All of my credit cards read MRS. HOWARD JEROME.

So I kept my mouth shut.

Even now, two years after Howard died, I never have to worry about money. I've got all that I need. Howard made sure I would always be taken care of, and I will always be grateful to him for that.

Still, what I wouldn't have given for a little romance myself in those times.

If there's any wisdom I've gained from reaching seventy-five, sadly, that's it.

Sex with Howard was fine. At least I think it was fine; I never knew it with anyone else. Howard was the only man I ever had sex with in my entire life. We never had crazy sex—just plain old Howard-on-top or me-on-top sex, three times a week, sometimes four if Howard felt like it, never me. I was never much for sex. I wonder, if I had ever been with anyone else would I have liked it more? Believe me, I was a pretty woman back then, with a cute figure. I could have gotten a lot of men in my time if that was my thing. How wonderful it would have been to have some-one in my life who wrote me love letters. Howard never wrote anything. His secretary even signed his name on my birthday cards. How marvelous it would have been to just have that thrill of someone else finding me attractive.

You know, it did almost happen once. I'm not saying I would have actually gone and had the affair, but once at a benefit for the Philadelphia Museum of Art, Russell Minden took me aside and told me he thought I was one of the most beautiful women he'd ever seen. He asked to take me to lunch. This was 1962, and I got scared out of my mind. I was sure that everyone at the ben-efit could hear my conversation with Russell. So I just laughed demurely, and then regretted not doing anything about it for the rest of my life. Russell died a few years back (the C-word, pan-creas). I saw the obit in the *Philadelphia Inquirer*. I sent a dona-tion to the Philadelphia Museum of Art in his memory, to thank him in my own way. I hadn't seen him for about twenty years, but I never forgot how beautiful he made me feel that night.

That's another thing I'm angry about. I never knew how at-tractive I was. When I look at pictures of myself back then, God I was beautiful. Everyone always said so, but I never believed it myself. I wish I had taken more advantage of my looks. In those days I looked good for Howard. I did my hair and ate right for fat-bald-run-around-with-other-women-behind-my-back How-ard. If I bought a new dress or a new perfume, it was for Howard to compliment. I should have been doing it for me. I only wish I had taken the time to feel good about myself.

So in a nutshell, take all that—no education, sex with one man, not knowing that the sun was bad for me, and not realizing how gorgeous I was—and that's why I'm jealous of my grand-daughter, Lucy. She's got her whole life ahead of her, and she lives in the perfect time in history. That's what I was thinking through my whole seventy-fifth birthday party: *I was born at the wrong time. I wish I was Lucy.*

You should have seen my Lucy sitting there at the party. She's got this mini e-mail contraption that she was using to talk to her friends the whole night about where they were going to go after she left my birthday celebration. "Texting," was what Barbara kept saying, as in, *"Lucy, it's Gram's birthday. Can you stop texting for two seconds to toast your grandmother?"* I winked at Lucy. It was okay with me.

All I wanted to know was who she was talking to and where she was going.

And the way she was dressed! Barbara kept saying all night, "She looks like a streetwalker." She had on a tiny minidress with platform heels and a jean jacket over it. I thought she looked like a movie star, and I wished I could wear something like that. Lucy has such a figure! She is so trim, not like her mother. Barbara takes after Howard's side of the family, with their big hips and ample bosoms. Barbara is constantly on a diet. (Ha! I think she cheats more than she diets.) Lucy and I don't diet. Sure, I watch my figure, but because of my metabolism I can afford to cheat, and so can Lucy. Sometimes Lucy and I have ice cream for din-ner. Just last week we got a big tub of Ben & Jerry's Chocolate Chip Cookie Dough and went hog wild. Lucy looks like I did when I was her age. I always had great legs, and a great tush like Lucy's. Everyone said so. I don't know what happened—my body just . . . *sagged.* It looks like . . . oh, you know when you put too much paint on a wall and it starts to drip down? That's what my body looks like. I'm thin, but saggy. But, oh, did I have a great behind! God I miss my cute rear end. I lost my tush somewhere between my forties and my sixties and I'm still looking for it. (And by the way, if you're reading this and you're much younger than I am, I have one word for you: *moisturize*. You'll still sag like a wet washcloth at seventy-five, but at least you'll look better than your girlfriends at the same age. At least I do. Oy, if you could only see Frida.)

Anyway, Lucy and I are very close. She only lives about four blocks from me in the city. I'm so happy we live close to each other. After Howard passed on, I had no desire to stay in that big house in the suburbs anymore. A few months after he died, I noticed that the water heater was leaking—just a little puddle, nothing dramatic. The water heater was located in the basement, just a few feet away from the washing machine. I only noticed the leak when I went to grab a new box of detergent. I always bought extra boxes of detergent and kept them right beside the heater. That's when I noticed the leak. I remember thinking to myself how funny it was that I never noticed that water leaked from the heater. I didn't know it wasn't supposed to leak. (Gladys, our dear housekeeper who died last year, was the one who always did the laundry.)

So when I went to take a bath a week later, there was no hot water. They had been doing some construction on Mrs. Lewis's house next door and I figured that had something to do with it. What can I say? It all seemed logical at the time. Later that day I went downstairs to throw some towels in the washing machine and the whole basement was flooded. Because I had those extra boxes of detergent by the water heater, there were soapsuds everywhere. *Everywhere!* It looked like a Turkish bath!

I was in such panic that I called Barbara, who came right over. When she saw the mess, she berated me for not having the sense to call a plumber. (Okay, *berated* is a harsh word, but she treated me like a child. So shoot me. I didn't know it wasn't supposed to leak.)

Anyway, that was it for me. I got a new hot water heater and put the house on the market the same day. I moved into a lovely apartment on Rittenhouse Square and I sold my car (word to the wise: when that "service" light that comes up on your dashboard, it is not there for decoration); and I'm so much happier as a result. My days are spent playing bridge or going to concerts at the Kimmel Center. At night I go out to restaurants with my friend Frida or other girlfriends who've lost their husbands. I bought in the same building where Frida lives and so we're always in each other's apartments. It's fun actually, and it's good that we can check on each other. My apartment faces Rittenhouse Square Park and nothing makes me happier than to go down there on a nice day and sit on a bench under a tree and read the newspaper.

Barbara didn't want me to move into the city. "It's too far from me," she said at the time. "Why don't you get something in the suburbs?" I'll tell you, I'm even happier that Barbara still lives in the suburbs. Barbara and I are close, too, but not in the way that Lucy and I are close. Lucy and I understand each other better. Barbara and I could never have that kind of closeness. Honestly, I don't think that's entirely my fault.

When Barbara and I talk, it sounds like an argument, but it's really a conversation. With Lucy, it's a plain old conversation. My daughter keeps tabs on me like I used to keep tabs on her when she was a teenager. I tell her, "For Christ's sake, Barbara, I'm a grown woman, and I can take care of myself!" She doesn't listen, though.

"Who is going to look after you if I don't?" she asks me.

"I can take care of myself," I tell her, even though I'm not quite sure that's true.

Lucy comes over about twice a week, sometimes more. She doesn't have laundry facilities in her apartment so she does it here. Those nights I'll make us a brisket and we'll eat and watch her reality shows while she does her laundry. Sometimes we'll leave the laundry and go to one of the quaint BYOs in the neighborhood. Lucy tells me all about her love life and her job designing clothing, and I listen. I listen to all her gripes about the boy of the week she thinks she's in love with. At twenty-five, Lucy has yet to have a serious boyfriend, and I'm so happy she hasn't. She has mentioned this boy Johnny lately, but I don't think there's anything serious to that. Who could take a person seriously when his name is Johnny, and not John or Jonathan? Barbara begs her to meet someone and settle down already, but I always pipe up and tell her she's got a lot of years ahead of her for that. I listen to her stories about work and who she's met and who she sold her clothing to and how much they bought. I love every minute of it. I always wanted to work with clothes like Lucy does. I used to know the inventory of Saks Fifth Avenue better than some of the women who worked there. My mother's best friend, Hester Abromowitz, worked there until she died. Hester outlived my mother and her friends by twenty-five years, and she always said it was because she worked. I loved Hester very much and think of her often. Before Hester's funeral, her daughter Diane, who was much younger than me, asked if I would say a few words about Hester, so I spoke about her time at Saks, since that was where I saw her most. I talked about how she took such great care of her clients, most of whom were at the funeral, and about her great style. People always said I had great style, and I thought so, too, and always attributed it to Hester. Over the years I thought about taking a job sometimes, but I had Howard and Barbara to look after, and even though we had full-time help—Gladys—I still had my role. Also, in my time, you were looked down on if you had a job. I brought it up to Howard a few times over the years, and he laughed.

"What are we, poor?" he'd say and smirk.

A lot of times, Lucy will go out after she visits me. She'll go to meet her friends in a bar in the neighborhood, and I can hardly keep myself from telling her I want to go with her. Sometimes I joke to her that I'm coming along, and she eggs me on, saying, "You'd be the coolest woman there! Let's get you dressed!" Once, just once, I'd love to go with her and see what her nights are all about.

Lucy is also much smarter than Barbara gives her credit for. Barbara wanted Lucy to go to law school, like Howard, but I know that's not my Lucy. Lucy went to the Parsons School of Design in New York City to learn how to design clothes. She worked for Donna Karan *herself* for two years as her personal assistant, and then she moved back to Philadelphia last year to pursue designing clothing on her own. Oh, and you want to know what else she did? She took my last name! Okay, Lucy Jerome looks a lot better on a design label than Lucy Sustamorn.

How horrible is the last name Sustamorn? When Barbara first brought Lucy's father home and he said his name was Larry Sustamorn, I thought, *Oh, that's just pathetic. It sounds like "such a moron" if you say it quickly.* Try it—say the word *Sustamorn* ten times fast and see what you get. Anyway, Lucy Sustamorn became Lucy Jerome, and although her mother was a little hurt by it, she came around. After all, my Lucy has her dresses in some of the best shops in Philadelphia—Plage Tahiti and Knit Wit and Joan Shepp—and the new Barneys CO-OP on Rittenhouse Square is interested in her dresses. Barneys!

I know. I'm such a proud grandmother.

One of Lucy's favorite things to do is go through my closet and pick out styles she can copy. I've saved everything through the years, and boy do I have a closet to show for it. By the time I moved from the house in the suburbs, I had filled every closet in the house. Barbara's childhood closet held my Chanel and Halston suits from the sixties and seventies. The guest room closet held all of my beautiful gowns. My furs (when fur was acceptable to wear, and you weren't in danger of having those people throw paint on you) and other winter coats were downstairs. I had my own closet for all my shoes and the clothes I wear now.

"You could put this stuff up for auction!" Barbara told me when I started to pack up the house.

There was no way I would do that, though. My clothes contain my memories of all the good times. I don't have scrapbooks full of pictures of old memories; instead, I've got the closet of a lifetime. My Oscar de la Renta pale blue taffeta suit from Barbara's wedding; my gorgeous James Galanos white sequined one-shoulder gown that I bought for a black-tie affair Howard and

I went to in New York once in the 1980s—Howard said he'd never seen me look more beautiful. I would never give up any of it. No siree, bob.

So I bought a three-bedroom apartment and turned one room into a closet. It took more than three months for the contractors to get it right, but when they did it became my favorite room in the world. Barbara doesn't understand it. Lucy does.

Lucy and I could spend hours in there together. She makes sketches of some of my dresses. She even copied a bright pink Lilly Pulitzer shift I bought on a trip to Palm Beach, Florida, in the 1960s, before Lilly Pulitzer was anyone in the fashion world.

Lucy calls it "the Ellie Jerome dress."

She named it for her grandmother.

When I think of my granddaughter, I glow.

And that's exactly why I'm jealous of her.

So tonight at my seventy-fifth birthday party at The Prime Rib, all I could think of was how much I wished I could go back in time and do it all over again in this day and age. Even for just one day. I wished that for one day I had my firm tush again, and my smooth, tanned skin. I wished that I could make mad passionate love to someone who only wanted to pleasure me. I wasn't asking for a lifetime; I didn't want to be piggish about it. I just wanted to have one day out of my miserable old-fogey life to experience the things that I missed out on and gain some appreciation for the things I took for granted. Do you know that I've lived for exactly 27,394 days? I figured that out on my calculator this morning. Out of all those days, would it really be a big deal to take one day off and really go crazy? What a wonderful wish! I thought it was highly creative. I would have shared the idea with someone, but of course you're never supposed to tell your wish or it won't come true. Ha!

So that's what I wished for when Barbara and Lucy came walking in with that big birthday cake.

"I could only fit twenty-nine candles on it," Barbara told everyone and laughed. Barbara can get on my last nerve sometimes.

So I wished on my twenty-nine birthday candles.

I wished to be twenty-nine again for one day.

If I had that one day, I would change everything.

This time, I would do it the right way.

And I would never regret again.

my word! i'm gorgeous!

The first thing I noticed when Barbara called and woke me up this morning was my boobs.

I always sleep on my stomach, so I have become used to waking up with my boobs hanging around my underarms. The first thing I do every morning is pull those mounds of flesh into a more comfortable position.

The phone was ringing when I came to, so I instinctively reached out to comfortably situate the first boob and noticed it was not in its usual spot. The boob was where a boob should be.

I didn't think much of it. It wasn't a big deal, and didn't jolt me into recognizing the changes that had occurred during the night. I only realized later that this should have been the tip-off.

As I opened my eyes for the first time to grab the boob (and the phone, of course), I looked at the digital clock beside my bed and saw that it was eight-thirty. I've been blind as a bat since I was fifty, yet I could read the clock. I thought that I'd fallen asleep with my glasses on. I've done that many, many times before, only the glasses never stayed perfectly on my face, especially since I sleep on my stomach. I looked at the clock again and then felt my face. No glasses. So I grabbed my glasses. Maybe I just *thought* I could see the clock. Obviously, I wasn't thinking with a clear head.

As the phone kept ringing, I sat up in bed and put my glasses on. The world around me suddenly became blurry.

So I took them off again.

The world was in focus.

So I put them back on.

Blurry.

Bernice Zankhower, a friend of my friend Lois Gordon, woke up one morning and found that her feet were a half a size smaller. I thought that maybe this was something along the same lines. What did I know?

Finally I picked up the phone, and of course it was Barbara.

"Did you have a nice time last night?" she asked.

"I had a lovely time, dear," I said, speaking my first words of the day. My voice sounded smoother, younger. Even Barbara noticed it.

"Well, if anything, you sound more relaxed today," she said.

"I feel more relaxed," I said.

I put on my slippers as Barbara babbled on, never noticing that my feet had no bunions from years of high heels, that my legs lacked the varicose veins I got when I was pregnant with Barbara. I did remark to myself that my pedicure still looked good after a week—a record for me. But the thought was fleeting.

"Didn't Lucy look awful last night?" Barbara droned. "What she puts on sometimes. I know you like some of the things that she wears, but honestly, Mother. And my steak was just a little too rare," Barbara went on complaining as I walked to the bathroom.

"Oh, for Christ's sakes, Barbara, everything was beautiful."

"Still, I thought that we waited a little longer for our food than we should have. Your friends seemed like they were ready to faint from hunger."

Truthfully, I had noticed Frida looking a little peaked from hunger, but Frida could stand to lose a few. She was a solid size eight before menopause, and then, poof! She was as big as a house, and she stayed that way for the next twenty-five years.

"Anyway, the reason that I'm calling," Barbara griped on, "is that I think I left my sunglasses in your handbag. Remember how they wouldn't fit in mine so I stowed them in yours? Are they still there?"

"Let me check," I muttered without glancing in the bathroom mirror.

I knew that I had left my bag on the table in the foyer, in front of the mirror Howard and I bought in a Paris flea market years ago. That mirror has always been one of my favorite items. I used to have it in the entryway in the old house, and now I have it in my foyer here.

"If you have them, I'm going to run downtown and get them," she said. "Maybe we'll have a little lunch?"

"Sure. How about we meet at . . ." I said, thinking of a place as I grabbed the purse and glanced at myself in the mirror.

And I saw myself for the first time.

"OH MY WORD!" I screamed louder than I can ever remember screaming before.

"WHAT'S THE MATTER?" Barbara screamed back through the phone.

At first I thought someone else was standing behind me, so I turned around and around, but no one was there.

"MOTHER, ARE YOU ALL RIGHT?"

"Oh my GOD!"

"MOTHER, WHAT'S GOING ON? DO YOU NEED ME TO CALL THE POLICE?"

I was suddenly speechless. Barbara was screaming on and on, and I just stood there, looking at this person in the mirror. *Who is she? I thought. What happened? Am I dreaming?*

"Barbara, everything is fine. I thought I saw a mouse," I said, thinking quickly.

"A mouse! On the twentieth floor?"

"I know, crazy. I'm crazy today."

All I could think was, *My arms, my arms! My arms are toned and tan!* Where was all the sagging old-age skin? I bought some new skin cream at bluemercury the other day for $120. The lady behind the counter said it was like a face-lift in a bottle—could it really have worked? Oh, please, like that stuff ever really works. But did it?

"Mother, I'm coming down there. I'm afraid you might be having a stroke!"

Maybe she was right. Maybe I'd had a stroke. Maybe I was dead and a ghost in some limbo universe that looked like my apartment. One thing was for sure: Barbara could not see me looking like this. What would she think?

"Barbara, on second thought," I said, deepening my voice—why did it sound so high? "On second thought, I just remembered I'm meeting Frida for lunch today. Why don't you come tomorrow?"

"But I need my glasses," she said.

"Oh, for Christ's sake, Barbara," I shot at her, "they're not even prescription. You probably have five other pairs that look exactly the same."

"So you don't want to see me today?" She paused, sounding melancholy.

I looked at myself in the mirror again.

"No, I think tomorrow would be a better day."

"Fine. You're welcome for the party," my spoiled fifty-five-year-old child announced, but I couldn't bother with her antics.

As you can imagine, I had more important things to think about.

"The party was the best thing that ever happened to me," I said and smiled into the phone. "I'll call you later."

I don't know how long I stood in front of that mirror in my nightgown, staring at my face. A half hour? An hour? It could have been only ten minutes, though. Time just stood still. I just kept saying, over and over, *How could this be?*

"Am I dead?" I asked out loud, pinching my arm, my face.

My face! The skin was smooth, with no wrinkles. The skin around my eyes was tight. There wasn't a crow's foot to be seen.

My hair, formerly thin and dried out from all the peroxide over the years, was now smooth and thick. I must have run my hands through my hair about fifty times before I decided to stop. Doesn't it fall out if you brush it too much? Or is that an old wives' tale?

"MY EYEBROWS ARE BACK!" I screamed, as I looked closer in the mirror.

I just want to take a moment to say to you young girls at home, *do not*, under any circumstances, pluck all your eyebrows until they're gone, even if it's the style. A little plucking here and there is fine, but *do not* remove them completely. They never grow back. I know this firsthand. Now I was staring at gorgeous, luxurious, natural eyebrows—without the help of a pencil. God knows how much time and money I've spent over the years trying to get the pencil to look like eyebrows. Then there was that experiment with the Rogaine. You get a smudge of that stuff on your forehead or someplace else hair shouldn't be and you look like someone who should be in the circus. The one thought that consoled me at Howard's funeral was that we were married for over fifty years and he never saw me without my eyebrows, not once. If he had, he would have dropped dead long before.

How did this happen?

Oh—the wish I made on those candles! The wish to be twenty-nine for a day!

I couldn't imagine any other way this could have come about. I tried to think: Had I taken any odd herbs that might have done this? I'd eaten at The Prime Rib many times before. I had some of the crab cake, a little bit of salmon, some salad, some birthday cake, and a glass of Champagne. I've had that meal many times at The Prime Rib and I never even got heartburn, much less became young again. Was it possible that the same thing happened to anyone else?

I picked up the phone and called Frida, my oldest friend. Was she twenty-nine again, too?

"Hey, Frida?" I said when she answered.

"Hi, Ellie," she said and yawned. Frida always slept late.

"Frida, how do you feel today?"

"Okay." She yawned again. "My back hurts, like always."

"So you feel the same?" I asked her.

"Are you checking to see if I'm still alive?"

"No," I said, but truthfully, I thought maybe I should start calling her every morning; Frida's kids were awful and never called. "I had a strange reaction from the meal last night and I wanted to see if you were having it, too."

"Nope," she said. "Maybe a little indigestion."

That was normal—Frida was always a little dyspeptic.

"Are you okay?" she asked. "Do you want me to go with you to the doctor?"

"No, I'm okay," I told her.

"Oh, okay." She yawned again.

"Go back to sleep, Frida," I told her.

"I'll come by and see you later," Frida murmured.

Okay, so Frida hadn't lost fifty years in her sleep like I had. Chances were that Barbara didn't get younger, either, or she definitely would have said something. This was all me.

This isn't right, though, I said to myself as I ran my hands down my smooth legs. It's not the way the world works. I'm *supposed* to be pissed off and sad about being seventy-five. Don't we all regret our lives in one way or another and wish we could go back and change them? Sure, I know what I wished, but I didn't expect it to actually happen. I knew that I could not stay this way, not even for a day.

Also, poor Barbara. What would she think when I told her that I woke up and was twenty-nine again? Barbara is such a fragile person, anyway; she'd have a nervous breakdown over this.

"No," I said out loud. "I've got to get back to the way I was."

I knew Barbara had bought the cake at my favorite bakery, the Swiss Pastry Shop on Nineteenth Street; that's where we've always gotten our cakes. I've had cakes everywhere—from Paris to Italy to New York to Philadelphia—and I've always said that nothing comes close to the Swiss Pastry Shop. There's just something about the lightness of the yellow sponge cake combined with the flakes of chocolate on the sides. The icing and filling aren't too sweet, or too dense. It's very soothing to the tongue and goes perfectly with a nice hot cup of coffee. Sometimes, even when it's not someone's birthday, I'll run over and get myself a piece of cake. That's not too often because I watch myself—even with my great metabolism, no one at my age can go too crazy. Once or twice a year is fine for that cake, but nothing more!

So I ran to my closet room to throw on a quick something and tie back my mane of hair so I could get over there. Luckily, Lucy had left one of her cloth rubber bands here. I had remarked on it one day when she was wearing it. She said it was called a . . . "scrungy"? Or was it a "scrunchy"? She said it was the type of thing you should never wear out of the house. How a hair band could ever be considered a fashion faux pas, I don't know, but my hair was all over my face and I couldn't see, so I'd have to buck the trends for a few blocks.

The first thing I grabbed was my pair of khaki silk-lined pants—the ones I always wear on planes. They are comfortable enough to sit for hours on a flight to Tokyo, and nice enough for first class. Then it occurred to me—*No, this is what a seventy-five-year-old woman would wear, not a twenty-nine-year-old girl.*

I knew I had a pair of jeans I'd bought a few years back when we went to a dude ranch in Arizona, so I searched the bowels of my closet looking for them. They were all the way in the back. I grabbed them from the hanger and threw them on under my nightgown. I was sure I'd look exactly like Lucy does in her jeans, and I have to admit I was excited when I ran over to the mirror to look.

Oh, no, no, no.

First of all, the jeans were now a size too big. My bottom belly was gone! I'd contemplated having that thing sucked out many times, but if you've ever had a face-lift and a brow lift and felt the pain of that, it makes you pause before doing anything else too invasive. Anyway, what did it matter? It was gone! A flat stomach with a cute little belly button was staring back at me in the mirror!

But I couldn't think about that; I had to concentrate on poor Barbara. I had to get back to my old self.

So I threw on a belt, grabbed one of my golf shirts, slipped quickly into my Tod's driving shoes, and ran out the door with my pocketbook. It was only later that I realized I didn't put on a stitch of makeup. Not even lipstick. I hadn't taken the trash out without throwing on a little lipstick in fifty years. My head was everywhere, I was so mixed up.

Now, for some reason, I don't know why, everyone on the

street was staring at me as I ran the five blocks to the bakery. Maybe it was the panicked look on my face. Maybe I didn't look as good as I thought without makeup, even if I looked twenty-nine. Okay, so my pants were too big. I've seen worse things on the street than that. And it was around the third block that I noticed I was still running without being out of breath. I felt amazing, free; I wanted to keep running past the bakery, it felt so good.

But I couldn't. I couldn't enjoy this, not even for one day. I had to get back to my old body. *Barbara*, I reminded myself, *think of Barbara*.

"Three birthday cakes, please!" I shouted, maybe a little too loud, as I opened the door of the bakery. There was only one other customer besides me, a nice-looking thirty-something man in a suit. I immediately noticed his blue eyes. I have a thing about blue eyes, I guess because everyone in my family has brown ones. I once got blue-colored contacts, but they made my eyes look scary, so I stuck them in a drawer and never wore them again.

"I'm so sorry," I said to him. "I didn't mean to take my turn in front of yours."

"Oh, no," Blue Eyes said, presenting the bakery to me with a sweeping motion of his arm. "Please, anything for a pretty lady."

Who was he talking about?

"Well, thank you, young man."

"Young man?" Blue Eyes laughed. "I think I'm a little older than you."

"Of course you are," I laughed, throwing my head back. "But no, please, take your turn. I'm sure you're in a hurry."

"Not at all, please. Beauty before age."

I have to admit I was sort of speechless.

"Well," I said, straightening my hair, "thank you." I smiled, walking in front of him.

"Three birthday cakes, with every candle you have in the store," I ordered with intensity, remembering what I was there for.

I left the store with three large boxes of cake in my hands. Yesterday it might have been agonizing to carry those big heavy things through the city streets, but today it didn't feel that way at all. I might as well have been holding bubbles in my hands from the adrenaline I was feeling over that compliment. And from such a handsome boy! Sure, it was just a tiny thing, but a tiny thing I hadn't experienced in more than thirty years.

Okay, maybe I would just have a little fun. I mean, I was going back with the cakes, anyway. Maybe I would just pop into a store and try on some clothes with my new figure. What could be the harm? And as I stopped in front of the window of Plage Tahiti on Seventeenth Street, I saw a cosmic sign. There, right in the window between the mint cashmere sweater and the halter top with the white slacks, was Lucy's Ellie Jerome dress.

"Can I help you with anything?" the kind, blond-haired woman behind the counter asked as I set the cakes down.

"Yes, actually. I was just walking by your shop and I noticed that very pretty dress in the window. It's gorgeous!"

"That's by a Philadelphia designer, Lucy Jerome."

I just couldn't keep back my excitement. It was killing me not to tell her. No one could blame me for being proud, could they?

"I know! She's my granddaughter!" I exclaimed.

"What?" The woman looked at me cockeyed.

"Oh, she's my cousin. Did I say granddaughter?" I tried to

laugh. "I got confused because she actually named the dress after her grandmother . . . my grandmother, too," I stammered. I've always been the worst liar.

"Oh, sure. You look just like both of them. You've all got such hot bodies. Your grandmother is such a pretty lady; she's so regal-looking. I see her in the park sometimes. I always think about saying hello, but she doesn't know me at all."

"Oh, she loves to sit in the park and read the newspaper," I said, getting excited. "You should go say hello to her next time you see her. My grandmother is really *cool*."

"She must be if Lucy designed this dress in her honor." The saleswoman smiled as she took the dress off the mannequin. "Here, this should fit you perfectly."

"Well, I'll just try it on. I'm in a hurry to get home with these cakes."

"For your grandmother's birthday?" she asked. "Lucy was telling me your grandmother turned seventy-five."

"I know! Can you believe it?" I exclaimed, going into the dressing room behind the curtain and taking off my clothes. "Can you believe my grandmother is seventy-five? She looks like she's fifty!" I waited for the compliment.

"It's hard to believe," she said as the dressing room curtain suddenly opened. "Now, let's see how the dress . . ." She paused.

"Oh, sweetheart," the saleswoman said and sighed. "You've got to get out of those granny panties and get some cute underwear for that figure of yours."

I was mortified. "I know. They're dreadful." I smiled sheepishly as I shut the curtain.

As I, Ellie Jerome, slipped into my Ellie Jerome dress, I

couldn't help but stare at myself in the mirror for just a few seconds. This was what I wanted to see; it was like seeing a child-hood friend after many years. Did I even look this good when I was twenty-five? Barbara was already nine years old by this point. No, I didn't look this good, because I already had varicose veins and stretch marks. So not only was I twenty-nine, but I was twenty-nine without the post-pregnancy body!

"How is it?" the saleswoman asked.

"I'll take it!" I shouted.

I went back up to the front desk as the saleswoman rang up the dress.

"I would think that your cousin would give you a discount if you got it from her," she confided.

"She would," I said, trying to think quickly. "But why not help with sales?"

"You're a good cousin," she said as I handed her my credit card.

"Oh, is this your credit card? Is your name Ellie, too?"

"Uh, yes. I was named for my grandmother."

"Oh, how sweet," she said as I breathed a huge sigh of relief. And just when I thought I was in the clear, the phone rang.

"Plage Tahiti?" The saleswoman smiled as I signed the receipt. I watched as she wrapped the dress in tissue and put it in a bag.

"Lucy!" the saleswoman shouted toward me with glee. "You're not going to believe this! Your cousin Ellie is here, and she just bought your dress!"

Oh, no. Oh, no. Oh god, no. Oh god. No.

Oh, I was in such a panic. I could see this poor saleswoman's face going from excited to shocked in about two seconds.

"Your cousin Ellie," she enunciated into the phone. "She looks just like you, and she says she's your cousin."

I was caught. How would I explain myself? There was nothing I could do. I had no choice.

So, like a crazy lunatic, I did what any normal crazy lunatic would do.

I ran.

I grabbed the bag with the dress and my three birthday cakes and hightailed it out of there, running down the street as fast as I possibly could. I ran clear past Walnut Street and nearly dropped everything when I almost ran right into the guy with the umbrella stand just past Lil Pete's restaurant. When I got to Rittenhouse Square, I turned back to see if the saleswoman was chasing me, but she wasn't.

What a morning.

I finally got back to my apartment building and said hello to Ken, the doorman.

"Excuse me, can I help you?"

Aw, crap.

"Yes, I just left here a little while ago? My grandmother is Ellie Jerome?"

"I'll call up," he said as he went to pick up the phone.

"No!" I stopped him. "Uh," lying again, I said, "she's in the bathtub. I must have forgotten to tell you when I left."

"Well, technically I'm not allowed to let anyone up."

"Oh, please." I stomped. "Can't you see that I've got all these packages? My grandmother will call down to you when she's out of the tub, I promise. Look, I even have her keys . . . and her bag."

"Well, like I said, technically I'm not allowed to send anyone up." He smiled.

As the kids might say, yuck! Ken the doorman was flirting with me! Believe me, if you ever saw Ken the doorman, you'd understand why I wasn't impressed.

"Technically?" I batted my eyes. If that's what he wanted, he was going to see the old pro at work. I may not have cheated on Howard, but I could bat an eye and get what I wanted better than the best of them in my day.

I swear it felt like hours until that man said okay.

"Go ahead." He smiled again.

"*Merci beaucoup*," I said and winked. Oh, how fun!

Finally I was back in my apartment. I placed the cakes on my dining room table for a moment. Before I returned to my old self, I wanted to try on my new dress one more time.

I went into my bedroom and cautiously lifted the tissue-wrapped dress from the bag and placed it on my bed. I slowly opened the tissue and admired the dress, neatly folded, with the words LUCY JEROME on the label. I threw off my clothes and carefully slipped the dress over my head. Then I walked over to the mirror.

Only now and never before. I can honestly say I now know what George Bernard Shaw meant when he said that youth is wasted on the young. How wonderful it would be if everyone could age backward like I did, if even for a moment. You can't imagine the feeling youth gives you when you haven't had it for some time. It feels like a treasure that should only be given to those who appreciate it, and not something that is given to people who don't know what to do with it.

Inside, I was seventy-five. The eyes I saw through were still seventy-five. I looked at this twenty-nine-year-old body like it was a sculpture. I took my finger and followed the delicate line from my chin to my neck that so recently was wrinkled and saggy but was now smooth and straight. I felt my chest and waist, which had only yesterday felt brittle and shapeless. How could I feel so sad and absolutely glorious at the same time?

This was a wonderful trip, a wonderful morning with the most wonderful gift I could ever receive, but it just wasn't right. Even though I felt I'd wasted my youth, it was all I should have had.

I walked into the dining room. I placed twenty-five candles on each cake and then lit each one. (Which, by the way, was a pain in the ass. Have you ever tried to light seventy-five of those measly candles? It's impossible to get them all lit at the same time; no wonder Barbara only put twenty-nine on the other cake.)

I shut my eyes and wished.

I wished that I could be seventy-five again.

For Barbara, for Lucy, and even for Howard.

I wished as I took a deep breath and was getting ready to blow.

"Excuse me!" a voice behind me suddenly shouted, startling me. "*What the hell are you doing in my grandmother's apartment, and what the hell are you doing with that dress on?*"

esus, Lucy, you almost gave me a heart attack!" I gasped, grabbing my chest and turning around.

"*Where is my grandmother?*" she bellowed, picking up the priceless Italian vase that Howard and I smuggled back in my suitcase so we wouldn't have to declare it on the way back from Tuscany that time.

"Would you put that down?" I insisted, walking over to her. But she swung it toward me, anyway. "It's me!" I shouted. "It's Grandma! It's your grandmother, Ellie Jerome!"

"You really think I'm that stupid?" she said, continuing to swing the vase.

"I swear, it's me. Look, put the vase down and listen to me. Look into my eyes. It's me, I swear it. Why don't you sit down for a moment? Let me get you something to eat. Are you hungry? I have leftover broiled chicken from the other night."

Then I remembered all the candles burning on the cakes; they were almost down to the nubs.

"Oh, for the love of . . ." I snapped as I started to walk over to the cakes. "Do you see what you made me do? Now I have to get more candles."

"*Stay where you are*," Lucy demanded as she went over to the cakes and blew the candles out herself.

"Lucy!" I ran over to her, but she backed up a few steps. "Oh, for god's sake. Your name is Lucy Morgan Sustamorn, but now you're Lucy Jerome. I thought Lucille should have gone on your birth certificate, but your mother insisted on just Lucy. She had a thing for the show *I Love Lucy*. I still think your mother was wrong, but that's beside the point. You were born on December seventh at Pennsylvania Hospital. It snowed that morning, and Poppy Howard put chains on the tires of our car so we could drive to the hospital and see you. You were named after your Poppy Howard's father, Leonard, your great-grandfather."

"Anyone could know that. I have a blog!" she screamed.

"You named this dress after me!" I said, pulling on the fabric to show her. "You constructed it after you saw the one I had my closet."

"Everyone knows that!"

"Okay, what about this? Your favorite television show is . . . Oh, what's the name of that singing program?"

"*Idol?*" she asked.

"No, the other one." I snapped my fingers, trying to remember. "*Star Search.*"

"No, the one where you have to sing where the music stops."

"*Don't Forget the Lyrics?*" she asked, looking at me sideways.

"Yes, that one!" I jumped.

"I hate that show!"

"You do? Okay, fine, how about this one: you say your favorite movie is *Citizen Kane* but it's really *Legally Blonde.*"

This made her stop.

"Who told you that?"

"No one! I've had to sit and watch that picture with you a hundred times. You think I enjoy it?"

"Wrong!" She pointed the vase at me. "You said it was your favorite movie, too."

She had me; I laughed. I love that movie, with the cute girl and the little dog.

"See, you know it's me! I tell people my favorite movie is *Little Women.*"

"And any Jane Austen adaptation."

"Yes, but that's actually true—especially the one with that actress, what's her name?"

"Anne Hathaway?"

"No, the other one."

"Gwyneth Paltrow?"

"No, Lucy think, think!"

"Keira Knightley?"

"Jesus, Lucy." I was starting to get annoyed. "No, the other one, the other one . . ."

"I'm not supposed to tell you!" she screamed. "You have to prove it to me!"

"Oh, come on. I may look twenty-nine, but I still have the mind of seventy-five-year-old. You know I forget everything. Oh, Emma Thompson!" I said, remembering the actress.

That did it for Lucy, I thought. She stood there wide-eyed, not saying a word.

"Is that her name?" I asked.

"Yes!" Lucy whispered.

She stopped for a long couple of seconds and just looked at me. "What was my favorite stuffed animal when I was little?" she asked.

"Oh, that's an easy one. It was that bunny." I smiled, remembering. "Rae-Rae, that was the name of the bunny. Rae-Rae. You were never without Rae-Rae. We had to buy extras just in case you lost it. And when we did lose Rae-Rae from time to time, you always knew the difference when we handed you a backup. Oh, Lucy, you were so smart."

She paused again and looked at me inquisitively. "Okay," she said, on the defensive again, "what was my Flubby?"

"Flubby?"

"Yes, what was my Flubby?"

I thought for a second. "Oh, it was your blanket."

"Wrong! My Flubby was my pink alligator. My blanket was called Scrubby."

"Oh, come on, how am I supposed to remember that? Give me something a little easier."

"Okay, fine. If you're really my grandmother, here is something that only you would know."

"Fine, but don't make it too hard."

"No, this should be easy. What did we have for dinner last Tuesday?"

"Lucy, how the hell am I supposed to remember what we had last Tuesday . . ." And then I did remember. "We had ice cream! Our secret meal! We had the one with the chocolate-chip cookie dough! No one knows that, now do they? We swore to each other!"

Lucy gasped and stood there in shock. Oh, the poor girl.

"Look," I said, trying to get near her, "before you start asking me what on God's green earth happened here, sit down and let me explain. And could you put that vase down? Your grandfather and I schlepped it all the way back here from Italy."

"Grandma?" She was staring at me.

"Yes, it's me, but it's only temporary," I said, walking toward her again. "I mean, I think it's only temporary."

"But this can't be." She spoke softly as she looked at me in shock.

Now, I'm not an emotional person. I haven't cried since I can't remember when . . . Oh, wait, I *can* remember—Howard's funeral. But other than that I never cry. When you get older, all those emotional outbursts that we women have—you know what I'm talking about? Well, they kind of go away. I don't know what it is; things just roll off your back easier. You become stoic about things. How odd it was that when faced with my youth I feared death the most.

"I know," I said, getting emotional. "I'm pretty sure I'm dead. I think I might have had a stroke and died in the middle of the night. What do you think?"

She walked over to me and touched my arm.

"Wouldn't my hand just go through it if you were a ghost?" she wondered aloud to me.

"How the hell should I know?" I grabbed a tissue and wiped the tears from my eyes.

"But I don't understand," she practically whispered, looking at my face. "This doesn't happen."

"How do you think *I* feel? This isn't right! What would your mother say if she found out?"

"Oh, Mom can never find out." Lucy shook her head. "No way."

"I know—she'd have a coronary, and at her age! Well, of course with the way Barbara never takes care of herself, frankly I wouldn't be so surprised."

She looked at me again, speechless.

"You really *are* my grandmother!"

"That's what I keep trying to tell you!" I threw my hands up in the air.

She just looked at me.

"You. Are. Gorgeous!" She smiled.

And then we hugged. She put down the vase first, carefully, of course, and on my good chair. We hugged and hugged, and then we just started to laugh. I couldn't remember laughing like that in years.

"But I can't stay this way," I told her.

"Why can't you?"

"Lucy, this is ridiculous. I'm a seventy-five-year-old woman. It's like defying God, or the universe, or something."

Lucy walked over to the couch and sat down.

"Okay, this is just really, really, really strange," she said, still staring at me. "How did this happen?"

So I told her the whole thing, or as much as I knew about it. I told her about the wish for one day, and then how I woke up in the morning and found myself this way.

"So that's the deal with the cakes?" she said, walking over and picking off a flake of chocolate and eating it.

"That's probably the first thing you've eaten all day, Lucy," I said. "Come on. Let me make you something proper."

"I'm sorry, but I can't obey you when you look like this." She laughed.

"Oh, I know, everything is backwards. You should have seen the look on the poor woman's face at Plage Tahiti when she saw my underwear." I lifted up my dress to show her, and then tugged the dress down and giggled. How indecent of me!

"Yeah, she mentioned it to me after you ran out of the store," she said. This made her laugh. "You really ran out of the store?"

"I couldn't think of anything else to do," I tried to say through my laughter.

"Well, one thing is for sure—before you go back to your normal self, you should at least get yourself some cute underwear to try on."

"You think that's something? You should see my bra."

"I don't want to, thank you," she said and laughed again.

"I've always wanted to wear one of those little lace bras with no support." I smiled.

"Jeez, Gram—uh, Ellie. I don't know what to call you!"

"I'm still your grandmother."

"No, you're not. You're like my drinking buddy, but that's not important right now. What is important is the actual wish. Are you sure you'll only be like this for one day?"

"How the hell do I know?"

"What exactly was your wish?"

"I can't remember anymore."

"Well, it's kind of important. Did you wish to be twenty-nine for the rest of your life? Did you wish for a week, or was it just a day?"

I thought for a second. "Oh, yes, I do remember what I wished, but it was a birthday wish. You're not supposed to tell birthday wishes, or they don't come true."

She stared at my twenty-nine-year-old self for a moment, until my brain caught up with what I was saying.

"Oh, so I guess since it came true, I can tell you what I wished for."

"Bingo." She clapped her hands together.

"It was one day. I wished that I could be twenty-nine for one day."

"So there you go. It's one day. So why don't you just be twenty-nine for the rest of the day? If it's that easy, let's just have some fun today."

I thought about that for a moment. Barbara would never have to know, and it would only be one day.

"You think I should do it?"

"Why not?" she practically shouted.

"I've always wanted to wear a bikini," I said, thinking out loud.

"So we'll get you one!"

"And I've always wanted to go to one of your bars." I smiled.

"So we'll go! Not in a bikini, though."

I couldn't stop thinking of all the things I wanted to do. Oh, what was I thinking, not allowing myself one day? Of course! It was only one day! I started bubbling with excitement imagining all the possibilities.

"I want to smoke pot!" I shouted.

"You're not smoking pot."

"Well, I want to do something crazy, and whatever I say goes. Whatever I look like, I'm still your grandmother," I warned her.

"Okay, fine," Lucy agreed. "So here's the agenda. First we're going to get your hair done. It looks awful, Gram. And why are you wearing that scrunchy?"

"I know what you said about the scrunchy, but my hair was all over the place. I looked like an animal."

"Okay, first, hair. Second, bras and underwear."

"Check," I said, running into the kitchen to grab the pad I always keep next to the phone.

"Third, lunch," she said, and then stopped. "Actually, let's have lunch after we get your hair done. I'm starting to get hungry."

"I've got that cold chicken," I reminded her.

"It's so weird." She laughed. "You're so my grandmother, but you're so not!"

And then we paused and stared at each other one more time.

"AHHHHH!" we screamed, hugging each other.

"Lucy?" we suddenly heard. It was Frida, looking all eighty-five years to her seventy-five. I tell her all the time, *Don't wear your housecoat out of the house*, but does she listen to me?

"Hi, Aunt Frida." Lucy tried to appear calm as she looked to me for what to do. What *could* we do?

"I was just stopping down here from my apartment to see your grandmother. I have a key, you know, so I'm sorry to barge in like this. She didn't sound right this morning so I just came to check on her."

"Oh, she went out," I said, trying to think of something believable.

"Oh, she did, did she?" Frida looked at me, and then came a little closer. "You know, it's the strangest thing, but your friend here looks just like your grandmother when she was young," she said to Lucy.

"This is my cousin," Lucy answered her. "This is Grandma's brother's granddaughter, uh, Michele."

"It's uncanny," Frida said, again looking at me closely.

"P-people say that," I stammered.

"It's like looking through time," Frida uttered.

"Everyone says that, too," I said.

Frida paused. "But I don't remember Ellie's brother having a granddaughter."

"Sure you do," I said confidently, knowing Frida as well as I do. Once, when we were kids, I convinced Frida it was raining on a sunny day. Frida was never very brainy.

"Well, now that you mention it, are you from Chicago?" she asked.

"Yes, Chicago," I said with certainty.

"Oh, of course. Well . . . welcome to Philadelphia." She smiled.

Poor Frida, who has known me my entire life and spoken to me almost every single day. No one in my family has ever lived in Chicago; where she got that from I'll never know.

"So where is your grandmother?" she asked.

"Oh, Gram went out to Mom's house," Lucy replied.

"Oh, okay. Well, as long as she's okay, I guess I shouldn't bother you girls any more," she said, turning away.

Something about Frida standing there in her housecoat got to me. She has always been a gentle, fragile woman I've always felt I had to take care of, starting when we were kids, right up to when she had a family of her own. Frida was never a great beauty, she never wore the right clothes; she was never young, even when she was young. I don't know what Frida would have done if I told her it was really me. She isn't strong like that. She never was.

"Frida," I said, stopping her. "Would you like to go to lunch with us?"

She turned around and looked at us and smiled. I knew that's all she wanted to hear.

"Thank you, but I've got too many things to do today." Lie. "Well, have a nice day," she said, turning again to leave.

"See you, Frida." I waved as we watched her walk out the door. My heart sank.

That really snapped me out of it. Frida. Barbara. Even Lucy saying she couldn't look at me as her grandmother. No.

I just couldn't go through with it, not even for a day. This just wasn't right.

"I can't do this," I told Lucy.

"What can't you do?"

"I have to get back to my own age. You'll never look at me the same again. Poor Frida, I lied to my best friend."

"You've lied to Frida a million times."

"When? When have I ever lied to Frida?" I demanded.

"Last week, when Frida called to ask you to come with her to the symphony."

"That was different," I argued. "It was Bach; you know how I feel about Bach."

"No, it wasn't Bach. You said at the time that you couldn't look at Frida for another minute. You were sick of her that day."

She had me. "Okay, maybe I did, but this doesn't justify me

prancing around the city all day, being twenty-nine years old. Think of your mother, sitting at home thinking I'm seventy-five."

"Would you listen to yourself for a second? Mom is not sitting at home thinking that you're seventy-five."

"Well, her life revolves around me. I can't keep this from her."

Lucy paused, took a deep breath, and put her hands on my shoulders.

"Gram, for once in your life, please, do something for yourself. For no one else but yourself, Gram. All you've ever done your whole life is think about other people before yourself. You had Poppy Howard for all those years, and Mom and me and Aunt Frida. When have you ever just done something for yourself, without thinking how it's going to affect other people? You've even said as much before."

"It's my generation." I shrugged. "That's the way we were brought up."

"Okay, so guess what? For one day, you're going to live in my generation . . . and believe me, it's the most selfish generation this planet has ever seen. All we ever do is think of ourselves."

"But Lucy, that's the point. I'm not *from* your generation. As much as I want to, I don't know how to think like you."

"So what's wrong with trying for one day? For one day in seventy-five years, take the day off from yourself. Take the day off from your generation, and live like people my age do. Don't you owe that to yourself?"

"No, Lucy," I said, holding my ground. "I don't deserve it. Why would someone deserve this? It's wrong."

And then she said something to me that made me start to change my mind: "So why did you wish to be young again for one day if you didn't really mean it? Why are you getting this gift if you're not going to use it? There's got to be some kind of logical reason for this. Maybe there's something you need to do. Maybe there's something you need to find out about yourself. All I know, Gram, is that you've got to do it. That's why I'll say it again. Gram—for once in your life, do something for yourself. And if you really can't do something for yourself, if you are really that selfless and your generation is so selfless, then I'll ask you this: Gram, do it for me."

She bewildered me. "What would this do for you?"

Lucy took a deep breath. "How many people in this world get to hang out with their grandmother when she's around their own age? Think about that for a second—how many?"

"Well, that's true. I'm assuming there's never been anyone else who's ever gotten that chance."

"Exactly. Do it for me if you really can't do it for yourself. Let me have this one day in my life to see my grandmother at twenty-nine years old, without looking at some old grainy black-and-white pictures. Imagine how much that would mean to me for the rest of my life. Imagine what I could learn from it."

"But I didn't really mean it when I wished it!" I asserted.

"*Really?*" she said, taking a step back. "I wished for a car on my sixteenth birthday, and I got a computer. Judging by looking at you, I should have wished a little harder."

That made me laugh. My granddaughter was right. What was I rejecting this chance for? Who was I to throw away such a gift? Screw Barbara. Screw Howard. And—even though I felt bad about even thinking this—screw Frida. For one goddamned day in my life, I was going to do something crazy. I was going to live for myself. I was going to live as a twenty-nine-year-old.

"You are a wise girl." I smiled at her.

"I get it from my grandmother." She smiled back, putting her arm around me.

"Okay, fine," I said. "But for one day only. This is it. I'm going to buy some more candles, and at midnight tonight I'm going to light them, and tomorrow this will all seem like a dream."

"I'm not going to argue with you." She raised her hands, surrendering. "I'm just asking for this one day in our entire lives." Then, taking my hand, she said, "Come here."

She turned me around and pulled me in front of the Paris mirror. We stood staring at the two young ladies reflected there.

"Look at you," she said. "Just look at how beautiful you are."

"I look like you," I said, wiping away tears.

We stood there for a long time comparing our faces.

"I never realized how much we look alike," Lucy said. "You really can't tell from those old pictures."

"Sure you could," I exclaimed. "Look at your jawline—it's exactly the same as mine. Look at your cheekbones."

"Hey, you're taller than me," she said. "I was taller than you yesterday."

"That's right!" I remembered. "I shrunk through the years."

"You mean you shrink as you get older?"

"Shrivel is more like it," I complained. "Lucy, if I ask one thing of you, it's this: please, drink milk. It's the best thing for your bones."

"I thought sitting in the sun was the best thing," she said, trying to be funny.

"Oh, no, never sit in the sun," I told her seriously. "Sitting in the sun is no joke. Lucy, it's a horror on your skin. My poor friend Harriet, with the malignant melanomas—"

"I know, you told me a thousand times." She put her hand to my mouth, stopping me. "I'm kidding."

"You see? I really am your grandmother."

"Maybe you're right." She laughed. "Maybe spending the entire day with you was not the best idea."

"Oh, no," I replied. "You convinced me, and now I'm your problem for the day."

"Jeez, Gram, it was just a joke."

"Okay, now, let's make an appointment with your hairdresser," I instructed. "I don't want to go to mine. He only knows from blue hair. Then we'll have lunch, and then the bras, and then"—I giggled when I said this—"then maybe we'll pick up some hot guys."

"Yuck."

"It's my day."

"Okay, fine." She shrugged.

"After all," I said, looking at myself in the mirror again, "today is my day of being selfish, and what I say goes."

"Now you're speaking like a person of my generation!" she declared.

"You bet your damn ass I am." I laughed.

"My grandmother's cursing?" She looked at me, shocked.

"Oh, please, that's just the tip of the iceberg. There are a lot of things you're going to learn about me today. Now come on," I told her. "Let's get this day started. Cinderella goes back at midnight!"

frida

Frida Freedberg was always a worrier.

She attributed this aspect of her personality to her mother, Hannah, who would wake her up every morning for school with such vehemence that it terrorized her for the rest of her life.

"Frida?" her mother would whisper as she walked quietly into Frida's bedroom.

"Frida?" She would say, a little louder.

"*Frida!*" she'd shriek. "*You're going to be late for school and then you'll never graduate or meet a nice man!*"

Frida's mother had been dead for fifty years, but she could still hear that penetrating shrill voice stab her in the heart each morning. Frida wasn't crazy about her mother, but she never told anyone, not her late husband, Sol, and certainly not her best friend, Ellie. Frida never shared such things like Ellie did. Ellie couldn't keep a secret if she tried. Frida kept things to herself.

Still, she couldn't deny that she was a worrier, and this particular morning was no different.

Ellie had called her that morning sounding shaken up. She'd asked crazy questions. Was this the beginning of Alzheimer's? Oh, God forbid. So she went down to check on Ellie. They lived in the same building, so it wasn't so difficult to just take the elevator down a couple of floors to make sure she was okay. Instead of finding Ellie, though, she found her granddaughter, Lucy, and a person Lucy claimed was a cousin. Frida knew that such a cousin did not exist. Frida had known Ellie her entire life, seventy-five years' worth of knowing, and this young woman was no cousin. Frida even tried asking if the girl was from Chicago, even though Frida knew that no one in Ellie's family ever lived in Chicago. The girl took the bait and said she was. Still, she did look a lot like Ellie when she was younger. Then again, that could just be a coincidence.

This was the tip-off that something was wrong. The other woman had to be a nurse or, worse, a social worker, brought in to help the family decide what to do with Ellie. Lucy was probably keeping this from her, fearing she wasn't strong enough to take the news. What would Frida be without Ellie? Ellie was her dearest friend, a sister in every sense.

Frida was a champion in the game of jumping to conclusions. A worrier like Frida was worried.

Then again, another side of her, the saner side, told her that maybe Ellie really did go out to Barbara's house like Lucy said. She would just call Barbara's house to find out. Besides, she'd been meaning to call Barbara, anyway, to thank her for such a lovely time at Ellie's seventy-fifth birthday party the night before. No one would suspect she was worried about Ellie. It was the perfect cover. Then, if Ellie was there like Lucy said she was, all the worrying would have been for nothing, case closed, on to the next thing. She had enough to do that day, anyway. There was the business of the bruised peach she needed to return to the grocery store. Maybe afterward she'd stop at that coffee shop on Walnut Street. Frida never bought coffee from that place. Who in their right mind would spend three dollars for a cup of coffee that cost less than ten cents to make? The reason Frida went in the shop was the heaps of Sweet'N Low packets that were ripe for the taking. Frida was running low.

Everyone, including her closest friend Ellie, assumed that Frida's husband Sol had invested poorly before he died and left Frida practically penniless. This was not the case at all, however. In fact, it was Frida who handled the investments, even when Sol was alive. Frida had over two million dollars to her name. Being the worrier that she was, though, she saved for the rainy day that never came. Frida learned the Sweet'N Low trick from her older sister, Gert, God rest her soul, who was old enough to remember the Depression. Gert died with enough pilfered Sweet'N Low to satisfy the diabetic sweet tooth of a small town.

Frida picked up her address book and looked up Barbara's number as she took a seat on the sofa. Should the news be bad, it was best to be sitting.

"*Hellew?*" The voice on the other end spoke in a high-pitched nasal-toned accent. Barbara's voice. Barbara's voice made everything she said sound like whining. Frida would never tell anyone this, though, especially Ellie. She didn't want to hurt anyone's feelings.

"Hello, Barbara, this is Frida, you know, your mom's friend?"

"Frida," Barbara said, somewhat perturbed. "I've known you my entire life, of course it's you, who else would it be?"

"I'm sorry, dear," Frida said, worrying she might have upset Barbara. *Never upset Barbara. Don't get on Barbara's bad side.* A flare-up from Barbara could make anyone back down. Her temper was like dropping the A-bomb on Hiroshima. "I just didn't want you to think it was a different Frida," Frida said, hoping to clear up the dreadful situation she'd gotten herself into.

"All I'm saying is that I know it's you, Frida. I saw you last night. How are you today?"

"Oh, I'm all right." She tried to segue into the real reason she was calling: "Actually, I was calling to thank you for last night. It was a lovely party."

"It was, wasn't it?" Barbara said happily. *Always compliment Barbara.* It was always the way to curb Barbara's irritation toward you. "Oh, yes, the flowers were just lovely."

"You didn't think the arrangements were too ornate?" Barbara asked.

"Oh, no, dear, they were exquisite," Frida lied, but it was only a white lie.

"And what about the food? Didn't you think we waited a long time?"

"Do I feel that I waited a long time?" Frida repeated. Frida had learned that when she didn't have an answer to a question it was best to stall by repeating the question. Truth be told, it did take a while for the food to arrive—about five minutes. Frida thought she might have fainted from the hunger. "Everything came on time," Frida lied again. *Remember, don't get Barbara started.*

"Didn't you find the crab cake to be a bit stringy?"

"The lumps of crab in it were very generous." (What Frida really thought: the crab cake was like paste.)

"Was the lettuce in your salad wilted?"

"It was as crisp as a cracker." (What Frida really thought: it was so wilted you could have slapped it on something like papier-mâché.)

"Was your steak too rare?"

"It was just the way I like it." Frida ate the entire contents of the bread basket, insisted she was full, had her steak wrapped up and took it home and stuck it under the broiler for another fifteen minutes.

"And my coffee wasn't hot enough," Barbara added.

"I burned my tongue." Frida got brain freeze.

"What about the cake from the Swiss Pastry Shop?"

"Oh, that was good?" Frida sort of asked.

"I thought it was too sweet," Barbara grumbled.

"Yes, now that you mention it, maybe a little."

"That's the last time I'm going to that restaurant." Barbara sighed. "I have two standing reservations, but after that I'm through."

"Good for you," Frida agreed. Barbara always said she was never going back to The Prime Rib, yet continued to eat there at least once a week. Barbara's husband, Larry Sustamorn, the dentist, loved it there and insisted on going regularly. He was a timid man, but when he believed in something, like food at The Prime Rib restaurant, Barbara took it to heart.

"Anyway, at least Mom had a good time," Barbara went on.

"She did. She really seemed to be having a good time." Frida perked up. She'd almost forgotten why she had called Barbara in the first place.

"Did she tell you she had a good time?" Barbara inquired.

Frida paused. "Did she tell *me* she had a good time?" she repeated.

"Yes, *you!*"

"She did. She said she had a good time, a wonderful time, a stupendous time." (Frida's translation: They hadn't really discussed it yet.)

"Well, she said nothing to me."

"Nothing?" Frida gasped. "No, that doesn't sound like Ellie . . . does it?"

"Frida, she said nothing. When I called her this morning she said that the party was just fine and then she screamed some nonsense about a mouse and that was that."

Frida became alarmed, but didn't quite know what to say next. Ellie never mentioned anything about a mouse. She must have been seeing things. "Maybe Ellie had a lot of things on her mind today?"

"Like what?" Barbara insisted. "Frida, really, what could possibly have been more important than thanking her caring daughter for the seventy-fifth birthday party she gave her? Do you know how much time and effort I put into planning that party for her? Do you know how many hours it took to get the right flowers, the right guest list, not to mention the seating arrangements, with the way your friends don't speak to each other. I thought I was going to scream. If I heard one more time, 'Don't sit Edie next to Lila because they're still fighting over that bill from Outback Steakhouse three months ago . . .'"

"I thought they had gotten over that, and Edie agreed to split the tip fifty-fifty," Frida interjected.

"No, she won't budge on forty-sixty," Barbara corrected her.

"Oh, what a shame."

"Frida, honestly, women your age act like little girls sometimes."

"We do, don't we?" Frida wholly agreed, sighing inside.

Frida fantasized about telling Barbara to stick it you-know-where. What did she know about the controversy over the Outback Steakhouse bill? Barbara knew nothing about a fixed budget. Lila always over-ordered when she split the bill, and all the other ladies were fed up. In Frida's eyes, it was right for Edie to stand up and fight. Lila had no right to get the soup *and* the salad *and* dessert and not pay a little extra.

"Well, all I'm saying is that it took a lot of time and effort, and what does my mother do? She makes up some excuse to get off the phone with me, and a dumb one at that. I even thought we'd have a nice lunch today. I thought she'd want to shower me with thank-yous today, but instead she's going out to lunch with you. Good for you, Frida. Please give my mother my deepest regards and tell *her highness* that I'm ready at her beck and call."

"Me?"

"Yes, you. It's time you stand up to my mother and tell her what's right."

"No, Barbara, what I meant to say was"—Frida took a deep breath, dug her fingernails into the arm of the couch, closed her eyes, and prepared for the ensuing drama—"I'm not having lunch with your mother today."

"*WHAT?*" Barbara roared. "She told me that you were

having lunch together, and that's why she couldn't see me! She has my very best pair of sunglasses that I left in her purse and she wouldn't let me even come down and get them. What do you mean she's not meeting you for lunch?"

"I-I . . ." Frida stammered.

"Spit it out!"

Frida wiped her brow. "Well, Ellie called me this morning and asked if I was feeling okay. She wanted to know if I had any reaction from the dinner last night."

"I knew the beef was too rare!" Barbara snapped.

"Well, I said that I was fine. A little dyspeptic, but I'm always dyspeptic."

"Get to it," Barbara prodded.

"Well, then I asked Ellie if she'd like to get together today, and she said that she was going out to your house."

"She didn't!"

"Oh, yes," Frida responded carefully. She ripped off a piece of the newspaper and started fanning herself. This was too much.

"So she lied to me?" Barbara was astonished.

"Well, I'm not quite sure. See, then I got worried. Ellie didn't sound right. Maybe she was keeping something from me. Ellie always thinks I worry about every little thing . . ."

"Which you do."

"Well, I'm concerned for those around me, of course."

"So then what happened?"

"So then I started to think about it a little more. There was something about the tone of her voice."

"It did sound high this morning."

"Yes, that's exactly what I noticed. So now you can plainly see why I was alarmed."

"Yes, of course! Any rational human being could see why you would be troubled like this."

"So then I took my key—you know that Ellie and I have each other's keys, just in case?"

"Yes, yes."

"So a couple of hours later I went down to see if she was okay."

"And was she?"

Frida brought the phone to her mouth so she could whisper her next words. "She wasn't there," Frida said as gently as she could.

"*She what?*"

"But that's not all."

"Frida, I can't hear anymore."

"Well, this is a very important part of the story."

"What is it?"

"Lucy was there."

Barbara paused. "What was Lucy doing there?"

"I have no idea. She was with another woman. They had some cakes lined up on Ellie's dining room table. Ellie would never have allowed that, and that had me a little alarmed. They didn't even have a tablecloth set up."

"Lucy put cake on my great-grandmother's table that grand-mother Mitzi oiled and salved every week of her life?"

"The very same," Frida answered and then regretted it. She didn't want to get Lucy into trouble.

"Okay, so let me get this straight." Barbara sighed, then took a deep breath. "My mother told you that she was going out with me."

"Correct."

"My mother told me she was going out with you."

"Yes."

"Lucy was with some strange woman in her apartment eating cake."

"That's right."

"You stay on the line for a moment. I don't want to lose the connection. I'm going to call Lucy on my cell phone and get to the bottom of this."

Frida heard Barbara put the phone down, and then the *clack clack clack* of her heels on the hardwood floors of the kitchen getting more distant. Then, just as fast as the *clack*ing stopped, it started again, louder and louder as Barbara *clack*ed back toward the phone.

"Lucy, this is Mom. Aunt Frida is on my landline, worried sick about Grandma. Frida told me you were in Gram's apartment this morning with some woman eating cake. Please give me a call. Aunt Frida is very worried." Barbara got back on with Frida. "Let me call Lucy's home phone. She never uses it, just the cell phone, but I'll try just in case."

Barbara called.

"Lucy, it's Mom. I know you never use your home phone, but Aunt Frida is very worried about Gram, and she needs to know if you've seen her. Please call me." Barbara picked up the land phone again. "I should call Lucy back and tell her to try me on both my landline and my cell phone. Hold on one more second,

Frida." She switched phones again. "Hello, Lucy? It's Mom. Try me on both my cell phone and my home phone. Aunt Frida is very worried."

Barbara picked up the land phone and said to Frida, "That was her home phone. Let me leave the same message on her cell." She put down the land phone again.

"Hello, Lucy? It's Mom again. Don't forget to try me on both my cell phone and my home phone. Aunt Frida is very upset. Love, Mom."

Barbara picked up the land phone again.

"Well, that's all I can do for now. Why doesn't Mom get a cell phone? I keep telling her it's very important."

"I don't have one, either, Barbara," Frida told her. "They're too expensive. If someone wanted to call me, they'd call me at home."

"Because situations like this could arise!"

"Oh." Frida pondered this. "Well, that's very true."

"So who was the woman Lucy was with?" Barbara inquired.

"A woman about Lucy's age, maybe a little older. But you know how these girls dress older, so maybe they were the same age."

"Well, with the way Lucy dresses . . . Did you see how she looked last night?"

"I thought the dress was a bit short," Frida agreed, which was one hundred percent true.

"Well, as long as she's making her own way," Barbara reasoned.

"And Ellie is very proud of her."

"The two of them speak their own language."

"Yes, I noticed that, too."

"Sometimes I just don't get the two of them, the way they think."

"I agree."

"What I wish is that Lucy would just settle down already. She'll be an old maid before she knows it."

"You'd think she'd have found someone already, with all of her good qualities."

"She says she wants to make it on her own first. She sounds like Mary Tyler Moore!" Barbara chuckled, and Frida followed her cue. Sometimes Barbara could make Frida feel at ease, but it didn't happen often. "I mean, sometimes Lucy can be so immature."

Frida continued laughing. "Barbara, you speak the truth. What I can't get past is why Lucy presented that woman in the apartment as her cousin from Chicago. You don't even have any cousins in Chicago."

Barbara stopped laughing. "What do you mean she said the woman in the apartment was a cousin?"

Frida paused. "Didn't I mention that?"

"No, you didn't! Frida, how could you leave out the most important part of the story?"

"I ... I ..."

"Well, what did Lucy say?"

Frida grabbed the paper and started fanning herself again. She'd never regretted anything more in her entire life than making this call. "Well, she said that the woman was Ellie's brother's granddaughter from Chicago."

"Why would she say that?"

"I don't know. That's why I was so worried."

"If you were so worried, why didn't you tell me this piece of information in the first place?"

Frida put her head in her hands. "Oh, Barbara." She sighed. "It's been such a crazy morning, with Ellie calling me and then her not being in her apartment and finding Lucy with the cakes. I guess it just got away from me."

"Hold on just a second."

Barbara put the phone down and dialed Lucy's cell number. "Lucy, it's Mom. Did you lie to Aunt Frida and tell her that the woman she saw you with in Gram's apartment was your cousin from Chicago? You know very well that we have no family in Chicago. Why would you do that? Call me back. Aunt Frida is very worried."

Barbara got back on with Frida. "Do you think I should call her land phone, too?"

"Well . . ." Frida thought about all the times her children seemed upset that she called too much. "Maybe it's best to leave it with just the one message."

"You're right."

"So what are we going to do now?" Frida asked.

"What are we going to do?" Barbara repeated tersely. "I'll tell you what we're going to do. I'm coming down there, and we're going to find Mom and Lucy and this strange woman with the cakes and we're going to get to the bottom of this."

Frida got worried again. To make Barbara drive all the way from the suburbs with the way gas prices were seemed crazy. Maybe Frida was making too much of it and calling Barbara had been a big mistake. Maybe Ellie was just running some errands. Maybe Lucy had a very good reason for lying. Frida heavily regretted getting involved.

"Now, Barbara, why don't we give it an hour or two? Maybe

Ellie went to run some errands. Maybe she *was* planning to have lunch with one of us today."

"She lied to both of us. Lucy lied to both of us. You know they're up to something, and I don't like it, given Mom's condition."

"Is there something wrong with your mother?" Frida grabbed her chest.

"Yes! My mother is seventy-five years old and she's all alone in the world and living in that big city. She can't take care of herself!"

Frida knew this wasn't true, and she knew that Ellie hated it whenever Barbara said anything like that. Still, she reminded herself, *Never make Barbara mad.*

"So what do you propose we do?" Frida asked.

"Here's exactly what we're going to do. First, Frida, you wait at Mom's apartment."

"Oh, I can't do that. I don't feel right being at your mother's apartment when she isn't there."

"Frida, how are we going to know if Mom comes back?"

"Well, okay."

"I'm grabbing my keys, and I'll be downtown in thirty minutes at the most."

"Got it," Frida said, wondering if she should write this down.

"In the meantime, should Lucy or Ellie call, or if Ellie comes home, I will have my cell phone. You have my cell phone number, right?"

"I'll take it down. Are you sure you should be taking a telephone call in the car, though, while you're driving on the expressway?"

"It's the twenty-first century, Aunt Frida. People have adapted to doing two things at the same time."

"Oh, I didn't know."

"Now here's the number. Do you have a pen?"

Frida rushed to the kitchen to grab the pad and paper she kept by the phone. "I got it, Barbara." Her hand was shaking as she put pen to paper.

"Okay, it's 5-5-5-2-5-4-2. Can you read that back to me?"

"It's 5-5-5-2-5-6-2."

"No, it's 4-2."

"555-2452."

"No, 555-2542!"

"Oh, 4-2!"

"Now read it back to me."

"The number is 555-2442."

"Frida! Are you going deaf?"

"Just say it slowly, one more time," Frida pleaded.

"555-2542. 555-2542. 555-2542, got it?"

"Yes. 555-2542."

"Good." Barbara sighed.

"And do I dial a one first?"

"Yes, and then the area code, which is 6-1-0."

"Oh, okay. So let me just read that back one more time: 1-610-555-2542."

"Finally, yes, Frida." Barbara sighed again. "Now, leave your apartment right now and go down to Mom's."

"I'll do it."

"I'll see you in a little bit."

"I'll be waiting. Good-bye."

"Good-bye."

Frida hung up the phone and looked around the room, wondering what to do next. A few moments on the phone with Barbara was more than she could ever handle. Far be it from Frida to say anything, but how could Ellie deal with her daughter on a day-to-day basis? Ellie was so calm and cool. How did she get a daughter like Barbara?

As Frida went into her bedroom to change into something more suitable to wait in Ellie's apartment, something occurred to her. Frida thought of herself as being a calm, cool person, just like Ellie. Sure, Frida worried sometimes, but who didn't? Barbara was just like Frida's mother all those years ago when she'd wake her up sounding like a lunatic. Why didn't she ever see that before?

"Maybe that kind of thing skips a generation," she said out loud to herself.

Normally, Frida never put on slacks, but today was different. If she was going to wait for Ellie, who knows for how long, she should at least be comfortable. Frida had a pair of pink sweatpants that she'd bought when she and Ellie joined that gym they never went back to. Frida thought the sweats were smart and cute, because they were pink. She also put on the matching pink sweat jacket. She went into her closet and found the sneakers she'd worn only that one day at the gym. She noticed immediately how much more comfortable they were than her regular orthopedic shoes. Maybe she'd start wearing them more often. Maybe she'd wear the entire outfit more often.

Suddenly her phone rang and she rushed to answer it. Maybe it was Ellie.

"Hello?" Frida answered.

"YOU HAVEN'T LEFT YET?" a high-pitched nasal roar came over the line.

"I know, I'm sorry. I'm going down now."

"Call me when you get down to Mom's."

"I will."

Frida was so startled by Barbara's call that she decided to leave her morning clothes sitting on the bed where she'd left them. This never happened—Frida was always neat as a pin. But there was absolutely no time to fold them up and put them away. What if Barbara called back? She walked as fast as she could out of her bedroom and toward the door of her apartment.

The phone rang again, stopping Frida in her tracks.

What if it was Barbara, and this was another test? She couldn't take it. This was one of those times she wished she had an answering machine. The answering machine her son bought her some years ago was still in its box, stored in the back of her closet. She could never figure out how to work it.

She hurried to the front door, opened it, and slammed it shut after her, making sure it was locked from the inside. She jiggled the door handle like she always did for a good fifteen seconds just to make sure it was locked. The phone continued to ring. But there was always time to check to see that the door was locked—even Barbara could understand that.

When she was finally content with the locked door, she scurried down the hallway to the elevator.

That's when a curling feeling went straight through Frida's heart.

Frida realized that she left her purse *and* Barbara's cell

number *and* her keys *and* the keys to Ellie's apartment inside her apartment.

As the elevator door opened, she found she couldn't move from where she was standing in the hallway. She watched as the elevator door closed without her inside. She continued to stand in the empty hallway, unable to think of what to do next. The only sound that could be heard was the telephone ringing on and on from inside Frida's apartment.

a woman of a certain age

I'll never forget the first time I felt discriminated against because of my age.

I had gone to get a facial at a chic spa that I had read about in *Philadelphia* magazine when I first moved into the city. I'm not going to tell you the name of it or where it is, though. I don't want them to lose any business because of my story. It's not that the spa treated me shabbily; on the contrary, they couldn't have been nicer. That was the problem. From the second I walked into the place, I could tell that they didn't usually deal with people from my age group. Personally, I was a little put off by the streamlined design of the place, anyway. Are masculine chrome walls and hard marble floors really soothing? Also, this awful flute music played constantly. When the aesthetician finished my $180 oxygen facial, she left the room and told me to "breathe in the aromatic scents" while concentrating on that flute music. I wanted to tear my eyes out after a minute, the aromatic scents smelled like the mentholatum I used to rub on Barbara's chest when she was home from school with a cold. Also, I don't know about you, but I've never found fountains to be a tranquil sound in the least. All they do is make me have to pee. But I'm getting off the track here. (Sorry, I do that sometimes. Howard always made a comment whenever I did that.)

As I was saying, it wasn't that the people at the spa were just nice to me. They were more than nice. They were *bend-over-backwards* nice. From the second I walked up to the desk, the woman behind the chrome counter spoke louder than I know her normal volume level really was. Believe me, no one shouts or enunciates like this woman did. The sound of her voice was deafening as she told me about the benefits of an apricot body scrub (I could tell that she knew as well as I did that I never would have taken off my clothes and gotten that done). Then, anything I said to the aesthetician, she laughed a little more than she should have. If I complained just a tiny bit about the way she was poking at my pores, she apologized profusely. I'm not saying she wouldn't have done this with any other customer; I'm just saying that she was pouring on the charm a bit more because she'd never before performed a facial on a seventy-something woman. And then, once I had paid and was getting ready to leave, I realized that I really had to pee from the aforementioned sound of that so-called *soothing* fountain dripping water on the stones. Both the aesthetician and the receptionist were standing there and I said, "Would you mind showing me where the powder room is?"

"*The powder room?*" the receptionist shouted, still thinking I was deaf. It was getting to the point where I wondered if I should just be rude and correct her. But any way I could have said it would have sounded rude, and frankly, I was already intimidated enough.

"She means the bathroom, the ladies' room." The aesthetician chuckled as if I had been speaking a foreign language, which I was: the language from the 1950s. Okay, I know the term *powder room* might be dated, but I still call it that. Calling it a *bathroom* makes it sound like a dirty stall at a gas station. So shoot me for trying to sound polite.

But I'm getting off the track again. Apologies.

Anyway, here's what I'm getting at: the aesthetician said she would gladly show me where the powder room was, so we walked back into the spa.

Well, she took me into the locker room. There were two doors for bathrooms. One door had no sign. The other door had a handicapped symbol on it. At first she opened the door with no sign on it.

"Here," she said, opening the door. Then she paused. She shut the door to that bathroom and opened up the other door. "Actually, you'll probably want to use this one."

I always like to use the handicap stall because it's roomier, don't you? Still, to this day, I know she thought I *should* have gone in that stall because I was old. It was the kindness in her voice that tipped me off, that temperate way that people talk to children and the elderly.

As lovely as she was, she pitied me for my age, and it hurt. I left that spa and never went back. I couldn't even go down that street for a while. I got a little paranoid thinking that they might have laughed at me after I left. Why would an old wrinkled prune (well, an old wrinkled prune with a face-lift, Botox, and Restylane) like me want a facial? It's a shame, too. I really enjoyed the facial.

From then on I went back to my facialist in the suburbs. It's lovely there. They've got comfy couches and powder-pink walls and I've known Sheila, the facialist, for years. I never even tried to get another hairdresser in the city. There are a couple of salons down the street from my apartment, but they look too overdone for me. I looked into the window of a place one time when I thought that maybe I'd just get a blowout. They don't even sit you in normal hairdresser's chairs. They sit you on stools! Can you imagine? Of course no one over the age of fifty goes in there. Whose back could stand sitting on that stool for so long?

"I think it should be cut shaggy, with lots of layers," Lucy commented as we left my apartment building.

"Oh, Lucy, I don't want to do anything too crazy." I pulled my compact umbrella out of my tote in preparation to walk on such a sunny day.

"Gram," Lucy said and laughed, staring at the umbrella, "come on, do you really need the old-lady umbrella today? You're wearing your Ellie Jerome dress! No one will be able to see you behind this big ugly umbrella."

"You're right, Ms. Smarty Pants." I laughed and handed it to her. "I don't need it today, but you do! It's about time that you start taking care of your skin. Trust me, Lucy, you will thank me when you're old. Come to think of it, though, since I'm only going to be this way for a day, I'm going to sit in the sun like I haven't done in years. Lucy, add that to the list of things to do today."

Lucy took out the list we'd made. "Do you want to schedule the sun time before your bikini wax or after you try on thongs?"

"After we try on thongs. My tush hasn't seen the sun in fifty years, so who knows?" I nudged her, laughing, but she didn't join in.

"Do you want to be arrested, too? That's another thing you've never done."

"Spoilsport." I smiled at her as she locked her arm in mine.

As we looked up, we saw Hershel Neal coming toward us.

"Oh, crap, here comes Hershel," I whispered to Lucy.

"Hi, Lucy," he said and held out his hand to her.

"Hi, Mr. Neal. How are you today?" she said, extending her hand to him. He took her hand in his and clasped it tenderly.

"Very good. How was your grandmother's birthday?"

"It was a really nice night." She turned to me. "Hershel, this is my cousin Ellie, uh, Michele, uh, Ellie Michele, from Chicago."

"Of course you are!" He smiled then took my hand and clasped it. "You two could be twins. Very nice to meet you. Ellie Michele—that's an interesting name. I guess you were named for your grandmother?"

"Yes." I smiled, but that was all I said. I couldn't stand him when I was old; he was the last person I wanted to talk to when I was young.

"By the way, Ellie Michele, that's a lovely dress."

I looked down and smoothed the dress.

"Thank you," I said, barely smiling.

"Please send your grandmother a nice hello from me," he said to Lucy.

"Will do."

As we walked past him, Lucy whispered back to me, "Hershel Neal says hello."

"Thanks," I said with a hmph.

"I don't see what's wrong with him," she said. "He's cute."

"Oh, please," I said, turning around to see the back of him. "Here it is, seventy-eight degrees outside, and Hershel is in a sports jacket. I don't think I've ever seen that man outside without a sports jacket on."

"Of all the people to complain about that—you're Miss Proper."

"I'm just saying that it would be nice to see him in something a little more comfortable. He's such a stuffed shirt."

"You like him," Lucy ribbed.

"Oh, please." I threw up my hands.

"You do, you like him," she egged me on.

"I like that he pays attention to me, but I told you before, I don't need another old man coming into my life who's going to tell me what to do."

"How do you know he'd be like that?"

"Believe me, I know. All men from my generation are like that. You know who he'd be better off with, don't you?"

"Who?" she asked.

"Frida. The two of them are so buttoned-up it wouldn't be such a bad idea if they unbuttoned together, if you know what I mean." I laughed. "God, for Frida to start dating someone, that would be a dream. No, there is no way I would ever go on a date with that man."

"You're being so closed-minded."

"Subject closed. I'm right."

"Fine." Lucy sighed.

"Oh, and another thing—let's figure out exactly what my

name is. Should I be Ellie or Michele? That Ellie Michele stuff sounded crazy."

"Well, I guess if we run into Frida again, your name is Michele. We'll have to call you Ellie, though, if you need to pay with a credit card. What if they ask for an ID?"

"Smart thinking," I said. "How did you get so smart?"

"It runs in the family." Lucy smiled and we continued walking, arms locked.

Lucy's hair salon was a place that never would have accepted me at my real age. On this day, though, I was exactly who they wanted in their shop. We walked over to the reception desk, which looked like a spaceship (and not to be rude, but the receptionist's hairstyle looked like it was from outer space, too, and I hoped they wouldn't do something like that to me).

"Now here's what I want," I told Lucy's hairdresser, Szechuan. (Szechuan! A name only a hairdresser would have, and only in a salon like this one. For this day, though, I accepted it wholeheartedly.)

"She wants sexy," Lucy interrupted.

"I want feminine sexy," I told him.

"She wants cool," Lucy continued.

"Yes, yes," I said, getting excited. "I want to be the sexiest, coolest, most feminine-looking woman who ever walked out of this place."

"I've got it." Szechuan nodded. "We'll do it all today. We'll get rid of your natural blah color and make it a little darker. Then we'll do highlights. Then we'll shorten it. I don't want to shorten it too much, but you have gorgeous bone structure, like your cousin, so you would look lovely if I cut some layers near the brow."

"All of that sounds good, Szechuan. Just as long as we can be out of here in an hour. We've got a full plate today."

"But all of that will take me at least three hours."

Lucy and I looked at each other.

"How about just cutting it really short and sleek?" I asked.

"Oh, you don't want that," Lucy protested. "If anything, you should get extensions."

"Actually, with her cheekbones it could work well," Szechuan mused.

"Come on, Gram . . . Ellie . . . Ellie Michele. You don't want short," Lucy said.

"I do, I want it short. I want something light and sleek. I've had the same hairstyle, that helmet bob, since Barbara was in pigtails. I want sleek and stylish. I want my head to feel weightless for one day."

"Trust me, you don't want short. No one wears their hair so short these days. It's all long layers," Lucy pleaded.

"Lucy, it's my day, and this is what I want."

"You're going to hate it."

"I've made worse mistakes in my life."

"Fine, but don't cry to me." Lucy pouted.

"Do you ride a motorcycle?" Szechuan asked.

"What?" both Lucy and I asked.

"The helmet."

This made us laugh.

"I promise you," Szechuan said, taking my purse from me, "you will both love it."

I took my purse back from him. "I trust you," I told him, putting my purse back on my lap.

"Ellie, I'll take your purse," Lucy said, taking it.

Lucy realized that I was doing what old ladies do—we keep our purses close to us. Barbara had mentioned that to me before. Hey, I didn't know this Szechuan or the shampoo ladies from Adam. Younger people are more trusting than people my age. So I gave Lucy my bag.

For years my hair has been just past my shoulders, when it's wet and without the aid of curlers or hair spray. When my hairdresser does it, it's teased and curled so it looks about an inch shorter. Howard always liked it like that. I always got the same cut because Howard liked it so much. And all those years, what I wouldn't have given to just cut it all off! After Howard died, though, it just got away from me.

"Short," I instructed, "and sleek."

"Short and sleek." Szechuan smiled at Lucy. "Actually, it's going to be nice to do something different than the same long shag."

"And is there someone who could put a little makeup on me?" I asked.

"Oh, sure!" Szechuan got excited as he called out, "Hortense! Lucy's cousin wants a little makeup put on."

With each snip, I could almost feel the weight of my life coming off me. Lucy buried her head in her e-mail contraption as I watched this Szechuan person have a go at me. I could see the tense look I didn't even know I had on my face become an assured, confident look. I puckered my lips a little more, accentuating my cheekbones. I was loving myself more with each snip.

"*Oh, crap,*" Lucy practically shouted. "Gram, with all that was going on this morning, I completely forgot that this was like one of the most important days of my life."

"What did you call her?" Szechuan asked.

"It's her nickname for me. I love graham crackers," I lied as I turned back to Lucy. "What's the problem?"

"Today is the day I go to the Barneys rep for the store on Rittenhouse Square. I have to leave you for a while."

"No, let me come with you. I want to see you work!" I said, excited at the thought.

"No, Gram, I have do this on my own. You'll be okay for a while."

"Come on, let me come with you. I promise I won't say anything. You can say I'm your secretary or something. I'll bring a clipboard and pretend to take notes."

"That's so sweet!" Szechuan said to me, awed. "You're so proud of your cousin!"

I smiled at Lucy like a grandmother smiles at her perfect grandchild. "You don't even know the half of it," I told him.

"Okay, fine," Lucy said. "But promise me you won't say anything."

"What?" I couldn't hear her because the hair dryer was in my ear.

"Promise you won't say a word."

"Oh, I promise," I said, drawing an X over my heart.

"How long did you say you were in town for?" Szechuan asked.

I paused and thought about it. "Just one day. I'm leaving tomorrow."

"What a shame," he said, turning to Lucy. "I like her."

"Thank you." I smiled.

"Okay, I'm done here," he said, turning me around so I couldn't see the mirror. "But I don't want you to see the finished product until Hortense finishes your makeup."

"I won't look, either," Lucy said, turning her back to me. "I want to wait for the finished product, too."

"It's a deal. What time is the meeting?" I asked Lucy as Hortense applied some powder to my face.

"In an hour and a half. So that gives us time to have a little lunch," she said.

"And the thongs?" I reminded her.

"Yes, the thongs, too." Lucy laughed.

"So did you two grow up together, like sisters?" Hortense asked as she lined my eyes.

"No, I'm older than Lucy."

"Oh, so you bossed her around?" Hortense teased me.

"No, I couldn't boss her around. Her mother took care of that."

I watched as Lucy's back pulsed with a laugh. "Ellie was the one who always stood up for me," she said.

"Isn't that sweet. Like a big sister," Szechuan said.

"Yes, kind of." Lucy laughed.

"How old are you?" Szechuan asked. "You can't be that much older than Lucy."

Lucy reached around without looking at me and pinched my arm.

"I'm . . . I'm a woman of a certain age." I smiled.

"Touché." Szechuan snapped his fingers.

"Okay, I'm done. Are you ready to look at yourself?" Hortense asked as she backed away for Lucy and Szechuan to see.

Szechuan grabbed his chest. "¡Ay, Dios mío!" he gasped.

"Gram. No. Seriously. Gram, that's not you!" Lucy exclaimed.

"Oh, for Christ's sake, you're so dramatic," I said to her as Szechuan turned me toward the mirror.

Okay, maybe I was a little gorgeous.

Okay, maybe a lot.

"Szechuan, do you think you could cut my hair short like that?" Lucy asked.

"I just love the ease of it," Szechuan said, combing his fingers through my hair. "I'm going to call this the 'Gram Cut.'"

"And you didn't need a lot of makeup," Hortense added. "I just made you look fresh."

"If people didn't turn and look at you on the street before, you're going to cause accidents now," Szechuan said.

That's when it occurred to me—the people looking at me on the streets that morning! I'd thought it was because I looked so strange in the clothes I'd been wearing. Was it possible that they were looking at me because I was attractive? No. Could it be?

I didn't even want to touch my hair; I was afraid that any small movement would ruin it. I was so happy I wanted to cry, but I was afraid that I'd ruin my makeup.

"So, what do you think?" Lucy asked.

"I think I need to take a moment," I said, and I really did. "Could you tell me where the powder room . . . uh, the bathroom is?" I asked Hortense.

"I'll show you," she said, taking my hand.

We walked through the salon, past the other chairs, and I glanced at the other young women having their hair done. All of them were under the age of thirty. No one thought it was strange that I was there. I was one of them.

Hortense led me to the restroom but as I unconsciously moved toward the door marked with a handicapped symbol, she put her arm on mine and indicated the regular ladies' room.

"Here you go." She smiled.

"Thank you." I smiled back and shut the door.

I stared at myself in the mirror, just as I had for so long earlier that morning. I thought to myself that if I didn't stop I'd turn into Narcissus and stand there for the rest of the day. I looked for just another minute, though—just one more minute. And then it was time for the rest of my day.

On the way out I kissed Szechuan on both cheeks, as I'd watched Lucy do a second before, and then did the same with Hortense. I decided that I would do that from now on, and not just when I went to Europe.

If I do say so myself, we looked like an ad in a magazine as we walked arm in arm down sunny Chestnut Street. Somehow everything looked different to me. It could have been because I wasn't feeling the pain of bunions or the way my back hurt when I walked a few blocks. I held my head high and looked in all the shop windows. I noticed people's faces as they walked by. I was starting to see things through the eyes of a twenty-nine-year-old.

"If I could take one memory from this day, this would be it," I said and smiled at Lucy.

"What, walking down the street?"

"Yes, just walking down the street with you, arm in arm." I pulled her in tighter.

"Me, too." She smiled, putting her head on my shoulder.

We walked half a block with our arms around each other and only stopped when Lucy's cell phone rang.

"It's Mom." She grimaced.

"Don't answer it."

"She'll keep calling if I don't."

"So let her."

Lucy put her phone back in her purse.

"Okay, so where should we eat?" I pondered.

"Johnny is working the lunch shift today. We could go see him."

"Is it a good place to eat?"

"It is—really cool. They've got outside seating."

"I only want to go places that are young and hip today."

"This place is young and hip. They've got cushy ottomans for chairs."

"What's with the youth and having no backs for chairs?"

"What do you mean?" She giggled.

"I mean every place that's hip and chic has no backs on their chairs."

"That's a good question," Lucy replied. "I never thought about it before."

Lucy's phone rang again. She dug into her purse and looked at the phone's caller ID. "It's Mom again. I told you she would just keep calling."

"That woman . . ." I threw my hands up in disgust. "She'll give up after a while."

"I should answer it," Lucy said, worried.

"No, it's my day, and I'm being selfish. Don't answer the phone."

"B-But . . ." Lucy stammered.

I gave her a look that shot her down.

"Fine," she said, throwing the phone back in her purse.

"So tell me more about this Johnny."

"Well," Lucy began, smiling again, "he's handsome."

"Yes."

"And smart."

"Yes. He doesn't want to be a waiter all his life, does he?"

"Yes, Gram. His dream is to be head waiter before he's fifty."

I looked at her in disbelief. Even in my young body I was still slow to pick up on jokes.

"I'm kidding!" She grinned. "He wants to open up his own restaurant. He's got some amazing ideas. And his best friend Zach created a Web site called couture.com. He has a ton of money; he's going to fund the restaurant."

"And what's wrong with dating the rich best friend instead of the waiter?"

"Jeez, Gram, we're twenty-five years old. We're supposed to have no money right now. We won't start making money until our thirties. Zach just has money because he got a good idea for a Web site and sold it for like fifty million dollars. Anyway, I'm not attracted to Zach. He's cute, but Johnny is more my type. Zach is the suit-wearing type. Johnny is jeans and sneakers."

"Just a moment. This friend has fifty million dollars?"

"Something like that."

"Lucy, marry the rich guy! You'll never have to worry about anything for the rest of your life!"

"Gram, I intend to make my own riches."

I was about to tell her that it was easier my way, that she wasn't thinking clearly, that she was too young to know better. But I realized if I did say those things, I would sound exactly like my mother. I immediately shut my mouth.

"You're right," I said instead. "If this Johnny makes you happy, that's what's most important. What do I know, anyway?"

And then Lucy's phone rang yet again.

"Oh, for Christ's sake," I said, stomping my foot. "Does this happen every day?"

"Yes, if I don't pick up the phone. She knows it's annoying to me, so she'll make something up and say, 'Daddy wanted to know . . .' or 'Daddy was thinking of you.'" She looked down at the phone again. "So should I answer it?"

"I don't know," I said, and this time I really didn't. "Do you want to?"

"I don't know. Maybe I should just see what she wants?"

"So pick it up."

Lucy pressed a button and spoke into the phone. "Hello?" She heard nothing and looked at the phone. "It went through to voice mail."

"Well, then, check your messages. Let me hear it, too; share the phone with me."

"I'll put it on speaker," Lucy said, pressing another button.

"It does that?" I was shocked. "You can do that on a cell

phone?" I asked as the recording on Lucy's phone announced that she had three messages.

"You can also take videos on a cell phone," she told me.

"Now you're teasing me again."

"I'm not. But it can only store less than a minute's worth of footage."

"You poor thing," I said, teasing her now. "We didn't even have our own phone line when we were younger. We had to share a line with the people next door. Oh, Frida and I used to listen to their conversations. Mr. Hampton from next door was impotent—"

"Wait, Gram, shh, here are the messages."

"Lucy, this is Mom."

"Like I don't know." Lucy rolled her eyes.

"Aunt Frida is on my landline, worried sick about Grandma. Frida told me you were in Gram's apartment this morning with some woman eating cake. Please give me a call. Aunt Frida is very worried."

"Do you see what I mean? 'Aunt Frida is worried,' not her."

"Oh, Frida." I grimaced. "Can she ever stop being such a fretter? I'm gone for two hours and she thinks I've been kidnapped."

"Wait, here's the second message," Lucy whispered.

"Hello, Lucy? It's Mom again. Don't forget to try me on both my cell phone and my home phone. Aunt Frida is very upset. Love, Mom."

"You see what she does? You see how it's not her that's worried, it's Aunt Frida?"

"I know that trick. I taught her that trick. That's not her fault."

"Wait, here's the third message."

"*Lucy, it's Mom. Did you lie to Aunt Frida and tell her that the woman she saw you with in Gram's apartment was your cousin from Chicago? You know very well that we have no family in Chicago. Why would you do that? Call me back. Aunt Frida is very worried.*"

"Oh, Frida!" I stomped my foot.

"I shouldn't have said you were a cousin from Chicago."

"Oh god. Your mother will have the police looking for me in another minute."

"We should call her," Lucy said. "Seriously, this is getting to be too much. You know how she freaks out."

"Okay," I gave in. Lucy dialed Barbara's number and let it ring.

"She's not there," Lucy said. "Should I leave a message?"

"Yes. Tell her you just saw me and I'm shopping and I'm fine."

"No, I can't." She shut the phone off.

"Why not?"

"What am I going to say about the cousin in your apartment? Why would I say something like that?"

I thought about that for a second. "Oh, I don't know. Tell her that you and your friend were having fun with Frida."

"She'll see right through that. That just doesn't sound right."

"Well, I don't know. Look, I'll call her later. This is wasting my day."

"What about Frida?"

"I'll call Frida. I'll tell her that I'm out shopping and then going to a movie by myself. If she asks me about Barbara I'll tell her I was planning to have lunch with her, but then I didn't feel like it. She'll believe me, she believes everything I tell her. I once made her believe it was raining on a sunny day."

"You've told me that story about a hundred times."

"Well, now it's a hundred and one, Ms. Smarty Pants. Now give me your phone."

I dialed Frida's number.

"God, I'm hungry," Lucy said.

"Me, too. Do they have pizza? I'd love to have a pizza."

"I don't think I've ever seen you eat pizza," Lucy said and laughed. "But yes, I'm sure they have pizza."

"Good. I want to eat like a twenty-nine-year-old. Oh, to live a day and not have to worry about how much fiber I've had."

"Yuck, Gram."

"You scoff, but you'll see. As you age regularity becomes your life." I laughed and then remembered I was waiting for Frida to pick up. "Where the heck is she?" I asked, listening to the phone. "She never leaves the house." I let it ring a few more times. "I don't know where she is," I said, handing Lucy the phone. "Here, I don't know how to hang it up."

Lucy touched a button and then shut the phone.

"Well, we'll get it all straightened out after lunch," I said.

"Yeah, let's forget about it for now. Mom will probably forget about it."

"And when she doesn't, we'll tell her where she can stick it."

Lucy laughed. "I don't think I'll ever get used to you today."

"I'm young, gorgeous, and a woman of the world," I said, swinging my arms and accidentally bumping into a handsome man. "I'm sorry," I said and smiled at him.

"It was my fault," he said, giving me the once-over.

Lucy grabbed me, urging me to come on.

"He was cute!" I smiled, looking back at the man, who was

still staring at me. "And finding a cute guy was one of the things on my list today."

"We've got a lot of hours left in the day. Don't worry," she said. "We'll find you someone cute."

"Someone with a nice tush." I laughed.

"Oh, Gram." Lucy cringed.

"Do men do that all day?"

"What?"

"Do they whistle at you and look you up and down and say nice things?"

"Yes." Lucy rolled her eyes again. "Trust me, you get sick of it."

"Trust me"—I put my hands on her shoulders—"if there's one thing you must never do, it's get sick of men whistling at you, even the ones you're not interested in. There will come a day when they don't do that anymore, and believe me, you'll miss it."

A hint of worry came into Lucy's eyes.

"I'm sorry, was that too depressing?"

"No," she said, smiling gently. "I guess we're both learning a lot today."

hubba hubba

The question I've grappled with, even in the years since Howard's death, is this: What would my life have been like if I had married someone I was *in love* with? What kind of person would I have become if I had married my soul mate? If I'd had the choice all those years ago, if my mother hadn't stood in the way and told me to marry Howard. If I'd married with my heart, would my life have been any better? What would my daughter have been like as a result? Would Barbara have been more independent?

What is more important in life? I don't know; maybe it's different for women today, like Lucy, because she can go out and make it on her own. Still, it is my belief that as long as this world is round, there's going to be that age-old question: Should you marry for love or security?

I've made it to seventy-five years old and I still don't know the answer; so much for that old-age wisdom.

"Johnny!" Lucy shouted across the restaurant as we walked in.

You should have seen Johnny's face when he saw Lucy.

Howard never looked at me in our entire marriage with such a smile.

"Excuse me for a second," I heard him say to the customers he was helping as he held out his arms for my Lucy and gave her a great big hug. "I thought you were showing your clothes to Barneys today," he said, looking concerned.

"I am." She smiled at him. "It's not for another hour, so I thought I'd pop in to see you for good luck."

He put his arms around her again and gave her a kiss on the lips. I looked away to let them have their moment. I have to say, Lucy has good taste. He might not have had a proper profession, but boy, was he handsome.

"I'm sorry," he said, extending his hand. "I'm Johnny."

"Oh, sorry," Lucy excused herself, turning to me. "This is my friend . . . er, my cousin from Baltimore, Ellie."

"Chicago," I corrected her.

"Did I just say Baltimore?" She laughed nervously. "I meant Chicago. This is my cousin Ellie, from Chicago."

"Oh, of course. Well, you look exactly alike," he said, shaking my hand.

"Everyone says that," Lucy and I said at the same time and chuckled.

"Come sit over here"—he motioned to a table—"Zach is here. Sit with him. I'll grab you some menus."

"Zach is the rich one?" I whispered, nudging Lucy.

"Yes, shh," Lucy said, nudging me back, seeming mortified. What? No one could hear us.

"Hey, Zach," Lucy greeted him.

Zach looked up from his menu. Why did he look so familiar?

"Hey, Lucy," he said, standing up and giving her a peck on the cheek. That's when he looked at me. "Hey," he said, looking as bewildered as I felt.

"This is my cousin Ellie, from Chicago," Lucy introduced me, getting it right this time.

"Don't I know you?" Zach asked, his blue eyes twinkling in the sunlight streaming into the restaurant.

"I think I know you, too," I said, scouring my memory.

"Oh!" He snapped his fingers. "You're that cute girl from the bakery this morning!"

"Oh, for goodness' sake! You're Blue Eyes!" I said, clapping my hands. "I don't believe it! Is this a small world or what?"

"What did you call me?" He laughed.

"Blue Eyes. The thing I noticed first about you was those blue eyes. Doesn't he have the most beautiful eyes, Lucy?"

I looked at Lucy, who gestured for me to calm down. It was such a small world, though, wasn't it? Evidently, older people are more shocked that the world is so small than younger people are. Maybe it has something to do with growing up with the Internet and cable TV. So—he was the young man from the bakery this morning, with the gorgeous blue eyes! How do you like that?

"Your hair is different."

"Yes," I said, patting it down. "I got it cut at Lucy's beauty parlor."

"It looks incredible!" he said, then chuckled. "I love that you said 'beauty parlor.' Only my grandmother ever called it that."

"I meant the hair salon." I giggled nervously. "I don't know why I said that." But I *did* know why I said that—I was crazy for those eyes, those eyes!

"That's what they call it in Chicago," Lucy interrupted, saving me.

"Yes," I bluffed.

"Like 'pop' for soda, I guess," he commented as he pulled out two chairs. "Here, take a seat with me."

"We'd love it, thank you," I said, sitting across from him. Lucy took the seat next to him. When he looked down for a second, I mouthed the words *hubba hubba* to Lucy. She put her face in her hands like she was embarrassed.

In addition to those blue eyes, boy, was he ever handsome! What a gorgeous head of hair he had! And he was tall and broad! If he wasn't so young, I would have thought that the phrase *tall, dark, and handsome* was invented for him!

"So why were you buying all those cakes this morning?" he asked me.

"Oh, um, well . . ." I faltered.

"It's our grandmother's birthday. That's why Ellie is in town," Lucy quickly chimed in.

"Oh, that's right. Johnny said you had your grandmother's birthday party last night. So you were picking up the cakes today?"

"Today is Ellie's birthday!" Lucy said, getting excited.

"Happy birthday!" Zach smiled at me. Goodness, he had nice teeth.

"Thank you!" I smiled back.

"So why were you picking up your own cakes?" He looked confused.

"Well, I was up early this morning, so I picked them up. No

big whoop." I looked at Lucy to see if this explanation seemed plausible. She shrugged and nodded.

"So how long are you in town for?" he asked.

"Just today," I said. "I have to go back to . . . I have to go back tomorrow."

"Then we'll all have to go out tonight and celebrate." He beamed.

I beamed back, and then looked at Lucy, who seemed to be pondering the idea.

"Sounds cool!" she declared.

"Sounds really cool!" I added as Lucy, again, motioned for me to calm down. What can I say? A couple of hours and I've already got a date with a wealthy, blue-eyed hunk!

"So what is everyone having?" Johnny asked, coming over to the table.

"Pizzas all around?" Zach asked us.

I immediately wondered if I had a Pepcid in my purse, but then remembered that my twenty-nine-year-old self would not be needing any heartburn medication for this meal.

"With extra spicy peppers," I added, excited.

"I'm loving your cousin!" Zach turned to Lucy and said.

"So am I." Lucy smiled at me.

"You know, there's this great little Italian place we could go to tonight," Zach said.

"For what?" Johnny asked.

"We're all going out for Ellie's birthday," he told him.

"Cool!" Johnny smiled.

"Why don't we meet for a drink before?" I proposed. "Lucy,

what about one of the bars you like to go to?" I asked hopefully.

"Excellent idea!" Lucy exclaimed. "Let's meet before dinner at our usual place, on Fifteenth Street. I've been wanting to take Ellie there."

"I'm in," Johnny confirmed.

"Me, too," Zach said and smiled, a hint of flirtation about him.

When the pizzas came and I took a moment between my second and third pieces, I put my hands under the table and pinched myself, like I had earlier that morning, to make sure I wasn't dreaming.

I was sitting in this restaurant talking about bands I'd never heard of. Zach spoke about his Web site, but I had no idea what he was talking about or how it made so much money. If no one paid to look at the site, how could it make money? I wanted to ask, but I didn't. No one else seemed to wonder, so I didn't pursue it.

What *did* matter was that I was one of them. I was young and free and life could not have been more exciting.

So I pinched myself again and reached for another piece of pizza.

Zach, however, stopped me mid-grab and took the piece off the platter himself and put it on my plate for me.

"Thanks, Blue Eyes." I smiled.

He smiled back.

I heard a ringing sound and Lucy looked into her bag and took out her phone.

It's Mom, again, she mouthed as she threw her phone back in her bag and we listened to it ring on.

F rida Freedberg was a wreck . . . and all before noon, too.

After she watched the elevator doors close, sans keys to her apartment and Ellie's apartment, money, and identification, which she was never without, she continued to stand in the hallway, unable to think of what to do next. Frida felt like she was going to faint. She needed smelling salts. It had been years since she'd used smelling salts, but she always kept some in her purse. For a worrier like Frida Freedberg, this was as bad as bad could get.

Frida knew she had no choice but to go downstairs and wait in the lobby for Barbara to arrive. Barbara had told her explicitly to go to Ellie's apartment and wait for Ellie to come home. Maybe she'd catch Ellie coming in and the whole crisis of the day would be averted, anyway.

"Hello, Ken," Frida greeted Ken the doorman as she got off the elevator.

"Hi, Mrs. Freedberg," Ken said and smiled. "You're looking pretty today."

Frida liked Ken, but in the back of her head, she always

thought that maybe he didn't like her. Ken was always happy to help with her groceries, but she always noticed that he seemed a little more outgoing when Ellie came in with packages. Ellie suggested once that maybe it was because Frida tipped only a dime when he brought up five bags of heavy groceries, but Frida was sure that couldn't have been it.

"Ken," Frida said, "I seemed to have locked myself out of my apartment."

"Oh, that's no problem," Ken said, turning around to grab her extra keys out of the spare key closet.

"No, you see, I leave them with my friend, Mrs. Jerome."

"That's right," Ken said. Was that a smirk she saw flash across his face? Frida decided that the next time she came in with groceries she'd up the tip to a quarter to test the waters.

"I was wondering if maybe you'd seen Mrs. Jerome this morning? Maybe as she was leaving the building?" She paused hopefully. "Maybe she's come in the building in the last few minutes?"

"Nope," he said, thinking about it. "I can't say I remember seeing her today. She could have left before I got here, but I haven't seen her since my shift started. I *did* see her granddaughters, though."

"Her one granddaughter; she was with a friend."

"Yes, the one who lives around here. But then the other one came in and out. I let her up."

"By herself?"

Frida could see that Ken was getting a little annoyed with her, but when something was as important as this, she couldn't help herself.

"Yep. She had some big boxes of cakes or something with her."

Frida couldn't hear any more. "Thank you, Ken. Well, Ellie's daughter is coming any minute, so I'll wait for her here."

"Mrs. Sustamorn is coming?" Ken said and pouted slightly.

"She is." Frida grimaced.

She took a seat on the lobby couch. It was so strange not to have anything to hold on to; Frida always had her bag in her lap. She took a deep breath and tried to relax.

She had never sat in the lobby before. Though she had been on the building's decoration committee for years, she couldn't think of a time when she had sat on the couch she'd helped pick out ten years before. The decoration committee was planning to get together again to discuss a new couch, and Frida was glad that at least she could now go back and report that she'd sat on it. There was no need for a new couch, in her opinion, though she did notice some wear and tear on the cushions.

Since she had nothing else to do, she watched Ken as he opened the door for people walking in, signed for packages, and petted a couple of dogs as they walked by. He was kind to let her sit there. Maybe she'd give him fifty cents the next time he brought up her groceries. She felt it wasn't right to always have to tip him since he got a salary, but Frida's husband had always said it was good to tip the help so they would feel bad if they wanted to steal something later.

None of the people walking in and out of the building was Ellie. However, when Hershel Neal walked into the building, Frida was happy to see a familiar face.

"Well, Frida, fancy seeing you here." He smiled as he saw her. He was always such a gentleman.

"Hello, Hershel. Good to see you, too." She smiled back.

"You look so sporty today. What a pretty color," he said, admiring Frida's pink sweat suit.

"Thank you." She smiled, feeling flattered.

"So what brings you to the lobby today?" he asked.

"Well, I've had a bit of unfortunate circumstances this morning."

"Nothing serious, I hope."

"Oh, no," Frida lied, not wanting to upset him. "I accidentally locked myself out of my apartment, and I'm waiting for Ellie's daughter to come downtown."

"Oh, that's nice. Isn't Ellie around?"

Frida tried not to make too much of where Ellie might be. Ellie never liked Hershel—though why, Frida could never understand, because he always seemed to have eyes for Ellie. She was even a little jealous and wished someone as handsome as Hershel might have eyes for her.

"Have you by any chance seen Ellie today?" Frida asked him.

"No," he replied. "I *did* run into her granddaughters just a short while ago. The one in from Chicago, and of course Lucy."

Lucy was going to have a lot of explaining to do, but Frida didn't want to confuse Hershel any more by telling him that the other woman was no cousin.

"You know, Frida, as long as I've got you alone for a second, I wanted to talk to you about something, you know, since you're Ellie's closest friend."

Frida gasped inwardly. Did he know something she didn't? "Sure. What is it, Hershel?" Frida asked calmly.

"Well, I don't know if you know this, but I've had a little crush on Ellie for some time now. I'd love to take her to a concert sometime. You know I've got tickets to the Kimmel Center. They've got some wonderful concerts coming up."

"Oh, I don't know if I should be the one you talk about this with," Frida said, shying away. How could she tell him that Ellie wasn't interested?

"If she needed a chaperone, I wouldn't mind getting another ticket, if you'd like to come along."

It was a marvelous idea. Frida always loved the Kimmel Center. Still, Ellie wouldn't have liked Frida sticking her nose in this kind of business.

"Well, I'll see if I can persuade Ellie, and I'll get back to you."

He placed his hand on Frida's arm and smiled warmly. "That would be wonderful. Thank you Frida." He continued to smile as he walked toward the elevators.

What was Ellie's problem?

Frida went back to watching Ken, who was standing at the door contentedly watching the day go by. Suddenly his expression tensed. Frida knew exactly what he had just seen.

She got up and walked toward the door. The woman was more than a block away, but with that hard *stomp, stomp, stomp* in her step, it was impossible not to know who she was. As she got closer, Frida noticed she wasn't wearing the usual large black bug-eyed glasses that practically covered her entire face. She was squinting into the sun. It must have been eighty degrees outside, and she was wearing black clothing from head to toe, long heavy gold chains around her neck, and big diamond rings on her fingers. Her hair, as usual, was held back tightly by a big black bow.

"Hi, Mrs. Sustamorn," Ken called out to Barbara.

Frida got a hot flash. How would she explain what she was

doing in the lobby? Frida watched as Ken put a fake smile on his face.

"Ken!" Barbara's called out in her loud, nasal accent. Ken clenched his smile a notch tighter. "I'm looking for my mother. Have you seen her?"

"I haven't, ma'am, but Mrs. Freedberg is right inside," he told her as he stood at the open door.

A shadow darkened the room as Barbara stopped through the doorway. Spotting Frida standing in the middle of the lobby, Barbara breathed in heavily.

"Didn't I say—" Barbara threw down her large Louis Vuitton tote and put her hands on her hips.

"Now, Barbara, don't get excited." Frida held up her hands like a boxer expecting a right hook.

"What are you doing down here in the lobby?"

"Well, I had a slight mishap this morning. I accidentally left my handbag in my apartment."

"You must have taken your keys."

"They were in the handbag."

"And Mom's keys?"

Frida had no more strength to answer.

"Oh, Frida," Barbara tsked. "I don't know how you survive. What would we have done if I didn't have the keys to Mom's apartment?" Barbara said, taking Ellie's keys from her purse.

"I don't even want to think about it. You're always thinking one step ahead, Barbara, always prepared, thank goodness." Frida sighed.

Barbara smiled lightly. *Always butter up Barbara.*

"Now, Ken," Barbara said, turning to him as Frida's smile

faded. "We have a serious situation on our hands here. I'm sure Mrs. Freedberg must have asked you by now if you've seen Mrs. Jerome this morning."

"I haven't," Ken answered, running over to the door and opening it for a couple walking in. "Like I told Mrs. Freedberg here, she might have come in before I started my shift."

"And what time was that?" Barbara inquired like a true detective.

"Six a.m."

Barbara breathed heavily again. Frida felt faint again.

Barbara walked closer to Ken and looked accusingly in his eyes. "Are you sure you haven't seen Mrs. Jerome?"

"I saw her granddaughter, if that helps," Ken replied, taking a step back.

"And did Lucy mention anything about my mother?" Barbara questioned.

"Oh, you mean Lucy. I saw Lucy, but I'm talking about the other granddaughter. The one staying in her apartment."

"The one from Chicago," Frida clarified to Barbara.

"Yes, thank you, Frida," Barbara said tartly.

"Yes, that's the one. She came in and out earlier today. She came back with some cakes, and I let her up."

"*You let a total stranger up to my mother's apartment?*" Barbara bellowed.

"Look, the young girl had already been in your mother's apartment," Ken began calmly. "I saw her leave. She looked just like your daughter. When she came back a while later, she had all these boxes in her hand. It was obvious to me that the girl wasn't up to any trouble. I have a sixth sense about people."

"Well, maybe your sixth sense should have told you that the young woman you saw today was of no relation to either me or my mother! She was an imposter who just might have something to do with my mother's now very apparent disappearance!"

Frida sat down and put her head between her legs, or at least tried to. She was able to get only halfway down.

"Look, I am very sorry that this has happened to Mrs. Jerome. I like Mrs. Jerome very much. I could only have assumed that this young woman was a relative since she told me she was, in addition to the fact that she left the building with your daughter."

Barbara looked at her watch and sighed. "Well," she said, "I suppose there's nothing I can do about this right now, but don't think for a second that I will forget this, Ken. Now, look, this is very important: What time did you see this woman leave with Lucy?"

"It was, oh, about an hour ago . . . no . . . maybe two."

"They could be anywhere by now," Frida said, her head still halfway to her knees.

"Frida, let's you and I inspect Mom's apartment to see if anything was taken." Barbara looked at Ken. "Ken, the keys, please."

"Well, technically, Mrs. Sustamorn, I'm not allowed to give keys—"

"KEN!"

Ken jumped and went to the key closet to grab Mrs. Jerome's keys and handed them over.

"Frida, let's go," Barbara said and stomped her feet toward the elevator with Frida trailing behind.

As the elevator doors shut, Frida tuned to Barbara.

"I thought you had the keys to your mother's apartment."

"Of course I have the keys to my mother's apartment! You think I'm going to trust them downstairs with that degenerate doorman anymore?"

"Oh, okay," Frida said and nodded.

Barbara straightened her oversized black sweater and slicked back her hair. For the first time that day, she noticed Frida's pink sweat suit.

"Frida, what the hell are you wearing?"

"I don't know. What I was thinking?" Frida said, wondering if that was the right thing to say.

Barbara said nothing and looked up at the numbers changing as they rode from floor to floor.

Once inside the apartment, the first thing Barbara noticed beyond her mother's Paris mirror in front of the door were those cakes.

"Disgusting." Barbara grimaced, grabbing the cakes off the table and taking them over to the trash can. She looked up to see if Frida was watching, which she was. Darn. The Swiss Pastry Shop cakes were her favorites. A little swipe of frosting might have tasted good right about now. She'd been planning to eat the leftover cake she'd taken home from the party before Frida had called. Maybe she really would start her diet today, like she was always planning to.

"Frida, take a look around and see if anything's been taken," Barbara instructed.

Frida walked into the living room.

"Oh, no!" Frida shouted, causing Barbara to run in with icing on her lips.

"What?"

"Ellie's prized vase from Tuscany. It's moved! It's on Ellie's good chair! Maybe she tried to use it to fend off the intruder. You know, when I came down here before, what if they had Ellie tied up in the bedroom?"

"Or maybe Mom moved it to clean it." Barbara balked at Frida's theory. Then, "My grandmother's pearls!" Barbara suddenly remembered and rushed into her mother's room.

Frida moved over to Ellie's baby grand piano. The piano was rarely played, but Frida always admired it just the same. On top of the piano sat dozens of photos in silver frames. It was her best friend's life laid out for everyone to see. In one, a young Ellie was at the beach with chubby Barbara. Barbara hadn't changed much, Frida noted, and Ellie had always had the best figure. And there was Ellie, holding baby Lucy, with the most joyous smile on her face; Frida and Ellie laughing at Frida's fiftieth birthday party; Howard dressed in one of his suits, God rest his soul.

Frida started to get weepy. What would she do if something had happened to her friend?

"Barbara," Frida called out.

"It doesn't seem like anything has been taken here," Barbara called back. "There are those jeans here from that time you all went to the dude ranch."

Barbara entered the living room with the empty Plage Tahiti bag and pulled out the receipt. "Looks like the imposter must have done a little shopping on Mother's card," she said, then noticed Frida's worried face. "What's the matter?" Barbara asked.

"Barbara, we have to find Ellie." Frida was starting to get upset.

"We will," Barbara said, permitting herself to be slightly comforting.

"Your mother is the only person in the world who cares about me. Next to my children, she's the most important person in my life."

Although it was completely out of character, Barbara put her arm around Frida.

"*There, there*, Frida. We'll find Mom. Don't you worry."

"I am very worried." Frida dug inside her sweatshirt arm cuff, took out a ragged tissue, blew her nose with it, and then tucked it back where it came from.

"Frida," Barbara said with a little more intensity. She put her hands on Frida's shoulders. "Frida, we will find Mom. I promise you we will find my mother today, but you've got to be strong. Can you be strong?"

"Can I be strong?"

"You can be strong."

"Okay, Barbara."

"Now, the first thing we're going to do is head over to the Swiss Pastry Shop. Maybe they can give us some clues. Then we'll go over to the Plage Tahiti clothing shop and find out who used Mom's credit card and what they bought."

"I think we have a pretty good idea who used this credit card," Frida said and nodded.

"Maybe she'll head back there. Maybe what she bought was too big or too small."

"Good thinking," Frida agreed. "Only . . ."

"What is it?"

"Well, I'm feeling a little ravenous right now . . ."

"Oh, Frida, how could you think of food at a time like this?"

"Well, my blood sugar gets low and—"

"I did notice you wrapped up your steak last night."

"I was so full from the wonderful salad and crab cakes," Frida lied.

"Fine. I'll call over to Lucy's boyfriend's restaurant. He'll wrap something up for us on our way to the Swiss Pastry Shop. That's actually a good idea—maybe he knows where my daughter is. I'll try Lucy's phone again and tell her we're headed over there."

Barbara went to her bag, got out her phone, and dialed Lucy. Again.

"Hi, Lucy, it's Mom. I haven't heard from you today and, like I said, Aunt Frida is very worried about Grandma. When you get a chance, please call us back. Also, we're headed over to your friend Johnny's restaurant for some takeout. Love, Mom."

"That's a good idea," Frida said.

"Though I really do think we should retrace the steps first," Barbara said. "Johnny probably hasn't seen Lucy today. She's always on the move, and of course she hasn't called me back. Maybe Mom has something in the kitchen we could snack on until then."

Frida walked over to the kitchen and opened the refrigerator. There was a broiled chicken inside. Ellie always made wonderful chicken; she was always able to make it so moist on the inside and crisp on the outside. All Frida could ever do was burn things. Ellie. How could Frida be eating anything at a time like this? She suddenly became upset again and shut the refrigerator door.

"No, Barbara, let's go find Ellie."

"But what about your blood sugar?"

"Forget my blood sugar."

"Well, okay," Barbara said. "Maybe Mom has some cheese and crackers I can grab. She always has a stash."

"Good thinking."

Frida walked over to the Paris mirror to fix her hair. What did Barbara know about style, always in her black outfits? The pink sweat suit was cute. And it was comfortable.

"Barbara, are you ready?" Frida called.

"I'm ready." Barbara's answer sounded garbled. "Here are the cheese and crackers." She handed a pack to Frida and put the rest in her handbag.

"Barbara?"

"What is it? Let's go!" Barbara rushed her.

"Nothing, it's just . . . I thought you threw out the cakes."

"I did. Come on, let's go."

"Oh. It's just that you have some icing on your lip."

"It's flour from the pantry. You know Mom is a slob! It must have gotten on my face when I opened the door," Barbara blustered as she wiped away the buttercream.

Don't get Barbara mad. Don't get on Barbara's bad side.

Sometimes, though, it was fun to rile her up just a little.

"Okay," Barbara said, grabbing the keys to the apartment. "Let's go."

They walked out of the apartment and into the hallway. Barbara shut the door and made sure the safety lock was on by jostling the door. Then she locked the three locks on the door and jostled it again for a few more seconds to make sure it was locked. She turned around and saw Frida looking at her sheepishly.

"What is it now, Frida?" Barbara moaned.

"Maybe I should use Ellie's powder room before we leave. What if we're never near a clean bathroom?"

Barbara grunted in disgust as she looked through her vast Louis Vuitton bag for the keys she'd just thrown in. "I can't find the keys. I'm too agitated. You find them." She threw the bag at Frida.

Frida looked into the bag and found the keys immediately.

"Do you have to go, too?" Frida asked.

"I never have to pee," Barbara protested. "I've got the bladder of a camel."

Frida unlocked the door to the apartment, placed her one pack of cheese and crackers and Barbara's purse on the table in front of the Paris mirror, and headed into Ellie's powder room. As she sat, she wondered when or if she would be sitting at all for a while.

"Frida!" Barbara called out.

This startled Frida. She finished peeing and flushed. As quickly as she could, she pulled up her control-top panty hose and then her sweatpants. *Never keep Barbara waiting.*

"Frida, the elevator is here!"

"I'm coming!" she shouted as she hurried out of the bathroom and through the apartment.

"Frida, let's go!"

"I'm here!" Frida shouted as she slammed the door.

It was then that she remembered.

She started at Barbara, who was standing with one foot in

the elevator and one foot in the hall. The door was about to close on her body so she pushed it to make it open again.

"Please don't tell me that you left my bag in Mother's apartment."

Fear paralyzed Frida. Again.

"Frida, please tell me you at least have Mother's keys in your hand."

Frida suddenly remembered the cheese and crackers. They were in the house. With Barbara's bag. Her blood sugar dropped another level.

"Jesus, Frida! What the hell is the matter with you? You are so stupid sometimes!"

Twenty floors below, Ken the doorman was standing outside the lobby elevator loading Mrs. Kristiansen's groceries when he heard the howl of Barbara Sustamorn's voice echo down the elevator shaft and through the lobby.

"What was that?" a startled Mrs. Kristiansen asked as she widened her eyes and stiffened.

Ken shrugged. "Mrs. Jerome's daughter Barbara is up there."

"Ah." Mrs. Kristiansen nodded, getting the picture. "Well, thank goodness she only visits. Could you imagine if that woman lived here?"

"There's a silver lining to everything, isn't there?" He chuckled.

"You said it." Mrs. Kristiansen agreed, handing Ken a five-dollar tip.

business before pleasure

Lucy and I skipped like schoolgirls down Chestnut Street. She didn't want to, but it was my day so I made her. I swear I could hear Gershwin's "Bronco Busters" or the melodic sound of a full orchestra playing "'S Wonderful" inside my head. Whenever I hear Gershwin in my head it means I'm having a good time. (By the way, if you're too young to be familiar with Gershwin, please get yourself some CDs. You'll thank me later.)

"So what should we wear for our dates tonight?" I asked Lucy, throwing her arm up and down along with mine in excitement.

"We'll pick you out one of my dresses."

"I want that black one—you know, the one with the sexy back."

"Gram, we're not going any place fancy, just a bar and to grab something to eat."

"Well, I don't care," I said as we headed up the stairs to Lucy's studio. "A handsome boy wants to take me out for a night on the town; the least I can do is look nice for him. What am I going to do, show up looking like some schlump? And then what?"

"You don't want him to think it's your first date, though. If you wear that dress it looks like you're expecting him to take you someplace more extravagant than where he's really taking you, which is a bar and an Italian place where you bring your own wine."

"Lucy, the job for the man is to show the lady a nice time. The job for the woman is to look like she appreciates it."

"Well, let's just hope he doesn't appreciate you to the point where he wants more in return," Lucy warned me.

"A little peck on the cheek never hurt anyone," I replied, though I knew exactly what she meant.

Lucy stopped me in front of her door. "Please don't leave my side all night, Gram. Men today are different than they were when you were younger."

"And whose fault is that?" I asked her.

"It's no one's fault. If a woman feels like having a one-night stand, she should be able to, as long as she has no regrets afterward. Men, though . . . Well, sometimes men think they're getting away with something."

"Are you speaking from experience, or is this something every woman your age knows?"

She stopped and looked at me. "Both."

I kept my mouth shut. This was something I didn't need to know about. The truth is, in my entire adult life, I was considered single for maybe a month before I met Howard.

"You don't think this Zach person will take advantage of me, do you?" I asked as she opened the door to her studio.

"Oh god no," she balked. "He's one of the nicest guys I know, next to Johnny. He's that guy who is too nice to women. A lot of women don't know how to handle it. A lot of them just use him." She laughed. "Maybe he's the one I should be warning." She paused. "Anyway, forget about that now. For right now, I need to pick out the dresses to bring to Barneys."

"Definitely the blue one," I said, pointing to an azure cocktail dress.

"You don't think it's too much?" Lucy wondered.

"Not at all."

"Here, try it on for me. Let me see if there's anything else I need to do with it. You should be the sample size."

I climbed demurely out of my dress.

"And after Barneys, we're picking up the underwear and bra," Lucy added. "Actually, here"—she reached under her dress and moved around, pulling her bra out of her sleeve—"put this on. We're about the same size."

I took Lucy's bra in my hand and turned around to put it on.

"It's like two coffee filters." I laughed.

"You'd be surprised. It gives a lot of support."

I slipped into the blue dress and stood on Lucy's tailoring box in front of the mirror. No matter how many times I looked at myself in the mirror that day I would never get over how I looked.

"I'm bringing it." Lucy smiled, standing back. "And you're going to be my model."

"Me?" I replied, shocked.

"You look amazing in that. You'll look amazing in everything. With your hair and makeup already done, why not?" She stood back and looked me over like an artist studying her canvas. "All I need to do is take in a little here," she said out loud to herself as she pinched the fabric by my waist and began to pin the dress. "This should take two seconds to sew, and then we'll get to the other ones. I don't know why I didn't think of this before. You're a perfect fit, Gram!"

I started to tear up again.

"If you keep crying like this you'll never enjoy the day," she joked.

"I don't think I want this day to end," I said and smiled at her.

"Me, either." She smiled back.

It was only a few blocks from Lucy's studio to the Barneys buyer so it was easiest for us to just put the dresses on a wheeled rack. I walked in the front and steered and pulled while Lucy took the back and pushed. We were having a heck of a time with the thing, and more than once we lost control of the rack as we went from one block to the next. I had read an editorial in the *Philadelphia Inquirer* about the fact that the handicapped ramps on the streets were dilapidated and crumbly. Now I saw that they were even worse than the article said. I'd also heard Mrs. Goldfarb complain about negotiating the sidewalks while pushing her husband in his wheelchair. Since we'd had rain a couple of days before, water had collected in the potholes, and I had to lift up all the dresses so they wouldn't get splashed.

As we approached our destination, Lucy stopped me.

"Now Gram, let me do all the talking."

"What if I have something to add?" I asked her.

"Gram? Nothing," she insisted.

I shut my mouth and mimed locking it for her. The last thing I wanted to do was ruin Lucy's day.

As we wheeled the rack into the elevator, Lucy took out her

phone. "Maybe we should just call Mom and tell her you're okay. She's called about five times now."

"Lucy, I don't want to hear about it. For one day I'm going to be left alone."

"I can just imagine how she's feeling, though. You know Mom."

"Here's the thing about your mother," I told her. "She can be a real bully sometimes."

"No, Mom is a worrier. She worries so much that she turns into a bully. Kind of like Aunt Frida just shuts down. It's funny how they're both these big worriers, but they show it in different ways."

"Sometimes I wish Barbara would get some friends."

"She'll never have friends," Lucy said, sighing. "She's just too confrontational."

"You know, I've always been afraid that one day you'll start to really dislike your mother for the way she acts."

"I understand her," Lucy answered. "I almost feel like I have to take care of her. Not the way she feels the need to take care of you, but I stick up for her when I have to."

For the second time that day, I realized my granddaughter was wise beyond her years.

"What?" Lucy asked.

"It's just that every day I know you, I love you more. How on earth did you get so smart?"

"Good genes." Lucy smiled as the freight elevator door opened.

"Okay," I said when we reached the buyer's office. "Let's call your mom."

"She's not at home," Lucy told me. "I'll call her cell."

She dialed and waited.

"No answer. I'll leave a message," Lucy reported. "Hey, Mom, it's Luce. I got your message . . . uh, messages." She looked at me and shrugged, not knowing what to say. We should have planned this out. "Uh, I haven't seen Gram today—"

"Yes you have! Yes you have, and I'm fine!" I whispered to her.

"Oh, come to think of it, I *have* seen Gram. I saw her this morning. She was going to get her hair done." She shrugged, wondering if that was a good excuse. "So tell Aunt Frida that Gram is fine and not to worry. Love you." She hung up the phone and put it in her bag.

"Satisfied?" I asked her.

"Yes." Lucy exhaled.

"Lucy Gorgeous!" the man shouted as he came out of his office.

"Rodney," Lucy greeted him with equal joy as they gave each other kisses on both cheeks. "I want you to meet my cousin and model, Ellie Jerome."

"What a pleasure." He greeted me warmly, with kisses on both cheeks. I wished that I had a gay friend. They don't have gay men in the Main Line suburbs of Philadelphia. Sure, I knew some here and there, like that nice decorator (though I never used him; I stuck with Myrna Pomerantz, who did a gorgeous job, until she developed Alzheimer's and died, poor thing). The furrier on Montgomery Avenue was gay, too, but he closed down in the early 1990s when fur wasn't the thing to buy anymore. When I moved downtown I hoped that I'd meet a nice gay man to become friends with. I haven't yet, but I think I'll start looking.

"You can change over here," Rodney said, taking my hand

and leading me behind a curtain. "What a lovely figure she has, Lucy," he said, "and her posture is unbelievable."

Lucy smiled. "I thought she would be a great model."

"Posture was the one thing my mother always insisted on, and I in turn instilled it in my daughter," I shouted through the curtain. "You can say lots of things about Lucy's mother, but you can't say she doesn't stand up straight."

"What?" I heard Rodney ask. "How are you related?"

"It's a long story," Lucy answered.

Although each dress made me feel more fabulous than the last, Rodney didn't comment on any of them. He looked studiously at how each dress fit and had me turn around slowly. Then he'd take some notes. Lucy would say something like, "I went for the straight collar here because I thought it would lay better," and Rodney would nod. I just did my job, like Lucy told me. I didn't say a word and tried the best I could to show the dress by extending my arms or resting my hands on my hips. I've seen a lot of today's actresses in Lucy's magazines, and when they have pictures taken on the red carpet, some of them stand to the side and lean back, resting a hand on their hips. Some lean too far back. I told myself not to go that far.

After the last dress was modeled, I went behind the curtain to change back into my Ellie Jerome dress.

"I love them all!" I heard Rodney exclaim.

"Yippee!" I shouted from behind the curtain.

I heard Rodney and Lucy laugh, which I thought was a good thing. Lucy had looked so nervous each time I came out with a new dress, a bit like Howard used to look when he was awaiting a decision in one of his cases.

"I want them all for spring," Rodney said. "Let's talk numbers. Normally," he explained, "with an outside designer, we work on consignment. For each article we sell in the store, you'd receive, shall we say, forty percent of the pretax retail price?"

"Well," Lucy said nervously, "I was kind of hoping—"

I couldn't help myself. For all the work that Lucy had done, no one was going to cheat my granddaughter. "We want at least seventy-five percent," I demanded.

"Gram!" Lucy shouted.

Rodney laughed, but I wasn't having any of it. I lived with Howard Jerome, King of the Negotiators, for fifty years. I figured Lucy could yell at me for years afterward, but she was going to get the right price if I had anything to do with it.

"Forty percent is fine," Lucy insisted, with a look in her eyes that said she was about to shoot me.

"No, it's not fine," I butted in. "Seventy-five percent, Rodney, or we take it all over to Bloomingdale's."

"You're serious?" he asked, looking at me. "The model also has a brain?"

"I will take my cousin's business elsewhere," I told him.

"Gram! Leave! Now!" Lucy shouted at me.

"I'm not going anywhere until you get what's coming to you," I informed her calmly. "Now look, Rodney, this girl works harder than anyone I know. She's more talented than anyone I know. She's worth a lot more than you're offering. I saw the look on your face each time I came out with a new dress, and you couldn't put it past me—you were in awe."

"Listen," Rodney said. "I'm not going to deny that Lucy's designs are fabulous, but forty percent is all I'm allowed to offer."

"So to whom do we need to speak in order to get more?"

"It's fine." Lucy clenched her teeth as she pinched my arm, then said, "Rodney, it's fine. My cousin doesn't know this business."

"I know a lot of things, Lucy. I've been around long enough to know that you should be getting more," I told her.

"*I swear to God . . .*" Lucy muttered at me under her breath.

"All right, hold on, let me see what I can do," Rodney said and left the room.

"Gram, I swear to you, if you screw this up for me I will never speak to you again," Lucy whispered angrily.

"Jesus, Lucy, what are you so afraid of?" I said in my full voice. "Don't you understand the art of negotiation? It's all about leverage."

"I have no leverage!" she responded furiously, though still whispering. "This isn't some little shop. This could be my entrée into all the big department stores. It doesn't matter how much they're paying me. If I can get my dresses into the Philly store and they sell out, they'll come back with a better deal. They'll want to put my dresses in their other stores. That's when I negotiate, not now!"

"This is where you're wrong, Lucy!" I countered, just as angry. I lowered my voice and crossly told her, "If they get your dresses for bubkes, they'll stick the dresses in the back of the store, where no one can see them. If they pay a little more for them, they're going to have to put them in a better spot."

"You're wrong!" Lucy grumbled at me when I knew all she wanted to do was shout.

"I'm right!" I shot back.

After that we sat in silence for couple of moments, until we heard Rodney coming back in.

"Well, we never do this with new designers, but I talked to the powers that be and they're willing to go to sixty percent. But this is highly unusual for us."

Lucy smiled. So did I. In my head, I thanked Howard.

"We'll take it!" I shouted, throwing my arms around Rodney, kissing him on both cheeks.

"You drive a hard bargain," he said, kissing me back.

"And one more thing . . ." I started to add.

"Gram?"

"No, it's not about this. It's a just a thought."

"What is it?" Rodney asked.

"Well, Lucy and I, we have a very hip grandmother. Why don't your stores ever sell anything that older women can enjoy, too?"

"Women of all ages can wear our clothing," Rodney said, offended.

"I think that's a discussion for another time," Lucy said, grabbing my hand and trying to lead me out.

"Who knows when I'll ever get a chance like this again?" I turned to her and said. And then I mouthed, *It's my day*. She let go of my hand. "Older women are cut differently. Boobs fall to the floor, skin sags," I began.

Rodney started to look like he was going to gag.

"They still want to look chic, though. How many pantsuits can a woman wear? All I'm saying is think about it."

"You know, I have some ideas for that," Lucy added.

"You do?" Rodney and I both exclaimed at the same time.

"If you met our grandmother, you'd know why," Lucy explained.

"Who is this woman of the world?" Rodney asked, getting excited.

"Maybe we'll all have lunch sometime," Lucy said and smiled.

"It's a deal," I said, feeling all keyed-up.

"I'm still pissed off at you," Lucy said, laughing, as we walked the rack through the streets back to the studio.

"Rule number . . . how many are we at today?"

"I don't know." Lucy laughed again. "Between us, four thousand."

"Rule number four thousand: Always have confidence. It gets you everywhere."

"But how did you know he wasn't going to say no?" she asked me, practically jumping up and down.

"Because I knew. I knew that your dresses were spectacular."

"That was what you went on?" She looked at me quizzically.

"That and the poker face he had on. No one looks that serious unless he wants something. If he didn't like what we were showing him, trust me, he would have said, *gorgeous*, *exquisite*, things like that."

"Damn, you're good." Lucy looked at me in awe, then stopped the rack for a second and came around to my side. "Thanks, Gram." She spoke sincerely.

"Oh, sweetheart," I said, kissing her on both cheeks, "believe me, it was my pleasure."

"So now the best day of your life is my best day, too," she whispered back.

"Any day I get to spend with you is my best day," I told her.

"That's such a grandmother thing to say!" She laughed.

"It's true, though," I said, kissing her on her forehead.

"Well," she said, walking back to her side of the rack, "we still need to do more for you today. We need to do something exciting, something you'd never be able to do at your age."

"What happened to the list?" I asked, suddenly remembering.

"It's back at my studio. We'll look at it there, but those are such basic things. Isn't there something you've always wanted to do? Something you've always wished you could have done when you were younger and never did?"

"We never got those bras and underwear," I said.

"No, something big, something bigger than a bra or a date with some guy."

"I'll have to think about it and get back to you," I told her. This was the truth. I couldn't think of much more that I really wanted to do. So far, it had been a hell of a day. And for the first time that day, I started to think that maybe I'd just stay twenty-nine forever.

Barbara Jerome Sustamorn was a terror even before she was born. Ellie loved to tell people that Barbara kicked her so hard while she was pregnant, she once told the doctor she was afraid that Barbara would kick right through her womb. Whoever she told the story to would laugh and laugh. "Barbara the bully," they'd say, then snicker as if this wouldn't offend Barbara at all. But who wants to be called a bully? Barbara hated it when Ellie told that story.

It's not that Barbara didn't know she could be difficult at times. She knew when she was going too far. Afterward, she'd be full of remorse and self-hatred, although she never said a word. Only Lucy knew. When she'd come into her mother's room after school to find Barbara lying in bed, she knew. Even when she'd been as young as eight, Lucy had known when to climb onto Barbara's bed and put her arms around her mother. Lucy was the only person Barbara would never bully. Though it was never said, she knew that Lucy was the only person who ever understood her.

Barbara felt she had gone through life with a mother who never understood her.

She wondered sometimes if she would feel better about herself if she never spoke to Ellie again. Yet she craved her mother's approval so much she couldn't leave her alone, even if she tried. She loved her mother dearly. Ellie was the person Barbara most wished she could be. She was also the person Barbara most wished she could please, and that was what made Barbara so angry, hotheaded, and just plain frustrated. And her behavior caused people, including her mother, to judge her. She spent her life trying and failing to please Ellie. If her mother would love her, then everyone else, including Barbara, would love Barbara, too. She was caught in an endless cycle of need and frustration.

Barbara had been trying to emulate Ellie her entire life. When puberty struck and it was apparent from her large breasts and hips that she got her looks and shape from her father's side of the family, she started eating nothing but carrots and celery so she'd have the figure Ellie had (and okay, when the aggravation of that scale never budging got to be too much, maybe she cheated, maybe a lot). Like Ellie, she married the first man who showed any interest in her, Larry Sustamorn, the dentist. Like Ellie, she never held a job, and concentrated on her family. Try as she might, Barbara never seemed to be able to make her mother proud.

Then she gave birth to Lucy.

Lucy was the shining light in everyone's eyes. She was Ellie's only grandchild, and as hard as it was for Barbara to take, Lucy was Ellie's doppelgänger. She looked and acted nothing like Barbara. It wasn't that Barbara minded that her mother and daughter were so close; it just saddened her that she couldn't be more like them, that the duo would never be a trio, and this only made her that much more cynical and disparaging.

A war raged inside Barbara's subconscious. It was *Maybe today will be the day my mother finally understands me* versus *Maybe this will be the day I finally don't give a shit anymore.* One side of her knew it was crazy to be fifty-five years old and still trying to please her mother. The other side couldn't stop.

"It's just another block," Barbara called out to Frida, who was a block behind her, panting.

Barbara stopped so that Frida could catch up to her.

"And I'll promise you this, that Ken the doorman has seen his last day at that building," Barbara continued the rant she'd begun earlier. "Who doesn't have another set of keys?"

"Well, we had all the keys," Frida tried to reason.

"Oh, please. What about the passkey?"

"Well, you *did* ask him that, and he *did* say that he could call a locksmith."

"Like I'm going to sit there all day and wait?" Barbara threw her hands in the air. "And wait where?"

Frida shrugged.

"No, you and I have a much more serious problem than being locked out without keys, a phone, money, or my car. My mother is missing."

"Maybe she showed up at home by now?" Frida hoped to get Barbara to change her mind.

"God knows where she could be by now," Barbara answered.

Just a block behind them, Ellie and Lucy were pushing the clothing rack across the street.

"Barbara, my feet are really starting to hurt from these sneakers," Frida said.

"When we get to the bakery you can sit down and take them

off for a bit," Barbara said, thinking to herself that maybe the bakery would give them a piece of cake for their troubles as well.

"Maybe they'll pity us and give us a piece of Danish," Frida added.

"Honestly, Frida, how you can think about food at a time like this is beyond me." She fumed as she rammed open the door to the bakery, causing it to bang against the adjacent wall, startling the ten or so people in line.

"Oh, crap, it's Mrs. Sustamorn," Flo, the woman behind the counter, muttered to her coworker as Frida and Barbara entered.

"This is an emergency," Barbara announced to the other people in line as she shoved her way in front of them.

"Mrs. Sustamorn, you're going to have to wait your turn," Flo told her flatly.

"Flo, I need to speak with you. My mother has gone missing."

"Oh, no!" Flo grabbed her chest. "With the party last night and all."

"Flo, this is very important. A young woman came in this morning and purchased three cakes. Do you remember her?"

Flo tried to remember.

"Flo?" Barbara couldn't wait.

"Yes, we did have a woman come in and buy three cakes."

"Did she say what she was doing with them?"

Flo paused. "No."

"Did she say where she was going with them?"

Flo looked at her coworker. "No."

"Did she pay cash?"

"Yes!" Flo got excited. "I remember, she paid cash! Does that help?"

"No, it doesn't." Barbara exhaled. "So that's all you can tell me?"

"I think a man flirted with her. What's the name of the guy who flirted with her, Sal? You remember? Look at his slip."

"Oh, Zach Pierson—that guy with the Internet site."

"Are you writing this down, Frida?" Barbara asked, looking over at Frida, who had taken off her shoes and made herself comfortable on the bench in front of the store window.

"With what?" Frida asked her.

"I'm sorry. My friend is very tired. We've had a rough morning, and we are both without cash. Is it possible for you to give her some sustenance?"

"Hi, Flo," Frida said and waved.

"Hi, Mrs. Freedberg." Flo reached into the display case and pulled out a danish. "Your usual?" she asked figuring maybe if she gave her a danish, Mrs. Freedberg would stop pilfering the Sweet'N Low all the time.

"That would be nice," Frida said, clearly pleased. "I'll pay you when I get my purse back. I only left it my apartment, and then, sadly, I left Barbara's purse in Mrs. Jerome's apartment. It's been a crazy day—"

"Frida, would you spare her the news?" Barbara interrupted.

"Can I get you anything, Mrs. Sustamorn?" Flo asked, hoping that maybe the next time she came in she wouldn't be such a complainer.

Barbara's mouth began to water. "A danish would be nice," she said. "I'll make sure you are compensated for it later."

Flo wrapped both danishes in a napkin and handed them to Barbara, thinking maybe now she wouldn't be so picky with the cakes anymore.

"Thank you, Flo." Barbara semi-smiled. "Well, I guess our business here is done. Frida, shall we?"

Frida, who had been massaging her feet, began to put her shoes back on.

"Let's go," Barbara called again, so Frida had no choice but to throw on her shoes without tying the laces. Maybe there would be a red light at a crosswalk, and she could bend down and tie them then.

Barbara shut the door to the Swiss Pastry Shop and urged Frida to walk a couple of storefronts away. "Do you think she was hiding something?" she asked Frida under her breath, as if Flo could still hear her.

"I can't imagine why she would." Frida rested her foot against a storefront and struggled to tie her shoe.

"No, I suppose not. I don't suppose that Flo from the Swiss Pastry Shop has anything to do with Mother's disappearance."

"Maybe Ellie ordered the cakes!" It suddenly dawned on Frida. She shot up from her bending position and turned to Barbara, who was opening her mouth to take the first bite of her danish. And as she turned to share this revelation, she knocked right into Barbara's hand, which made Barbara drop both danishes on the dirty sidewalk.

They looked down at the pastries. Both were thinking the same thing, *five-second rule,* but neither said a word.

"You know, Frida, sometimes I could just shoot you," Barbara said and sighed.

"Maybe Flo will give us another. We could ask if maybe the young girl mentioned if Ellie was the one buying the cakes."

"I'm never going back there again." Barbara pulled Frida away from the store front. "Come on. Let's go to Plage Tahiti and find out what they know about the receipt for that dress."

Tired and hungry, the ladies walked the next few blocks up Seventeenth Street slowly, with their heads down. Barbara picked up her head only when she noticed the sign for Plage Tahiti. She rang the bell. The blond lady inside pressed the buzzer, unlocking the door.

Entering the shop, Barbara looked longingly for a second at a cashmere sweater she wouldn't even be able to fit her left arm into. Frida was glad that she wearing her sweat suit—at least she didn't look so out of place in a fashionable store like this.

"Can I help you?" the blond woman asked.

"Hi, I'm Barbara Sustamorn, Lucy Jerome's mother, and this is our friend Frida Freedberg."

"I'm a dear friend of the family," Frida added. "Lucy even calls me Aunt Frida, we're so close."

"Enough, Frida," Barbara snapped. "Now, we're very tired and very hungry here. My mother seems to be missing. Frida and I searched her apartment and came across a receipt from a purchase at your store this morning."

"Oh, I've been so worried all day!" the blond lady exclaimed. "I had no idea the young woman this morning had stolen Mrs. Jerome's credit card. I was going to report the transaction, but I never heard the rest of the story."

"I knew it!" Barbara said, coming to life.

"I mean, she looked just like Lucy. She could have been a younger version of Mrs. Jerome. I see Mrs. Jerome in the park. She's a very attractive woman." She paused, taking a scrutinizing look at Barbara. "You're Lucy's mother? Mrs. Jerome's daughter?"

Although the saleswoman didn't mean it to come out that way, Barbara was still a little hurt. She pulled at her black sweater to cover up her protruding stomach and straightened her slacks.

"Yes, she is!" Frida backed Barbara up.

"Anyway, the girl this morning seemed lovely. I didn't think anything was up when she said that Lucy was her cousin. If you had seen this girl, you wouldn't have blamed me for thinking—"

"Spare us your apology," Barbara broke in. "Just give us the facts. We're very worried."

"To tell you the truth, now that I've thought about it a bit, I should have known from the way this young woman was dressed. Her jeans were two sizes too big, and"—she leaned in and whispered—"frankly, her underwear looked like nothing I've ever seen on a young woman like that."

"The jeans on the floor," Barbara gasped at Frida. "She must have been wearing all of Mother's clothing!"

"Even her underwear?" Frida wondered aloud, shuddering at the thought.

"That's it." Barbara threw her hands up in the air. "We're going to the police." She slammed her hand on the counter. "Thank you very much."

"Please let me know what happens," the blond woman begged. "I've been very worried. I feel as if I've done something wrong. Should I call and report the stolen credit card?"

"No, this isn't your fault, and yes, we should have my mother's cards frozen. But don't worry. You shouldn't feel bad. This young woman is just a con artist who has done something with my mother. We'll straighten it out."

"Will you please let me know?"

"We will," Barbara said. "We're off to the police now. By any chance, do you know where the nearest police station is?"

"It's on Twelfth Street, just five blocks down."

"Five blocks?" Frida said, quivering.

"Five blocks," the blond woman repeated.

"Thank you again," Barbara said as she shut the door to the store.

Fifteen minutes later, Barbara and Frida had gone only two blocks.

"It's only three more blocks, and I'm sure they'll have some coffee at the police station!" Barbara called to Frida, who was again half a block behind.

"Barbara, please. I'm not as young as I once was, and this sweat suit might have been too much to wear on such a warm day." She lowered her voice so as not to upset Barbara. "Would you mind just walking a little slower?"

"After this, we're getting you on a treadmill every day. If you have this much trouble walking a couple of blocks, I'm worried about you, Aunt Frida."

"Yes, Barbara," Frida consented. Barbara was really getting on Frida's last nerve, but the main thing was never to add to Barbara's hostility.

Frankly, Barbara was quite tired herself and didn't exercise as much as she told people she did. She would never admit it, though.

"When we get to the police station, I'm sure they'll have a nice seat for us, and a hot cup of coffee," Barbara reminded Frida.

"Let's hope," Frida said, unzipping her sweat jacket.

* * *

An hour later, two cops stood inside the precinct and watched as two women, one middle-aged and one elderly, walked feebly up the steps.

"Get a load of this," one said to the other.

"Lost suburbanites," the second one said and laughed under his breath.

"Can we help you ladies?" the first cop said.

"Yes, you can. We need to file a missing persons report," the plump middle-aged one with the gobs of jewelry and black attire announced.

"Officer Fairholm takes care of that," the second cop answered as he opened the door for them.

"Then that's who we'd like to speak to, pronto. Time is of the essence."

The cop pointed over to an attractive middle-aged female officer at a desk.

"What can I do for you ladies?" Officer Fairholm asked as they approached.

"In short, my mother is missing."

"Have you been to her home?" she asked.

"What do you think?" Barbara responded.

"When was the last time you spoke with her?" the officer asked as she wrote the information on a pad of paper.

"This morning!" Barbara answered, as if this had been ages ago. "We both did."

"Yes, I spoke to her as well," Frida confirmed.

"Was there anything suspicious in her home to make you think that she might have been kidnapped?" Officer Fairholm asked without any compassion.

"Yes! Some pants that she never wore were lying on the floor," Barbara cried out.

"And it's not possible that she might have just thrown them on the floor herself?"

"Oh, you don't know Ellie," Frida answered. "Ellie's clothes are very important to her. She would never just leave something lying on the floor. I'm the same way. We're both very neat."

"I'm sorry, and you are?" Officer Fairholm asked.

"I'm the missing person's best friend."

"So the only thing suspicious was a pair of pants left on the floor?"

"Trust me," Barbara said, "my mother never leaves anything on the floor."

"Anything else?" Officer Fairholm asked with growing skepticism.

"Yes! My daughter was there when Mrs. Freedberg went to check on my mother."

"She complained about a mouse," Frida added.

"No, she complained to me about the mouse. She just asked if you were feeling okay."

"Oh, that's right. My mistake."

"Look, she probably just went out somewhere. Chances are she's back by now," Officer Fairholm told them. "Why don't we try phoning her?"

"We know she's not there. That's why we came here," Barbara told her. "Look, what kind of a place are you running here? We know that my mother is missing, and we need you to find her."

"Yes, and if we could have a cup of coffee while we're waiting, that would be lovely," Frida said and Barbara shot her a livid look.

"Well, I'll tell you what. On your way out, please feel free to grab a cup of coffee in our break room. If your mother isn't back in twenty-four hours, I'll be happy to help you, but I'm sorry, there's nothing I can do about it until then."

"Nothing?" Barbara was seething.

"Nothing," the officer answered. "Let me just get your name, Miss . . ." Officer Fairholm started to write.

"It's Sustamorn, Barbara Sustamorn."

Officer Fairholm stopped writing and looked at Barbara. "Barbara Jerome?" she asked.

"That's right," Barbara said, eyeing the officer a little closer.

"Do you have any idea who you're talking to?" She smirked.

"I thinking I'm talking to someone who isn't going to help me one iota while God knows where my mother is," Barbara fumed.

"Close!" Officer Fairholm answered, as if this were a game they were playing. "It's Bea Lonagin, from Harriton High School."

"Barbara went to Harriton High School!" Frida said, excited.

"Oh," Barbara uttered. Memories of torturing Bea Lonagin flooded back. There were all the times she'd called the cutest boys in her class, saying she was Bea, and the many times she'd tripped Bea in the hallway, and that time Bea failed home economics because Barbara switched Bea's oven to broil during the corn cake final exam. Still, popular girls never liked Barbara.

"Yeah, hi, Barbara," Bea said, giving Barbara the once-over.

"Hello, Bea." Barbara smiled feebly.

"Do you ever see the old gang from high school? I'm still close with all of my friends."

"Sometimes," Barbara muttered. In truth, Barbara had no friends from high school, and she knew that Bea knew that. Bea looked like she was enjoying this little taste of revenge after all these years. Sadly, Barbara was not.

"Well, it's good to see you," Bea said through gritted teeth.

"You, too," Barbara gritted back.

"Now, like I said, of course I'd like to help such an old friend, and I remember your mother—nice lady—but rules are rules." Bea stood up.

"Oh, that's okay, then. I understand rules. We'll be back in twenty-four hours. So we'll see you then," Barbara said, taking Frida's arm.

"I hope it won't come to that." Bea grinned.

"Come on, Frida," Barbara said.

"What about the coffee?" Frida asked.

"We'll get some later," Barbara answered as Bea continued to stare her down.

They walked out of the police station.

"I'm surprised you didn't put up more of a fuss," Frida said, trying to keep up with Barbara as she rushed down the street.

"Shut up, Frida," Barbara answered, pained.

"Were you friendly with that woman?" Frida asked.

"No. She went to my high school, that's all."

"She really seemed to know you, though," Frida said, not getting it.

"Yeah, we went through school together, but I don't want to talk about it."

"You would have thought that an old friend like that would have helped us," Frida mused. "You'd think she would have just bent the rules a little for us."

"Yeah, you would have thought," Barbara answered as she kept walking.

"I think we should have at least taken the coffee she offered," Frida said, still trying to keep up.

"Yeah, well, we'll find some someplace else, okay?" Barbara was still in her own mind, thinking.

"Barbara, do you think you could just slow down a little bit?"

"Jesus, Frida! How are we going to find Mom if we walk so slowly?" Barbara barked.

"Well, where to now?" Frida said and threw her hands in the air. "Because I'm getting tired, and I'm out of ideas." Frida was starting to get perturbed, which was very un-Frida.

Barbara stopped. Frida was sure she was going to get it now, and that made her cower like a little girl. Frida had never raised her voice to Barbara, ever. Who could? Today, however, she could really take Barbara over the edge.

"Wait, where are we?" Barbara said, turning around and looking at the street.

Frida stopped and looked around, too. It was far more run-down than her neighborhood, and the street was noticeably dirtier than any block she normally walked down.

"Didn't you look at where we were walking?" Barbara asked Frida.

"I was trying to keep up with you!" Frida answered, getting agitated and, for the first time, not caring about upsetting Barbara. "Oh, wonderful, we're lost! That's it. That's all we needed." She panicked.

"How could we get so lost in just a couple of blocks?" Barbara asked her. "Frida, you've lived just beyond this neighborhood for over ten years. Don't you ever walk anywhere?"

"Do I look like I ever walk anywhere?" Frida angrily placed her hands on her bulging thighs. She turned in a full circle, trying to find something that looked familiar.

"Even so! In all this time you've never looked out the window when you were riding by?"

"I'm too busy watching my bag when I'm riding the bus. You wouldn't know about a thing like that, living in the suburbs. And by the way, if you're so smart, and you've lived here all your life, how come you don't know where we are?"

"You just said it. I don't *live* downtown." She stuffily raised her head and straightened her gold chains. "I live on the Main Line."

"Well, maybe you need to get out a little more," Frida said angrily.

"*I* need to get out more?" Barbara shrieked. "That's a crock!"

"Maybe if you didn't walk so fast I could have watched where I was going. I told you to slow down, Barbara!"

"I walk too fast?" Barbara shot back. "Frida, you're so slow we probably missed Mom ten times today."

That was it for Frida. *Get on Barbara's worst side. Make Barbara infuriated. Get on Barbara's last nerve. Make. Barbara. Mad.*

"*Look, you!*" Frida yelled, pointing in Barbara's face. "I've had just about enough of you! I've had fifty-five years' worth of your hemming and hawing and complaining, and I'm not going to take it anymore! Your mother is probably back home right now having a cup of tea and a cookie, which is where I should be! I've had it with you, Barbara. I'm done with this. I'm going home!"

"*Me? What about you?*" Barbara shouted back. "Your whole life you've been nothing but this fragile little shell who is too afraid to complain about anything. You're such a miser. God, Frida, I wouldn't be surprised if you had five million dollars in the bank!"

It's only two million, Frida thought to herself. "Well, *guess what?*" she yelled back. "I'm not going to be that person anymore. From now on I'm going to start saying it how I think it should be, and I'm going to start with you. Barbara, whatever has been bugging you your whole life, *get over it!*"

"*You better believe I'm over it!*" Barbara shouted.

"Fine!" Frida countered.

"Fine!" Barbara ended it.

That's when Barbara felt the jab in her back.

"Give me your jewelry," she heard a voice say.

Frida froze. She stared at the man who had come up behind Barbara. There was something in his eyes that told her immediately he had had a bad childhood and was not to be trifled with.

"Excuse me?" Barbara answered calmly, as if she had merely misunderstood the instructions. She had never felt a gun in her back before, but it was safe to assume this is what it felt like.

"Give me your jewelry," the deep voice repeated.

"Give the man the jewelry!" Frida rasped, shaking.

Barbara began to take off her gold chains. She handed them to the person she couldn't see.

"And the rings," he muttered.

"The rings, Barbara, give the man your rings!" Frida gasped. Frida had watched an episode of *Oprah* where the guest expert advised viewers to just give a mugger whatever he wanted. Don't put up a fight. Life is too precious. "Do you want my ring, too?" Frida offered as she began to pull it off.

The man cast a look at her tarnished ring with its cloudy stone.

"Just this fat lady's rings," he said, continuing to hold the gun in the small of Barbara's back. Barbara's heart broke a little. Why did the subject of her weight always have to work itself into every situation? Why couldn't he have said "Just this younger lady's rings"?

"*Give him the rings!*" Frida shouted this time.

"My hands seem to be a little swollen from the hot day," Barbara nervously explained.

Frida grabbed Barbara's hand and, with all her might, pulled the five-carat diamond ring off her finger and handed it to the assailant.

As quickly as it had appeared, Barbara felt the pressure of the gun disappear from her back. She heard the thug run off in the opposite direction. Frida and Barbara grabbed each other, relieved to be alive. When they saw their attacker turn the corner and disappear, Barbara peeled Frida off herself. Her eyes narrowed.

"*Give him the rings?*" Barbara roared at Frida.

"What the heck did you want me to say?" Frida said as she wiped her brow. "He looked dangerous. And he had his finger pointed in your back!"

"His what?"

"His finger. Why, what did you think it was?"

"*I thought it was a gun!*" Barbara hollered.

"Oh, God forbid it was a gun," Frida said.

"*Frida!* A man demands my jewelry in broad daylight, he's got no gun, and you just help him take my things? What, are you working with him?"

"Barbara, he could have killed us!"

"How? By poking us to death?"

"Don't you dare blame me!" Frida was coming to a boil. "I almost lost my ring here, too. I'm hungry and I need something to eat! I'm going back to the police station to get a ride home! I told you, *I'm through with your shenanigans!*"

"WE'RE NOT GOING BACK THERE!" Barbara yelled as she watched Frida walk away.

"*Just watch me!*" Frida replied. "I don't care what you did to that police officer when you were young. I'm going back!"

Barbara watched Frida as she walked down the street, took off her pink sweat jacket, and threw it over her shoulder.

Just look at the trouble she'd caused. Her mother had probably gone to get her hair done, gone shopping, or done something else that day. So what if her mother didn't want to spend the day with her? Why did she always have to control everyone? Why couldn't she just let things be? When would she just stop and let her mother live her life? When would she finally begin to live her own life?

"Frida!" Barbara called out. Frida stopped and turned around, and Barbara yelled, "Hold on. I'm coming with you!"

the point of no return

A moment comes in everyone's life when they realize they're old. I'm not talking about the day you see your first gray hair or the day you see the hint of a crow's foot. What I'm talking about is the day when you realize you've grown out of being able to adapt to something new.

It's the kind of thing that creeps up on you. Take music, for example. One day you're listening to the latest tune that comes on the radio, and then the next day you can't relate. It's too loud. You can't keep the beat. You say to the person next to you, "That's singing?" So you start listening to music that you know, and you stop listening to the new stuff. Pretty soon your kids are talking about bands you've never heard of, bands you never knew existed. You should have seen the look on Lucy's face when I told her I'd seen that Bono on television and that I never heard of the band U2.

"That's old-school," she said.

"It's what?" I asked her.

"It's not a new band."

And it's not just music I'm talking about. That's just an example. Look at these phrases the kids are saying today. I never even heard of this phrase *old-school* until Lucy said it. Where does that derive from? Does it mean that it's something dating back to when the person went to school, or is the word *school* abstract, as in the particular school of thought? I don't know—you tell me. This is just what I'm saying, though. Do you see where I'm going with this?

One day you realize that you've had the same hairstyle for the past fifteen years. It's not something you've thought about. It's just what looks good on you, so you keep getting it cut that way rather than trying something new. I almost had a heart attack when Lancôme stopped making my favorite lipstick. I was on the phone with Lancôme for three hours, with four different operators, trying to get to the bottom of why they discontinued my color, when the last person finally said, "No one wears that color anymore, ma'am."

"I do!" I said.

That wasn't even the thing that made me realize I was officially old. The thing with the lipstick happened long after the revelation, but it's just another example.

Milestones in your child's life should also make you feel older but, truthfully, that didn't happen to me. I was always the youngest mother in Barbara's school. I was always the prettiest one, too, but that was my own observation. Whenever I went to any of Howard's class reunions, I was always the youngest bride. Of course the last year we went, for his fortieth reunion, Howard's old friend Jerry Young (no pun intended) brought his new girlfriend, who could have been his daughter's daughter. She didn't make me feel old, though, she just looked ridiculous being with such an old man.

The latest music and the latest catchphrases didn't bother me, either. When my hairdresser started using a different dye on my hair to cover up the gray, even that really didn't get me.

What finally did it, what finally made me know that I was old, was when I realized I couldn't wear a miniskirt. It wasn't that it didn't look good on me, it was that it wasn't appropriate for my age. I swear to you, I still shudder when I think of it.

In the early 1970s, Howard and I were invited to a Christmas party, and I wanted to get something special, as I was always wont to do. I went downtown to Nan Duskin, an upscale department store in Philadelphia that closed in the mid-1990s. I bought most of my dresses and suits there. These days you can't find anything close to the fabulous collection of designers they had. I'm still mourning the loss. At that point, though, Nan Duskin was in its glory days, and all the saleswomen knew me by name.

I was looking for something to wear to the party and Barbara was getting something for a formal she was invited to. I'll never forget the dress I picked out for myself. It was a gorgeous gold George Small minidress with an eyelet lace overlay. How I loved that dress. Meanwhile, poor Barbara didn't have very good luck. It took three saleswomen to zip up the only long dress that would fit her, but the George Small mini fit me perfectly.

A few days later Howard and I were heading out to the party and I put the dress on. I thought I looked like something out of a magazine. My hair was just right, my makeup done just so. It started out to be a night like any other.

And then we got to the party.

All the other ladies there had on longer dresses—garden

dresses is what we called them, but the girls call them maxi dresses now, though today they're more acceptable for the younger set. I was the only one in a mini. No one had to say a word to me—I knew. At forty, I was dressed like a teenager. That was the first time I ever felt embarrassed by what I was wearing. I wasn't dressed appropriately for my age. I thought I heard a few whispers here and there, but that could have been my own paranoia. I don't think so, though. Frida set me straight when I asked her about it later.

"Well," she said gently, "maybe it's something for one of Barbara's friends."

My days of miniskirts were over. I never wore that dress again.

That was when I knew there was no turning back. I was officially older.

Until today, of course.

"Oh, Lucy." I stopped her as we approached her studio. "I have to run to the bank before it closes."

"What do you need money for?" she asked me.

"For tonight." I smiled, batting my eyes. "A girl always needs to bring some cash, just in case. In my day it used to be a dime so you could call your father to come get you if the boy started any funny business. Today, though, I guess you need a lot more than that."

"So we'll just head to the ATM on our way over."

"Oh, I don't go to those," I told her.

"What?" She looked perplexed.

"The ATMs. I don't trust that sort of thing. I like my girl at the bank. She knows me."

"Well, I don't think she's going to know you today," Lucy reminded me.

"Oh, that's right. How can I get money?" I was suddenly so worried.

"I'll give you money, Gram. Don't worry about it."

"No, you know what? I've got some cash stashed away in my lingerie drawer. Let's drop by and pick that up. I don't want you to be low on cash."

So we dropped off Lucy's dresses at her studio and grabbed our outfits for the night.

"We forgot the bras and underwear!" I suddenly remembered.

"I have some here," Lucy said, going into a drawer. "I always keep some here, just in case."

"Just in case what?" I said and winked.

"Just in case I have a model who needs underwear better suited for what she's wearing. Jeez, Gram, can you get ahold of your hormones? I'm really hating that."

"Sorry," I said, a little embarrassed. "I'm not used to having all this estrogen."

We grabbed the lingerie and walked back to my apartment.

Now, I could see Ken's face from a block away (how I loved not having to wear glasses!) and it looked a bit ashen. I didn't say anything to Lucy, but I knew something had to be up.

"Lucy," Ken called out.

"Hey, Ken," Lucy called back.

"You know, your mom and Mrs. Freedberg are out looking for you both. They seemed pretty worried."

"Your mother just can't leave me be for two seconds, can she?" I said, turning to Lucy.

"Hold on." She stopped me. "Ken, do you know where they went?"

"All I know is that both Mrs. Freedberg and your mother locked themselves out of both apartments, with no keys, so they went looking for you." Then he turned to me. "By the way, I got in a lot of trouble because of you. You said you were Mrs. Jerome's other granddaughter."

"I am," I answered in a way that made it quite obvious I wasn't.

"You think I was born yesterday?" he asked me.

"Ken, this is very important," Lucy broke in. "Do you know where my mom and Mrs. Freedberg went?"

"They didn't say. Your mom was in a big huff, and she dragged Mrs. F. with her."

"Oh, for Christ's sake. Let's go up and see if they left a note or something." I motioned to Lucy and grabbed my keys out of my bag. "I'll take it from here. Thanks, Ken," I said as we walked to the elevator and pushed the up button.

"But who are you?" Ken asked. "What do I tell them if they come back?"

"Tell them that you saw Mrs. Jerome, and that she's out looking for them, too," I said as the elevator door opened.

"But where is Mrs. Jerome?" he asked.

"She's out looking for them," Lucy and I answered at the same time as the elevator door shut.

My heart sank when I walked into the apartment. Sitting

right on my table in front of the Paris mirror was Barbara's bag. Frida's blood sugar must have dropped, because there was also a pack of my cheese and crackers. You don't even want to know what goes on when Frida's blood sugar drops. The woman turns into a crazy person. If she was anywhere with Barbara right now, Barbara was probably seeing a side of Frida she never knew existed.

"Oh, I feel awful," I said, taking a look in Barbara's bag. "Her keys are in here. Her cell phone. Where could they be? Do you think we should just call the guys and cancel?"

"I should at least," Lucy answered, grabbing her cell phone.

"Well, then, I should, too. Let's call it a day."

"Why should you cancel?" she asked me. "How are you going to explain yourself?"

"I'll tell them the truth. I'll tell them that I woke up and I was twenty-nine years old. I'll prove it to them the way I proved it to you."

"Gram, you're not going to do that. You're going to go on the date."

I took a seat on my sofa. I noticed that Barbara had taken the cakes off the table and thought she had probably thrown them out. No doubt she took a little piece before she did, but that was neither here nor there.

"Lucy, enough is enough. It's obvious I can't do any of that now. Your mother is probably at the police station filling out a missing persons report. Knowing her, soon she'll have the entire Philadelphia police force looking for me."

Lucy stood in front of me, seemingly deep in thought.

"No. I will handle Mom. You are going on your date."

"I can't do it," I said and put my head in my hands.

"You'll do it, just like we said you would, and I'm going with you. This is your day, not Mom's, and tomorrow you can deal with her."

"But your mother—"

"Should grow up already," Lucy insisted. "And Gram, you need to take a stand and stop treating her like a child. She is a middle-aged woman. It's about time she started acting her age."

"You know I hate that phrase."

"Gram, it's true."

"You don't understand, though. No matter how old your child gets, she's still your child."

And then Lucy walked over and joined me in the chair. "Not today, Gram. Not today."

My head was swimming. My child. Frida. Me. What was I going to do? How would I explain this to Barbara and Frida, anyway? They would never get it like Lucy did. It goes back to what I was saying before: there comes a point in a person's life when they stop accepting new ideas. Lucy wasn't at that point yet. Frida and Barbara, however, were. They would never accept the fact that I was twenty-nine years old.

Maybe Lucy was right, maybe there *does* come a point where the parent has to stop caring for their child's every feeling. There comes a time where you just have to stop and say, "My days of teaching and worrying are over. It's time for you to stop relying on me to take care of you. It's now up to you to start living your own life. I can't give you the answers anymore." *Was* Lucy right? As a smart as she was, Lucy didn't know what it meant to be a mother. From the moment they put that child into your arms, you deal with this quandary. How much do you give? How much *can* you give, when your heart keeps telling you to mother your child, no matter how old she is, but your head tells you something different?

And then I went back to the other side of the argument. *Today, I'm Lucy. I'm not seventy-five-year-old Ellie. Today I'm selfish.* No matter what my heart told me, if I was going to live as a twenty-nine-year-old woman, even for one day, I should start thinking like one, too. Or at least try to. So today would be my day to be selfish, to remember who I am outside of being a mother. Tomorrow there would be a whole lot of change.

"What are you thinking?" Lucy asked me.

"I'm thinking that I'm going to do what you said. I'm going to continue with my day. I'm going to go into my closet and pull out my makeup and spruce myself up for tonight. I've got a date."

"But I still think that I should look for Mom and Aunt Frida."

"Lucy, what was it that we said in the beginning?"

"It's your day."

"That's right. It's my day, and I want to spend it with you, okay? End of story. Change subject."

Lucy went silent. Now she was the one thinking.

"Tomorrow, Lucy," I said. "Tomorrow."

"But . . ." she started.

"And that's the last time we're going to discuss it today. Let your mother deal with her own problems." I took her hand. "Now, let's continue with *my* day. We don't have that much time left."

Truthfully, despite the things I said, I don't know how much of that I really believed, but I had to try. If I was going to look the part, I was going to try to act the part, too.

Lucy took my hand and we went to my closet.

I put on Lucy's underwear and bra and slipped into the black dress and took a look at myself in the mirror.

"I think I'm going to hem it just a bit," Lucy said, taking a look. "It will make the dress look less sophisticated and more playful."

"Yes!" I exclaimed. "Hem it a little shorter! I want to show off these young legs."

Lucy went to pull out my sewing machine. She was the only one who ever used it anyway. The thing must have been thirty years old. It's a good thing I had it.

After we picked out a nice three-inch heel (I wanted to wear my old four-inch platforms from the seventies, but Lucy protested), Lucy pinned the hem. I was about to put on my robe to walk into the other room, then I decided against it. I left Lucy in the closet to sew and walked through my apartment in the bra and underwear, taking a look at myself in the Paris mirror as I walked by, and headed into the kitchen to make a little something to tide me over.

"Gram," Lucy called from the closet, "maybe after today you could start coming with me to buyers—you know, as kind of an agent."

"I'd love to!" I called out, feeling flattered.

I took the cold chicken out of the fridge and cut it up and grabbed some bread. A nice chicken sandwich would be just the thing, I thought. I put the food on a tray with two glasses of iced tea and walked back to the closet, taking a look at myself once again as I passed by the Paris mirror.

"A little something to tide us over so we don't eat like savages tonight," I announced.

"We're going out for dinner," Lucy said, thinking she was reminding me.

"Oh, I know, but who eats on dates?"

"I eat on dates," Lucy said and laughed.

"A lady should never show a large appetite on a date."

"Why not?" she asked.

"It's not proper," I told her.

"But why?" she asked.

I thought about it. "You know what?" I smiled. "I have no idea."

I put the chicken back in the fridge, took out a bottle of Champagne, and grabbed two glasses. I always keep a bottle in the fridge; you never know when an occasion might arise. Lucy couldn't fault me for that.

I went back into the closet.

"Now you're talking," Lucy said, laughing, as she finished the hem.

"Just a little something for our nerves," I said.

"And of course to celebrate."

I popped the cork, poured the Champagne into the glasses, and handed one to Lucy.

"What should we toast?" I asked her as I stood stripped nearly down to my twenty-ninth birthday suit.

"To us?" she asked.

"To us, and to youth!" I toasted.

We clinked our glasses and took a sip.

"Okay, try this on for me," she said, unzipping the dress and handing it to me.

"Do you think I need stockings?" I asked her, heading toward my lingerie drawer.

"No, Gram, you don't need stockings." She balked as if I were talking nonsense.

"Of course I don't." I smiled. "I've always envied that you never wear stockings. I'll never get used to this day."

I slipped into the dress and Lucy zipped me up. I put on the black heels.

"Stunning," Lucy whispered.

"Now you," I urged her.

Lucy got out of her clothes and put on her dress, a red halter. Hers, however, hung to her knees.

"What do you think?" she asked.

"Stunning." I smiled back at her, taking her hands in mine.

"I need to take a picture of this," Lucy said, running out of the closet.

"Yes!" I shouted, then stopped. "Do you think that I can even be photographed?"

"What do you mean?" she asked, coming back in with her bag and taking out her cell phone.

"Well, I'm not real today," I told her.

"Oh, you're real." She laughed. "Besides, only vampires can't be photographed."

"Where's the camera?" I asked her.

"In the phone," she said.

"The phone has a speaker *and* a camera?" I asked.

"Yes, Gram." She sounded a little agitated.

"Well, I didn't know," I said.

"Well, if you're going to start working with me, you're going to have to get one of these newfangled cell phones."

"There's so much I have to learn," I said, nodding.

"Just when you think you know it all."

"So true," I said.

Lucy stood next to me and pointed the camera at our faces.

"Maybe we can get the guys to take a picture of us later," she said.

"That's a good idea, but let's get this one now so we'll have it."

We put our arms around each other and stuck our heads together.

"Now give me a big smile, Lucy. You never show your teeth in pictures."

"I have a look I like when I take pictures," she said.

"Yes, and it's boring. I want one picture with a full smile."

"No," she said adamantly.

I grabbed her side and proceeded to tickle her. A grandmother always knows the tickle spots.

Lucy howled with laughter. Her laughter made me laugh.

That's when she snapped the picture.

"I hate it!" she said, taking a look. "Let's take another one."

"No," I said. "I love it! Can you make a copy of it? Does the phone come with a printer?"

"No, it doesn't." She smiled at my naivete.

"Just when you thought all the technology was past you."

And with that, we went into the living room to finish the rest of our champagne.

"Where do you think they are now?" Lucy asked.

"Who knows?" I shrugged. "We'll take Frida's keys and Barbara's bag down to Ken. He'll return them when they come back here."

"You think they'll come back?"

"If I know your mother, she'll want to move in with me after this."

"Boy, I'm not looking forward to the time when we see them again."

"You and me both."

This made us laugh. Again.

I looked down at my watch.

"It's almost seven," I told Lucy.

"We better leave. We don't want to be late."

"Oh, they'll wait. If there's one thing I know, it's that it's good to keep them waiting."

"Is that what you used to do with Grandpop?" she asked.

"The poor man wasted half his life waiting for me. He was happy in the end, though."

"Do you still miss Grandpop?" she asked me.

I took a deep breath.

"All the time," I told her.

"What do you miss the most?" she asked me.

I thought about it. "I miss moments like this. I miss the look on his face when he'd see me come downstairs all dolled up."

"If I ever get married, I hope I have the relationship that you and Grandpop had."

"What makes you say that?" I asked her, feeling a little shocked.

"He really loved you. I always loved the way he talked about you when you weren't around."

"What did he say?" I asked, genuinely curious.

"Whenever we were out together, like if we were having lunch, he'd say, 'I'm going to order a dessert to bring home to your grandmother.' Or other little things, like when I'd go to change the radio station in the car and he'd say, 'Don't ruin the buttons. They're the stations that Grandmom likes.' And when he always said how pretty he thought you were: 'Grandmom is the prettiest lady in the world.'"

"Well, I tried, you know, for him." I said, not knowing what else to say. You must understand—Lucy would have never understood if I told her how I really felt about Howard.

"I don't think you ever had to try for him," she said. "I think he meant how beautiful you were on the inside, too."

"No, he never felt that way," I said.

"You think he never noticed how wonderful you were? Don't tell me you went through your whole life without noticing how in love with you he was."

Thoughts of Howard started pouring through my head. Not big things, either. Just little things like Lucy was mentioning, like the way Howard got up and made me fresh-squeezed orange juice every morning, and put the coffee on. He never made a bed or changed a diaper, but he always made sure I took my vitamins in the morning. He was always worried about that. He always opened the car door for me, always. He was always worried that I wouldn't be warm enough in what I was wearing (I never was), and he always had a shawl of mine in the back of his car. At night when we went to bed, Howard always got my sleep mask for me.

I could never sleep without my mask. But no, I wouldn't think of those things tonight. I wouldn't think of the good things. I would think of the things I really thought, of Howard as he really was, how I really knew him. I wasn't about to start feeling guilty now. After all, when Howard was having his affairs, did he feel guilty?

"Darn you," I scolded her.

"What?" She laughed.

I started to tear up.

"I'm sorry," she said, putting her arm around me.

"Nothing in life is perfect," I said, brushing her off. "Except for tonight. Tonight is going to be perfect."

"Well, let's hope." She smiled.

"Lesson number four thousand and one. This one is very important, so really take note."

"I'm listening," she replied.

"Never give up on wanting to learn new things."

"Like what?" she asked.

"Whatever it is, never get set in your ways. Always try new things, even if you don't want to."

"Okay, I won't forget to learn new things."

"Even if you don't want to."

"It's a deal."

I looked for my bag and headed over to the Paris mirror.

"Okay, how do we look?"

"We're gorgeous," Lucy said, taking my hand and standing in front of the mirror.

I patted my hair down a little.

"Are you ready for the night of your life?" she asked me.

adena halpern

"I grabbed the cash out of my lingerie drawer, right?" I said, looking in my purse.

"Yes, I saw you do it," she said as I saw the cash. "Now, are you ready?" she asked again.

"Bring it on!" I cheered.

"Where did you learn that phrase?" she asked.

"I'm old, I'm not oblivious," I told her.

Lucy opened the door and we walked out.

"Wait," I said, taking her arm.

"What?"

"What's the name of the boy I'm going out with tonight?"

"Zach," she reminded me.

"Zachary." I smiled.

B ut you were only a block and a half from here. How could you get lost?" Officer Bea Fairholm laughed, dumbfounded.

"I never come to this neighborhood," Frida said and shrugged.

"It's four blocks away from where you live!" Bea laughed again.

"Look, Bea, we know we were stupid. It's been a crazy day, what with my mother going missing, and then both Frida and me without keys or money or phones or our purses."

"We're really up a tree here," Frida whined. "Do you think we could just fill out the robbery report and then maybe a police car could take us back to my building? I'll have my doorman call a locksmith."

Bea looked at Barbara. Barbara had been pathetic in high school, and she was even more pathetic today.

"You say that the man who stole your jewelry ran south?" she asked.

"Yes," Barbara answered.

"Okay," Bea said, "let's fill out the papers and then we'll have a squad car drive you up."

"Thank you," Frida said and sighed. "And do you think I could get some coffee?"

"Oh, darn, the coffee urn is on the fritz," Bea answered. "It happened right after you left."

Frida took a seat in Bea's desk chair. She could have fallen asleep right there.

"Thank you for being so kind," Barbara told Bea.

"I think you have a pretty good idea that I wouldn't be so kind if it wasn't my job."

Barbara looked at her, unable to say anything. "I do," she finally uttered, softly.

"Like I said before, I am sorry to hear about your mother. If she's still missing tomorrow, come back and we'll begin a search."

"Yes. Thanks, Bea," Barbara said.

By the time Barbara finished the robbery paperwork, Frida was snoring. Bea called over a couple of police officers and instructed them to take Barbara and Frida wherever they needed to go.

"Aunt Frida," Barbara said as she shook her awake.

"I can't move another muscle," Frida responded in full voice, her eyes still closed.

"We're going home now," Barbara told her, and Frida grudgingly opened her eyes. The police officers lifted Frida under her arms and she groaned.

"You two really must have put yourselves out today," Bea said to Barbara.

"She walked a total of nine blocks," Barbara answered.

"Hopefully your mom will have come back and you won't

have to come in tomorrow. That's usually the way these things go," Bea told her.

"Let's just hope," Barbara answered. "And Bea?" she added.

"Yes?"

Barbara didn't know how to say it. How does a person even begin to apologize for something they did more than thirty years ago?

"I hope life has been good to you," Barbara told her. "I really do."

"It has, thank you." Bea smiled, a hint of surprise in her eyes.

The police officers continued to practically carry Frida as they left the station and headed to a squad car. It had started to rain. Barbara put her hand over her head, but Frida couldn't have cared less at that point and let the rain fall on her face.

"Where to, ladies?" one policeman asked as they climbed into the car.

"Home," Frida muttered.

"Just a couple of blocks from here, on Rittenhouse Square," Barbara told them. Then, "No, wait!" Barbara shouted, startling Frida. "Take us to Twelfth and Walnut!"

"For what?" Frida opened her eyes.

"Johnny! Johnny will know where Lucy is. It's our last chance."

"Oh, no, I'm done. Drop me off at Rittenhouse Square," Frida instructed them.

"Don't tell me you're giving up on Mom!" Barbara said to her.

"This is going to be the death of me!" Frida answered. "I can't go another minute."

"After all this?" Barbara countered. "Have you forgotten why we're out here? You're going!"

Frida had no energy left to fight. "Okay," she said. "For Ellie. I'll go to Johnny's restaurant, and then I'm going home."

"Twelfth and Walnut," Barbara instructed again, as if she were in a taxi rather than a police car.

It was pouring by the time they got to the restaurant. In the time it took Frida and Barbara to get from the squad car to the front door, they were drenched.

The restaurant was pretty crowded when the two sopping women entered. Frida immediately eyed the pasta on a nearby table.

"I'd give them five dollars for one spoonful," Frida said to no one in particular.

Just then, Johnny noticed the duo.

"Mrs. Sustamorn," Johnny said, visibly surprised by her be-draggled appearance. "I'm just about to leave to meet Lucy and her cousin."

Frida snapped awake. Barbara's eyes widened.

"We're coming with you!" Barbara told him.

"Um, are you sure you don't just want to call her?" he asked.

"No," Barbara answered, seething. "We need to find Lucy's grandmother. We've been unable to speak to Lucy all day."

"And that cousin is no cousin," Frida interjected.

"Well, okay," Johnny answered, unable to make sense of a word they were saying. If it was going to be easier to clear this up by bringing them along and then going on with their night, so be it. "I'm just meeting her a couple of blocks from here for a drink, and then we're going to a restaurant."

"More walking," Frida said and sighed.

the jig is up

The bar was dark and packed and the music, which Frida figured must have been punk rock (it was Maroon 5), was blaring. A Phillies baseball game was playing on the television in the back of the bar. Frida, who always prided herself on having an excellent sense of smell, immediately recognized the aroma of beer flowing from the tap. It made her think of mussels steaming in a bowl of spicy garlic and tomato gravy. The only time Frida ever had a glass of beer was when she ate mussels. She wondered if this place served mussels. As she followed Barbara through the bar, she envisioned a long, crusty piece of Italian bread that she could dip into the spicy garlic and tomato gravy.

"Here's a table for us," Johnny shouted to Barbara and Frida as they both took a seat. "Can I get you ladies something?"

"Do they serve mussels?" Frida asked him.

"Of all things, she wants mussels," Barbara said, giving her a strange look. "Thank you, Johnny, but we're not staying long. We've got dinner waiting for us at home." Barbara told him.

"Sure, okay. I'll just get something for myself, then." He smiled and walked over to the bar.

Barbara turned in Frida's direction. "If that boy gets us anything, he'll think he's part of the family. I'll be paying for that bottle of beer for the rest of my life."

"What?" Frida shouted over the music. "I think I saw someone eating a sandwich when we first walked in."

"*I-told-him-we'll-eat-at-home.*" Barbara enunciated, looking at her watch.

Both Barbara and Frida sat with their arms crossed, hoping that Johnny would come back soon.

"Excuse me, is someone using this chair?" asked a woman in a white tank top as she started to pull it away.

"Yes!" Barbara pulled the chair back angrily. "All of these chairs are taken."

"You don't have to scream at me, I was just asking," the young woman answered.

"What?" Frida shouted to the woman, having missed Barbara's comment amid the din of the music.

The young woman looked Frida up and down and laughed at her as she walked away.

Frida had once seen an episode of *Dr. Phil* in which he said that if you're in a situation you don't want to be in, you should just take your mind out of it. Frida pictured the ice-cream shop she and Ellie went to as teenagers. Frida would always order a burger and fries accompanied by a chocolate milkshake, because then, of course, cholesterol and calorie counts were unknown concerns. The boy who ended up being Frida's husband, Sol, had an after-school job as the busboy. She knew he fancied her when he slipped her a cherry Coke one day. A smile crossed Frida's weary face as she remembered dancing a jitterbug during Sol's break. Then Frida felt something cold drench her already wet hair. She leapt up and turned around.

"Sorry," a young man in a ripped T-shirt called out as he scooted behind her with two glasses of beer in his hands. Frida felt the back of her head. Her hair was sticky and matted.

"Watch where you're going!" Barbara shouted at the boy.

"Hey, I said I was sorry!" he shouted back as his tablemates snickered.

"Mrs. Sustamorn, this is my friend Zach," Johnny announced, coming back to the table.

"You're Lucy's mom?" Zach asked.

"I am. And this is our friend Frida," Barbara introduced her, but Frida was still trying to comb the beer out of her hair with her fingers.

"They're waiting for Lucy," Johnny told Zach as they sat down.

"We're meeting your niece here, too. Nice girl," Zach said as he took a sip of his beer.

"Oh, she's not . . ." Frida started. "Oh, forget it." She sighed and went back to work on her hair.

"Can I get you anything to drink?" Zach said, leaning into Frida.

"Yes, I'd love a nice—" she started to say.

Barbara interrupted and shouted. "*There they are!*"

Frida watched Ellie and Lucy laugh while trying to get through the crowd. Like the Red Sea parted by Moses, men formed a path on either side of the two beautiful young women, something the girls didn't even notice.

"*Lucy Sustamorn!*" Barbara shouted as she stood up.

But Lucy couldn't hear her through the crowd.

"*Lucy! Yoo-hoo!*" Frida shouted, but the young women still couldn't hear them. A man had stopped Lucy's friend and was asking her something. She could see the friend shaking her head no as Lucy grabbed her hand and proceeded to walk through the crowd.

"Yo, Luce!" Johnny shouted, but Lucy was bending down to say hello to a bunch of people sitting at a table in the front. She was introducing her cousin to the table. The cousin nodded to each person.

"I'll go get them," Zach offered.

As the song playing over the speaker system ended, Barbara snagged the opportunity, yelling, "*Lucy Sustamorn! You get over here right now!*"

The entire bar suddenly fell silent. Lucy and Ellie looked to the back of the room, where Barbara, Frida, Johnny, and Zach stood.

Barbara began to shove her way through the crowd.

"Make a break for it!" Lucy cried, pushing Ellie toward the door.

It was a moment I had dreamed of for so many years, walking into that bar with Lucy in my short little black dress. The bar was alive with young people, all in their twenties, some still dressed up from work. A lot of the men had taken off their ties and unbuttoned the top buttons of their shirts. Some of the women were in little shift dresses. They had taken their hair down. The rest of the younger people were in jeans and T-shirts.

Lucy seemed to know everyone in that bar. Even with my newly restored hearing, I couldn't make out a word she was saying to anyone, so I just nodded, a smile plastered on my face. The bar was packed with more people than I'm sure the fire code allowed. All of these young men made way for us as we passed by, like Moses and the Red Sea. I couldn't believe it!

"Hello, beautiful!" a young man said to me as I walked by. I smiled as I nodded to him.

"The music is so loud," I shouted to Lucy, and she laughed.

"Lucy!" a table of men called out and she bent down to give one of them a peck on the cheek.

"This is my cousin!" she said, pointing to me. At least I think that's what she said. I just nodded and smiled again. You would not believe how loud the music was. But I didn't really care.

Those few moments, walking through that bar—that was what I needed. I felt so young, so full of energy. I felt more beautiful then than I had the entire day.

And then I heard the last voice in the world I wanted to hear.

"Lucy Sustamorn! You get over here right now!" the voice came booming across the bar.

We both looked in the direction of the voice. Practically the entire bar looked in the direction of the voice.

Standing in the back of the bar were Barbara and Frida, looking as if they'd been dragged behind a city bus for several miles. They were wet and disheveled. Frida looked like she was close to collapsing.

"Make a break for it!" Lucy said as she pushed me toward the door.

Now, believe me, I've seen Barbara angry. You don't want to get on my child's bad side. I've seen fury come out of her that no rational person should have. Barbara's wrath could scare the bejesus out of the strongest man.

I thought about running out of the place. What could I have said to her? How would I explain the situation?

But then I saw Zachary.

That boy was so handsome, smiling at me as he stood there next to the two drowned rats. And what was with Frida's hair?

I had two options: make a break for it, as Lucy proposed, or stand up and face the situation.

Barbara continued to shout, and Frida looked like she wanted to cry.

"Mom, Aunt Frida, let me explain," Lucy said as she walked toward them.

Frida looked straight into Lucy's eyes. "Where is your grandmother? We have been looking for her all day!"

"Do you see how upset your Aunt Frida is?" Barbara said. "Look at her!"

"She's a wreck," I said, dumbfounded. I've seen Frida overreact about things, but this level of hysteria was something I'd never seen before.

"And who the hell are you?" Frida asked me. "Why are you using Ellie's credit card all over town?"

"Jesus, Frida! It's because I am—"

"Hold it!" Lucy stopped me. "Let's take this outside, where we can hear one another."

"Is everything all right here?" Zachary asked, unsure as to just what was going on.

"Luce, what the hell is this?" Johnny asked.

"I think tonight is over," Lucy said to Johnny. "I have to go and talk to my mom and my aunt."

"Do you have to go, too?" Zachary asked, taking my hand.

I didn't know what to say. I looked over at my daughter, who was completely beside herself. I looked at Frida—oh, Frida, in that dreadful sweat suit. I told her she looked like a powder puff when she bought the thing. I kept looking back and forth, from my daughter, to this handsome man, to my best friend, thinking about my one day off from life.

"I'll meet you back here in one hour," I said to Zachary. "Just give me one hour."

Barbara and Frida and Lucy were already pushing their way

through the crowd and I hurried to follow them. Right as the doors opened and we got outside, Barbara laid into Lucy in a way I've never seen before.

"Where is your grandmother, and who is this person who has been using Grandma's credit card all day long?" she shouted, pointing at me.

"Mom, you need to get a hold of yourself," Lucy said in an attempt to calm her.

"No, Lucy, you have no idea how sick and worried your mother has been," Frida interjected. "We were so out of sorts that we locked ourselves out of both my apartment and Ellie's. We're starving. We've been robbed. It has rained on us. Someone just dropped a bottle of beer down my back. We've walked miles and miles for one answer. Where is your grandmother?"

The three of us just stopped and stared at Frida. This was not the Frida I knew.

"Look, first things first: let's get you both back to the apartment and out of these dirty clothes and give you a hot meal," I said, taking Frida's arm.

"NO!" Frida shook off my embrace. "I want to know who you are, and where Ellie is."

I looked to Lucy for an answer, but she didn't have one. I signaled to her that maybe I should just tell them. Lucy shook her head no.

"This is my friend Michele," Lucy answered them like she wasn't making it up. "She didn't steal Grandma's credit card; Grandma told her to get the stuff she wanted."

"She told her to get three cakes?" Barbara asked her.

"And to put them on Ellie's mother's table without a table-cloth?" Frida added.

"Yes, she did!" I told them, like it really happened.

"Well, why would she need to try on and buy one of your dresses?" Barbara asked.

"Because . . ." I had no answer and again looked to Lucy for help.

"Because she's my model and I was out of that dress," Lucy quickly lied.

"So why did you tell me that you were cousins?" Frida demanded.

"We were just playing with you!" Lucy told her.

"Why on earth would you play with me?" Frida asked. She must have been really upset, or she wouldn't have used Lucy's slang.

Lucy just stood there, unable to answer her. Maybe Lucy wasn't such a good liar.

"Look, let's just get you back to Gram's apartment and out of these clothes. We'll get you both something to eat," Lucy told her.

"Yes," I agreed, helping Frida as Lucy took her mother's arm and we started to walk. "There's a chicken in the fridge."

"Just get me home," Frida said, taking my arm. "Just get me back there."

You wouldn't believe the stamina you need to hold Frida up, even if you're a twenty-nine-year-old. My apartment was only a few blocks away, but believe me, in those few blocks I resolved I was going to get Frida to lose some weight. We walked in silence through the streets of Philadelphia. At one point, Lucy and Barbara were already a block ahead of us.

"I just want to find my friend," Frida said to me softly.

This broke my heart. "You will, Frida, I promise you will."

"You're not a bad person, are you?" she asked me as she took a look at me. "You haven't done away with Ellie, have you?"

"Of course not."

"You're not a nurse, and Ellie isn't hurt, is she?"

"Now you're talking crazy, Frida," I said and shushed her.

She laughed. "You sound like Ellie."

"I promise you, wherever Ellie is, she's fine."

"I just hope you're right." She was breathing heavily. "I don't know what I would do if Ellie was hurt."

"I promise you, she's fine," I repeated.

"I'll tell you something." She stopped me. "These women are not just my friends. They're my family. And they've done nothing less than treat me as family. I've gone all day long without food or a bathroom or even water, and I'd go tomorrow, too, if I thought Ellie or this family was in any kind of trouble."

"I'm sorry you had to feel this way all day," I told her. "I really am. All I can say is that things will work out, and everything will be explained."

"Are you sure?" she asked with sadness in her eyes.

"The most important thing now is getting you upstairs and out of these clothes and putting some food in your body. Your blood sugar must be at zero right now."

"It's in the negative numbers. You can't imagine the depths it has sunk to," she said as she began walking again.

"What do you think Ellie would say to you if she knew that you hadn't eaten anything all day?"

She stopped and looked at me again. "She'd be very worried."

"That's right," I answered as we continued on.

"You know, you remind me of Ellie a little bit," she said.

"I've been hearing that all day."

"I even thought . . ." She started to chuckle. "I even thought, when you and Lucy were kidding me and saying you were her cousin, that you looked like Ellie. I thought you looked just like her when she was younger. You know, it's uncanny how much you look like her when she was younger."

"Yes, I've been told that, and that's why we played that little trick on you. I'm so sorry we did that to you. You didn't deserve that."

"That's okay. I should have known better."

We continued to walk.

"It's just . . ." She stopped again and looked at me. "It's just . . . your eyes. I know those eyes. That's what got me confused."

She stared into my eyes for a few moments, and I stared back into hers. In a way, I was hoping she'd just say it. I hoped that she'd figured it out. I thought Frida would understand, that Frida would be happy for me in a way only a true friend could be. She wouldn't be jealous or let out my secret. Later I'd be able to tell her everything—what I did with my day, the things I saw and experienced. She'd love to hear about it as much as I'd enjoy sharing it with her.

"No," she said, gesturing. "That's crazy."

"What's crazy?" I prodded.

"I'm an old lady. I get crazy thoughts in my head."

I continued to walk my dearest friend back to our apartment building.

Now let me tell you something: I always knew that Frida was the truest friend. A lot of people wondered why I spent my life taking care of her; a lot of people couldn't understand how two women who were so different could have been such close friends. Through the years, some women would tell me to forget about Frida, to not invite her to things. "She's a bore," they'd tell me. The hoity-toity ones would say, "She's really not our kind," when Frida wasn't wearing the latest styles or when she took out a pad and paper to add up her part of the dinner bill. I never listened to them. You want to know why? The answer is very important, and it's something that you should know if you don't know it already, so listen up: Friends come and go in your life. Friends go in different directions for different reasons. Most times it's because they choose different paths. Frida and I have fought over the years about the way our lives were going, but we've always stuck it out with each other. We have always been by each other's side 150 percent when no one else was. Husbands are wonderful, but some of them stray. A true friend? She's the only one who will never let you down.

It's wonderful to have a lot of different friends, but it's most important to have one friend who will be there for you through good times and bad. If something grand happens in your life, she's as happy for you as if it happened to her. If you are sad, she'll stay by your side until everything is better.

My mother had a saying she used when speaking of her

own best friend, Hester Abromowitz, the one I told you about who worked at Saks, the one I gave the eulogy for. I've always remembered this one thing my mother said about her, and I always thought it applied it to Frida: *It's not the friends who ride up with you in the limousine, it's the one who comes home with you on the bus.*

Today, Frida took that bus, and then some.

We walked in silence for the rest of the way back to the apartment.

When we finally arrived, Ken took over and helped me into the elevator with her. Frida collapsed in his arms as I continued to hold her hand.

"Mussels in spicy garlic and tomato gravy," Frida mumbled.

A little to the left," Frida instructed as I massaged her shoulders. Frida always has pain in her shoulders. It's the way she carries the world.

We were back in my apartment and no one was talking. The second after I put my keys in the door (you've never seen Barbara and Frida happier than when they saw me take my keys out of my purse), I grabbed two of my bathrobes and gave them to Frida and Barbara. Then I ran to the refrigerator and put that chicken on a plate.

"Some bread?" Barbara requested as she tore into the chicken and ravenously stuffed it in her mouth like a caveman.

"And soup. You need more sustenance, Barbara," I said, running back into the kitchen. I always have a can of soup handy for moments like these. As I waited for the soup to warm, it occurred to me that no one was questioning how I knew where these things were. That was how tired Barbara and Frida really were.

"Oh, my shoulders," Frida cried now, so I continued to massage her. "Now really dig in there," Frida instructed me as I massaged her other shoulder. "Yes," she said, breathing heavily. "Oh, the pain, the pain!"

"Oh, Frida, these knots," I exclaimed as I dug in. "It's a wonder how you do this to yourself. Now what else can I do?" I asked. "How about your feet? Your bunions must be killing you."

"Yes, some warm water for my feet," Frida cried softly. "Ellie has a pan she uses . . ."

"I'll get it." I ran into my kitchen and grabbed my large roasting pan and filled it with hot water.

"Now, how's that?" I asked her as she dunked her feet and ate her soup.

"Better, but not much," she said.

"Do you want me to take you up to your apartment?" I asked her.

"No," she said. "I don't want to leave here until Ellie gets back. I'll be up all night worrying."

Silence filled the apartment. I was out of things to do, but when your family is sick, you just want to keep doing and doing. Also, I didn't want the commotion to stop for fear of what would come next, which it inevitably did.

Lucy took the plate from Barbara, who was literally licking it clean.

"Lucy," Barbara called to her as she took the plate into the kitchen. "We have to get to the bottom of what is going on here. I'm going to ask you for the last time. Please tell me that you know where your grandmother is."

Lucy looked at me for any kind of clue as to what to say, but I was out of lies.

"I don't know," she said in a tone I hadn't heard her use since she was a child.

"You know," Barbara snapped at her, pointing, "you know something, and I don't want to be kept in the dark anymore."

"Mom, I really don't know," she told her.

"I'm going to count to three. If you don't tell me the information you know about your grandmother I will never speak to you again."

"Now come on, Barbara, don't you think you're being just a little dramatic?" I butted in.

"*You stay out of this!*" she jumped up and roared at me.

Oh, boy, did *that* shut me up.

"But as long as we're on the subject, just who the hell are you? Lucy has never mentioned you to me before. And do not call me Barbara. I am Mrs. Sustamorn."

"They were playing with me when they said she was the cousin," Frida interjected, sounding hurt.

"All that I know is that the trouble started the second you came into the picture." Barbara now glared at me.

"Mom, you need to calm down."

Barbara started breathing heavily, unable to stop.

"Jesus, Lucy, she's going to have a heart attack," I said, panicking.

"I have some smelling salts in my bag. If I had my bag. Or if I could move a muscle in my body to go to my apartment and get my bag," Frida mumbled, tired but concerned.

"Lucy, this is too much," I said. "Barbara, you need to calm down." But she just kept breathing erratically. "Barbara," I instructed her again, "pull yourself together."

"Stop." Lucy waved her hand at me. "She does this. I know what to do." Lucy calmly went over to her mother and helped her back into her seat. "Mom, you need to sit back down and take a few deep breaths, because you're getting to that place you don't like. Take a deep breath for me, Mom, in . . ."

Barbara looked into Lucy's eyes and took a deep breath.

"And out . . ."

Barbara exhaled.

And then I witnessed something I've never seen in the entire time I've known my child. Barbara started to cry. Sure, she's cried before, but not in this way. Barbara was heaving and sobbing in a way that was completely new to me.

Lucy took Barbara in her arms as Frida and I looked on.

"I don't understand what's going on here. Why can't anyone give me a straight answer as to where my mother is?" Barbara moaned.

"Mom, breathe, just like we always do. Breathe in . . . and out . . . and in . . . and out." She continued to cradle her mother in her arms.

This wasn't the daughter I knew. This wasn't a person I was familiar with. But Lucy knew her. Lucy knew exactly who this person was.

"If anything has happened to your grandmother, I swear to you, Lucy, I'll go out the window. I swear it to you," Barbara cried.

"Mom, Grandma is a strong woman, and so are you. You must know deep in your heart that she's fine. She's fine, Mom, she's fine."

"She's fine!" I shouted. "She's fine! She went away for the day and she didn't want anyone to know!"

"But who are you?" Frida asked.

I looked at Lucy again.

"She's my friend!" Lucy answered. "How many times do I have to tell you? You know, Mom, you don't know everything about my life. Did you ever stop to think that maybe I have a friend you don't know?"

Barbara thought about this for a moment.

"But we talk every day," Barbara replied.

"Look," Lucy said, pointing to me. "Does she really look like someone who did something bad to Grandma? For god's sake, be rational."

"But it was so strange this morning," Barbara told her. "Mom saying she saw a mouse, and then lying and saying that she was having lunch with Frida."

"And then telling me that she was having lunch with Barbara," Frida added.

"So that means that she was kidnapped? That means she is hurt? That means you have to go to the police?" Lucy asked both of them.

Barbara and Frida had nothing to say. Their worrying really did sound crazy when Lucy put it that way. I wanted to tell them to leave me alone, to stop worrying and being so ridiculous. But I could also see the hurt in my child, and I wanted to make that right. It was my day. My one day. And chances were if I tried to tell them the truth, I'd spend the rest of it locked in a mental ward.

"Mom, Aunt Frida, I'm going to say something to you right now that you might hate me for, but I have to say it."

"Maybe you shouldn't say it then, Lucy." Frida sounded worried.

"No, I'm going to say it even if it hurts you, Aunt Frida."

"Well, I don't know why you'd want to hurt me, especially with what I've been through today, but if you feel you have to . . ." Frida went on, cheerless.

"Well, it's not going to hurt you that much." Lucy smiled, patting Frida's shoulder.

"Well, okay."

Lucy turned away from us as if she were preparing her words. When she turned back around, she was dead serious.

"Mom, Aunt Frida, get a life!"

"What on earth is that supposed to mean?" Barbara asked, offended.

"Mom! You put yourself and Aunt Frida into a tailspin today, and for what? So what if your mother wanted to get away for a day? What is it to you anymore?"

"Exactly!" I exclaimed. "Thank you, Lucy."

"Now watch it!" Barbara said to me. "You have no idea what you're talking about. This is my mother we're talking about."

"Exactly. She's your mother!" Lucy shot back. "She's your seventy-five-year-old mother. If there's anything I see in Gram that I don't see in you, it's that she's got a life of her own. You're a fifty-five-year-old woman who is still obsessed with trying to do right by your mother. Don't you think it's time that you just cut that out already?"

"I think 'obsessed' is overstating it just a bit," Barbara told her.

"No, Mom, I think that's the perfect word," Lucy said with a bit of anger.

"Well, I think really what Lucy's saying is," I put in, "maybe this family should stop looking at one another as daughter, mother, and grandmother, and start looking at one another as people."

"Yes, that's exactly what I mean." Lucy threw her hands up. "Mom, would you take a good look at yourself? Do you know what it was like coming to that bar and seeing you there? And for what?"

"I wanted to know what happened to Grandma. You wouldn't pick up your phone all day!" Barbara cried.

"Because I had a very big day today! I had probably one of the biggest days of my life, and I didn't have time to talk to you. I should have that right."

"When I told you that I was worried sick about Mom—"

"No, you didn't say that you were worried sick. You said that Aunt Frida was worried sick."

"Which I was," Frida said.

"And you're just as bad, by the way," Lucy said to Frida.

Barbara looked at her daughter with tears in her eyes.

"Mom, I'm telling you this because I love you."

"Well, I love you too, Luce."

"But Mom, you have to grow up already. You just have to grow up."

"I mean"—Barbara paused as she thought about it—"I suppose that maybe I could start to look at things from another point of view."

"That's all I'm asking here," Lucy said. But I knew there was another person who could take Lucy's advice: me. I knew that the best thing I could do was cut the cord with my daughter. She would always be my child, no matter what age she was, but

I needed to stop judging her. I needed to try to see things from her point of view. I needed to act more like her friend than her mother.

Barbara and Lucy fell into a hug as Frida and I looked on.

"And how often do you call your mother?" Frida asked me as she massaged her legs.

"My mother died a long time ago," I told her.

"Oh, I'm sorry."

"Thank you," I said. "But to tell you the truth, she was a lot like you, Mrs. Sustamorn," I said, turning to Barbara.

"I'm hoping that's a compliment," Barbara said.

"She had a lot of love for me," I replied. "She worried about me a lot. The one way Lucy is different from me, though, is that I really listened and minded what my mother told me to do."

Frida stopped massaging her legs and looked at me.

"See, she listened to her mother." Barbara nodded at Lucy.

"But I should have done what Lucy has done. I shouldn't have let my mother's word be the last word. I should have used her advice as part of weighing my options. Lucy and I are very different people," I said. "Lucy has the sense to think for herself."

Frida stared at me, extending her neck as if she wanted to get a better look. Barbara smiled and patted Lucy's head.

"I hated my mother," Frida spoke up out of nowhere.

"What?" We all turned to Frida.

"My mother was a bossy woman who never made me feel good about myself." She looked squarely at me. "She died a long time ago, too."

I know, I thought to myself sadly as we looked at each other.

"I wish that I'd had the guts to stand up to her," Frida said softly. "She's been gone for thirty years, and I can still hear her rants. I wish she'd cared more about herself than about running my life. You know what? I'm glad Ellie took this day for herself. Maybe I'll take one, too. I've spent too many years worrying when I should have been living for myself." A tear ran down Frida's face. "Maybe it's time I start thinking for myself, too," Frida said.

"And I'm sure you will now," I said.

I smiled at Frida, so proud of her, and she smiled back.

"I'm going to start spending my money!" Frida suddenly declared.

"Don't go crazy now, Frida," I told her, getting a little worried that she might be taking my advice too far.

"Oh, no, I don't have to worry. I've got more money than King Solomon had gold in his mines."

"You do?" we all asked her in unison.

"Yes, I do," she answered firmly. "And I don't care how much it costs, I'm going to do something I've always wanted to do."

"Go to Paris!" I exclaimed. Frida always wanted to go to Paris.

"Buy yourself a new wardrobe?" Lucy guessed.

"I'm going to buy a cell phone!" Frida proclaimed.

This made us all laugh. We laughed and laughed. When the laughing quieted, Barbara took a deep breath and put her arms around Lucy.

"You know, I hate to admit it, but you're right," Barbara told me. "When Mom comes back, I'm not going to harp on her for not calling. I'll just ask her if she had a good day."

"She'll think you had a lobotomy," Frida said, perking up.

"And Aunt Frida, what can I say? I'm sorry that I dragged you around all day," Barbara told her.

"And I'm sorry that I yelled at you before," Frida said to her and smiled.

"What?" I blurted out. I couldn't help myself; had Barbara really pushed meek little Frida to her breaking point? Frida's stare was drilling holes in me, but Barbara didn't notice my outburst.

"What's the matter, Frida?" I asked her.

"Would it be okay if I spoke to you alone for a second?" Frida asked, again looking me squarely in the eyes.

"Sure," I said.

Frida nudged my arm as we began to walk. She led me into my bedroom and slowly shut the door as I took a seat on the bed. Then she sat down next to me.

"Go," she said, taking my hands in hers.

"Oh, no. I can't leave you all here in such a state."

"Go," she said again, squeezing my hands. "Go and enjoy yourself."

Now, I could have taken this conversation in a lot of ways. Frida might not have trusted this stranger; maybe Frida thought this stranger was up to no good and wanted her out of their lives. Maybe she was telling her: *Go, leave, and don't come back.*

Then again, maybe Frida felt that a young woman who didn't know this family shouldn't have to deal with their problems. Maybe the young woman had problems of her own and Frida was saying: *Go, you don't need this.*

But of course what she was saying was obvious, now that I thought of the way she'd been looking at me earlier: *I know it's you. I want you to enjoy this gift you've been given. I understand. Go.*

"Everything is fine here. Sometimes we all just need some time without questions or problems to solve for everyone else," she said softly. "Sometimes we just need to shut out the world and take some time for ourselves."

I took a deep breath. "But if I leave now, I don't know if I'll ever want to come back," I told her. This was the truth. Up until all the family drama started, this had been the best day of my life.

"You'll have to figure that out for yourself," she told me as she stroked my arm. "Personally, I know that you have too much here not to come back. For right now, though, you just need to go."

My friend was now staring into my eyes with an intensity I'd never seen before. She knew the truth and we both knew it.

"Do you know?" I finally asked her.

"Of course I know it's you," she said matter-of-factly.

"What was the tip-off?" I asked her.

"Well, I was sure this morning. Thought I was nuts. Then you knew about my bunions and my blood sugar. And there was the whole speech about your mother tonight; I knew that woman all too well. The clincher, though, was your reaction when you heard I'd finally stood up to Barbara. I still think I'm nuts, though."

"Well, you *are* nuts." I laughed, and she laughed with me. The cat was out of the bag. God, that felt good. "I would have thought that you'd have some kind of a coronary if you knew," I told her, exhaling.

"When you get to be our age, does anything really shock you anymore?"

"Good point. But, this one really threw me for a loop."

"But how?" she asked as she looked down at our hands, mine

smooth and free of bumps and wrinkles, hers looking its age. "How did this happen?"

"Frida, if I knew, I'd bottle it and sell it on the black market. When I woke up this morning and looked into the mirror, I thought I was dead."

She paused, looked down, and squeezed my hands. "Do you feel that?" she asked me.

"Of course I feel it," I answered.

"Then maybe *I'm* dead," she said. "I went through hell today, so it wouldn't surprise me."

I squeezed her hands. "Do you feel this?" I asked her.

"I'm not dead." She smiled. "Let me look at you for a second," she said, cupping my face with her hand.

"What do you think?" I asked her.

"It's like going back in time," she whispered as she felt my cheekbones. "I'm looking at you, and all I can see is myself at that age."

"Maybe it's a virus. Maybe you'll wake up at this age tomorrow," I joked.

"Oh, I hope not," she said swiftly, taking her hands off of me as if she might have caught something already.

"Why?"

"Well," she said, "because I lived that life. I don't need to go back and do it again."

This took me by surprise.

"You're telling me that if you were given this chance you wouldn't take it?"

"Ellie," she said calmly, "that's where you and I have always been different. I don't need to be younger or look younger. I've never minded getting old. Besides, I would miss my Sol too much. I couldn't be that young without Sol by my side. At that age it was Sol and me against the world. It wouldn't make sense to me without him. No . . ." She shook her head. "This is your wish, not mine."

"But Frida, to be free of physical pain and to look beautiful again and feel like you could take on the world—don't you want that chance?"

"Who says I can't look beautiful now?" she asked me, straightening her shirt. "I don't like feeling old. And I don't mean how I look on the outside, I mean on the inside. I'm tired of feeling this way, and I have the chance to change that. That I can do. That I'm going to do. The other stuff? I've done it already. You know me—I don't even like reruns on television. I've seen it already. What's done is done."

"You mean to tell me you have no regrets at all?"

"Ellie," she said, taking my hands again, "you're not dead. You're not dreaming. You're not in some other world. You know what I think?" she asked as she put her hand on my cheek.

"What, Frida?"

"I think you're taking a look at your life, trying to answer a question that has bothered you for many years. If a question has been on your mind for that long, it begs to be answered."

I looked at my friend, perplexed. "What's my question? I have a lot of questions."

"Well, that stuff about being young again, that's all a bonus. Really, though, knowing you as well as I do, I know there's one thing that's always bugged you. It's bugged you so much that somehow, some way, you've been given a chance to answer it."

"But what is it? Don't beat around the bush."

"You really don't know?" She looked surprised.

"No, I really don't."

"Well, I don't want to be the one to tell you. I think that's something you need to figure out for yourself."

"And that's why you think this happened to me?"

"You made a wish. Wishes come true all the time. It's not as crazy as you think it is."

"And what if I figure out the question, the answer? What if I have the power to stay this way?"

"Then you'll come visit your old friend sometimes."

"And you won't be angry with me?"

"How could I be angry with you? Ellie, I want what you want." She smiled and I knew it was true. "I only want what's best for you. As long as I know you're safe. As long as I know what you feel in your heart is right, and you're content, then that's all I want."

Frida and I embraced each other for a long moment. Then we looked into each other's eyes one more time.

"You have a pretty open mind for such an old lady," I told her.

"Hey," she said with a little slap on my hand. "You're older than me."

"By a month."

"A month and two days." She laughed, and I laughed with her.

"The thing that gets me is, why do you think Barbara hasn't figured it out?"

"How could Barbara know it's you?" Frida asked. "Barbara never knew this person. She only knew her mother."

"She's seen a million pictures of me. She was around when I was this age the first time. How can she not remember?"

"Pictures never tell the whole story. You know that," Frida explained.

"You know, I didn't think about it that way. It's just what Lucy was saying before: Barbara has never looked at me as a person, only as her mother. Just like I've only thought of her as my daughter." We smiled at each other one more time. "Okay," I said, clasping her hand in mine once more.

"Now go," she said again.

"Are you sure?" I asked her.

"I'm not going to tell you again. It's exasperating already." She poked me.

I looked at my friend and smiled again. "Thank you."

We got up and walked arm in arm into the living room, where Lucy and Barbara were still sitting.

"If it's okay, I have to be off right now," I told the ladies.

"Where are you going?" Lucy asked me, looking like she was asking far more.

"I just don't want to be a bother to this family more than I already have been. I'm sorry if I've caused any trouble."

"I'm sorry, too." Barbara looked at me. "I'm sorry you had to see us this way. Maybe you'll come over another time and meet Lucy's grandmother."

"Yes, that would be nice. I feel like I know her already."

Frida snickered to herself.

"But where are you going?" Lucy asked me.

"I'll call you later," I told her.

"She has things to do," Frida said as she slowly sat down

beside Barbara. "She's a young woman." She smiled, looking at me. "Let her be on her way."

"Barbara," I said before I walked out.

"Yes?" she answered.

I was at a loss for words at that moment. I wanted to tell her everything, how sorry I was, how proud I was. I wanted her to know who this person really was. "It was very nice meeting you," I said after a moment.

"It was nice meeting you, too. I hope we'll see each other again under less complicated circumstances."

"Yes." I smiled at her. "I hope we do."

I walked out of the apartment and into the hallway and pushed the down button on the elevator.

As I stood in the elevator watching the numbers go down, I wondered what this question was that Frida was talking about. Would this evening finally give me the answer I'd been looking for all these years?

the night of my life

I ran down Walnut Street like my life depended on it. Maybe it did. I was heading toward a night I'd always dreamed of.

All I wanted to do was find Zachary. If I could just get to him, if I could just recapture that feeling of being without a care in the world, everything would be okay. In less than twenty-four hours, all of my priorities had changed. I needed to find out what this adventure was all for. If it wasn't to see myself in cute under-wear or to sit in the sun, what was it for?

Block after block I sprinted in my heels past young people eating outside and shops that were open way past the time I usu-ally went to sleep.

And then I saw him.

He was standing under a streetlamp like Frank Sinatra in some old movie.

And when he saw me, those gorgeous eyes lit up.

"Why are you running?" he asked, laughing.

"I don't . . . I don't know!" I giggled as I ran into his arms.

"You were that excited to see me?" He smiled, looking into my eyes.

"Yes." I smiled back.

He took my hands and stretched out my arms to get a good look at me. "God, you're beautiful," he said.

I had no words. I just smiled back.

"So what's on the agenda for tonight?" he asked as he put his arm around me and we started to walk.

"I want to do everything!" I declared with a skip in my step.

"Everything, huh?" he echoed.

"I want to see every bit of this city that I've never seen before."

"Well, let's get started."

"I'll let you be the guide. You tell me where," I told him.

"Is this your first time in Philadelphia?" he asked me.

"Well, I've been here before," I tried to explain, "but never like this."

"You mean you were always with your family?" he asked me.

"Exactly," I told him. "Tonight is the first time I've just been free to do whatever I want in this town."

"Well, then," he said as he gestured to a motorcycle in front of us, "your chariot awaits."

I looked at him, and then at *the thing.*

"You want me to get on that?" I asked him, a little shocked.

"It's the best way to see the city," he said, handing me a helmet. "Come on, what are you, scared?"

"Oh, no." I waved my hands. "I'm not getting on that thing. You can be sure of that."

"I promise you," he said, strapping a helmet on my head, "I'm a very skilled driver. I spent two months last year driving this same kind of motorcycle all over Rome. Believe me, if I can

maneuver this thing through the streets of Rome without an accident, I can get down JFK Boulevard."

"Aren't the Italian drivers crazy?" I asked him. "My . . . my
boyfriend Howard and I once rented a car to drive to Tuscany. I
sat there with my hand over my eyes from the Colosseum until
we were at least twenty miles out of the city."

"You trusted Howard, and you won't trust me?" He smiled
with those blue eyes. "Besides, I thought you wanted to go crazy
tonight."

"But I'm in a dress, and heels," I protested.

"We're not going dirt racing," he pointed out.

"Well, okay," I finally agreed. He held out his hand to help
me on. "I mean, what's the worst that can happen, right?"

Truthfully, when I really thought about it, what *was* the worst
that could happen? What if, God forbid, we were in some sort of
accident? Could you imagine what would happen if the hospital
found my ID? Could you imagine Lucy and Frida trying to explain to the hospital people that it really was me? Oh, that's funny.

Now, if you've ever been on one of those things in a dress,
maybe you'll be able to tell me how you can straddle the seat
while keeping your miniskirt at a respectable length. Oh, I
was mortified at the thought of Zachary catching a glimpse
of anything he shouldn't have. I remembered one time when
Lucy hopped into a cab for dinner and she was wearing one
of her short dresses. She climbed into the backseat with her
underwear right out there for the world to see. I scolded her
for getting into the cab in such an unladylike way. She apologized, saying she didn't know she was "pulling a Britney." Then,
of course, she told me all about that Britney Speards (that's

the name, right, Speards? Or is it Spears? I have no idea) who showed her privates in every magazine on the stands and on the Internet. Tonight, the last thing I wanted to do was "pull a Britney Speards."

Zachary climbed on in front of me then took my arms and secured them around his waist. I sat with my body pressed up against his back as he revved the motor. My bare thighs were against his legs. My mother was turning over in her grave.

And then we were off. I swear to you that I could feel the grim reaper on my shoulder (or maybe it was my mother), so I dug my fingernails into Zachary's waist and shouted, "*Not so fast! Don't go between the cars, sweet Jesus, Mary and Joseph—you're too close to that car! Oh my God, we're going to die!*"

When we finally stopped for a second, Zachary turned around and looked at me. "You know, you're going to draw blood in a second." He laughed. "Relax, enjoy the ride."

I shook my hands around to get the blood flowing in them again and wiped the clamminess off on my dress.

"Maybe we should just park this thing and take a cab from here," I said.

"You're safe with me," he spoke above the revving motor. "I promise."

And with that we were off again.

After another few blocks, I started to calm down. After six blocks I was able to open my eyes again. In another six blocks, I had an itch on my nose, so I took one hand off Zachary's waist and scratched it.

"You're getting the feel for it?" he asked when we stopped at another red light.

"I think I am," I said.

"You ready to go faster?" he asked.

"NOOO!" I shouted.

This made him laugh.

Zachary had driven us all the way down to Penn's Landing, and then back up to Old City. I have to admit I was starting to enjoy myself as we passed Independence Hall. Zachary was telling me the history and I was trying to listen, but the bike was too loud so I just nodded. It was beginning to be fun to watch the people on the streets as we passed by. It was much different than seeing everything from a car. I loved feeling the warm night air blowing on my face.

"Are you cold back there?" he asked me, getting off the bike and then helping me off.

I shook my head. I was sure I'd have a chill, but the wind on my shoulders actually felt good.

"Come here, I want to show you something." He walked ahead of me toward a white glass building as I took off the helmet and fixed my hair and straightened my dress. Zachary knocked on the window of the building and waved to someone inside.

"It looks like it's closed," I said.

"I've got the situation under control," he told me confidently.

As I caught up to him, I saw that he was waving to a security guard, who pointed to the side of the building.

"You can't come to Philadelphia without seeing this. I wouldn't be a good guide if I didn't show you."

"What is it?" I asked.

"Thanks, Gus," Zachary said as the guard opened the door.

"Take all the time you need," Gus told us.

"It's the Liberty Bell!" I squealed.

Can you believe that in the entire seventy-five years that I've lived in Philadelphia I've never once seen the Liberty Bell? I've seen sights all over the world, but never in my own backyard. How crazy is that? Of course I'd seen models of it in the airport gift shop and pictures of it all my life, but I never once saw it up close.

The bell was housed behind a waist-high steel fence, but when Zachary asked, Gus said we could walk around it as long as we didn't touch it.

"It's like all priceless pieces of art—even the natural oils in your hand could damage it in some way," I educated them. I was on the planning committee for years at the Philadelphia Museum of Art. Did I mention that to you?

"That's right," Gus said, nodding.

"It's bigger than it looks in the pictures," I said, amazed.

I got closer to the bell so I could read what it said.

"Can you see that?" Zachary asked.

"I can't make out the words." I squinted (and then of course remembered I didn't need to squint with my 20/20 vision).

Proclaim LIBERTY throughout all the Land unto all the
Inhabitants thereof
Lev. XXV X
By Order of the ASSEMBLY of the Province of
PENSYLVANIA for the
State House in Philad[a]
Pass and Stow
Philad[a]
MDCCLIII

How apropos for me at that very moment, with all that I had on my mind. The Liberty Bell was the symbol of independence, liberty and independence from myself. It was such a shame I hadn't seen these words until now—what a waste! I wondered what other landmarks I'd missed all these years.

We stood in silence and gazed at the bell a bit longer.

"I don't know how we got to do this, but thank you for bringing me here," I said.

"It's my pleasure." He smiled.

"Thank you, Gus, for allowing us to come in," I said to the guard as he opened the door for us to leave.

"Pleasure," he said.

As Gus locked the doors behind us, I asked Zachary again, "How did you do that?"

"I donated a lot of money. They let you do things like that if you've donated a lot of money."

"Enough said," I replied, understanding completely. "My boyfriend Howard always got right into the emergency room at Pennsylvania Hospital because he gave a lot for research."

"So Howard is from Philly?" He stopped me.

"Oh, yes, he was, but that was a long time ago. He moved," I said, thinking quickly. "To Chicago."

"How old was he when he gave all this money?" he asked, handing me the helmet.

"Oh, uh, well, it was his family," I lied.

"Oh. What's his last name? One thing about Philly people, we all know each other."

"Oh, you wouldn't know his family," I replied quickly, putting on my helmet. "They moved, too."

"Oh," he finally conceded. "So, you hungry at all?" Thank goodness he'd changed the subject.

"I'm famished!" I cried out. "What are you thinking?" I asked him.

"Well, we could pop into one of the finer restaurants in the city, but I'm thinking you might want some genuine Philadelphia flavor."

"A cheesesteak!" I shouted. "Oh, gosh, I haven't had a cheesesteak in years!"

How perfect. Of course I'd been to all the restaurants he could have taken me to.

"You watch your weight?" he asked as he gave me a once-over.

"No." I shook my head. "Fear of cholesterol."

"Good for you," he answered with a chuckle. "You're never too young to start worrying about that stuff."

"Well, I do watch my weight, of course. But I've got a good metabolism. My . . . my . . . my sister . . . she got my father's genes. She's always on a diet, but I think she cheats more than she diets. Not Lucy and me, though. We can pretty much eat what we want."

"Your sister must hate that," he replied.

I thought about that for a second. "You know what?" I answered. "I bet she does."

I was already climbing on a motorcycle for the second time in my life, thinking, *If the motorcycle isn't going to kill me, neither will the cholesterol in a cheesesteak.*

"You're a girl after my own heart," he said. "But if you're going to have your first cheesesteak in years, it better be the best."

"JR's, on Seventeenth Street?" I asked.

"Pat's, in South Philly!" he shouted.

"*I'm in!*" I shouted back as the motor revved and we were off again.

A few blocks in, we hit a red light.

"How are you doing back there?" he asked me.

"You can go faster if you want!" I shouted.

"I would like a Philadelphia cheesesteak sandwich, please," I ordered through the window when we arrived at Pat's.

The man behind the partition gave me a quizzical look.

"She'll have a Whiz," Zachary broke in. "Do you want fried onions?"

"Oh, yes." My mouth watered.

"Whiz, wit," Zachary told the man. "Two Whiz, wit, inside out."

"What is that you told him?" I asked as we moved down the line.

"Cheesesteaks are ordered in a different language here," he told me. "I ordered us steak sandwiches with Cheeze Whiz and fried onions."

"And that's a Whiz, wit," I confirmed, enunciating my words, which he chuckled at. "Oh, but I'd rather have Swiss cheese. Can you tell him that?" I turned back to the man at the partition.

"Oh, no," he said, taking me aside as if I'd said something off-color. "They won't serve it with Swiss cheese. They'll kick us out."

"Oh! And what was the *inside-out* part?"

"The sandwich is better if they take out the bread from the middle," he explained.

"Oh, that's smart," I said. "And less calories. I'll have to tell my sister," I added, but then again, why get Barbara angry by bringing something like that up?

I grabbed a whole bunch of napkins from the counter as Zachary secured two seats at one of the picnic tables outside the building. I handed him half of the napkins as I spread one out on the table like a place mat.

"Wow, you're really dainty," he remarked with a chuckle.

"I guess I am," I admitted. "But who knows who's been sitting at this table?"

"Good point," he said, putting my cheesesteak in front of me and then taking a napkin and spreading it out, *daintily*, in front of him.

As I took the first bite of my cheesesteak, uh, Whiz, wit (which, incidentally, tasted magical), I tried my best not to get any of the onions on me, as they dripped from the other side of the sandwich.

"Messy, but good," he said, taking another bite.

"You said it," I said.

"Now you can officially tell your friends back in Chicago that you ate your cheesesteak from *the* place to eat cheesesteaks. I guess that's like Giordano's for you?"

"It's what?"

"Like Giordano's, for deep-dish pizza. Don't tell me you live in Chicago and you've never eaten at Giordano's."

"Of course I have!" I exclaimed, hoping he wouldn't ask me any more questions. What the heck was Giordano's, and what was deep-dish pizza? "So tell me about your Web site," I said, quickly changing the subject.

"Well, you know, I'm sure a stylish girl like you has bought things from my site before."

"No." I shook my head. "I never buy anything off the Internet. I don't even have a computer."

"You what?" He looked at me like I was living in the Dark Ages (which I was).

"I don't have a computer. I don't believe in typing in my credit card so the world can get ahold of it. Knowing my luck, someone will steal all my money."

"You know, most sites have software that protects you from that. Not only that, buying things off the Internet is safer than buying things over the phone."

"Oh, come on." I balked. "I'd rather give my credit card to a live person than type it in blindly over the Internet!" I told him, thinking it made total sense.

"You really have no idea about my Web site?"

"No, why?"

Zachary shook his head. "It's just that when most women find out that I started couture.com, they get visions of Versace dancing in their eyes. It's like being a rock star. Girls all want a piece of me. Unfortunately, I have a hard time figuring out which they like better, me or the Web site."

"I find that very hard to believe," I said, taking in all of his handsomeness. "I mean, with those stunning eyes and that gorgeous smile, you mean to tell me that you actually get taken advantage of?"

"You'd be surprised. Lucy tells me not to give them so much that they'll just use me for it, but I can't help it. Call me old-fashioned, but I think that when you take a girl out on a date, you should treat her nicely."

"I said the same thing to her earlier!" I exclaimed.

"I'm glad you think so," he said.

"Trust me," I said, "if a girl is stupid enough to just use a man like you for free clothes or a dinner, she's not worth it."

"I like the way you speak," he said, taking another bite of his sandwich.

"Although I might use you to walk up there and order me another one of these sandwiches after I finish this one."

"You can use me for that." He laughed, looking at me a little longer than he should have. He kept on staring as I took another bite.

"What?" I asked him, covering my mouth, which was full of sandwich.

"So you've really never heard of my site, and you've never bought anything off the Internet."

"No," I told him. "I told you: I don't trust buying anything online. But tell me what the site is all about. I've heard of Amazon.com; is it like that?"

"Well, yes, but Amazon is more like, say, Woolworth's five-and-ten-cent stores, which you're probably too young to remember. That was a place that sold everything from goldfish to televisions."

"I think I've heard of it," I lied, remembering countless hours I spent in my youth at the Woolworth's on City Line Avenue.

"Well, couture.com is more of a department store. It's a site where you can shop for all the latest styles, from stockings to dresses to gowns and coats, but the thing is, everything is tailored to fit your style."

"But how?" I asked, perplexed.

"Well, there's a place on the site where you can store all your information, your likes and your dislikes and your size. It takes about twenty minutes to fill out. We've got a long, detailed list of questions. And then you get e-mails once a week, or once a month, or every day if you're a big shopper, with pictures of outfits that have just come in that fit your profile. Whether you're looking for jeans or a couture gown, the site chooses what you would like according to your taste, price range, and what fits your body."

"That's incredible!" I exclaimed.

"Oh, it's really successful," he went on. "And then, if you download a picture of your full body, we can overlay each outfit onto the picture so you can see what you'd look like in it before you order the merchandise."

"So if I go to the site and I see a blouse I like, I can just put it on my picture?" I asked.

"Well, you're the model in the picture."

"I am?" I was puzzled.

"Well, on your page. You know when you look at a catalog and you see the model in the outfit?"

"Sure, sure."

"Well, on the site, it's *you* wearing the outfit."

"But how do you get everyone in the clothes? How does everyone who goes on the site get to see themselves, and not someone else?"

"That's the beauty of the Internet," he said, matter-of-factly.

"That's ingenious!" I screeched. "That's the most brilliant thing I've ever heard. And you can do it right in your own home?" I was beside myself at this news.

"Of course. I mean, this is old news. A lot of sites do it now. We were just one of the first. I can't believe you've never heard of it before."

"No wonder all these ladies clamor for you. You've made their dreams come true!" I tried to take it all in. "So let me get this straight. It's kind of like the olden days, when I was younger and my grandmother used to tell me how all the saleswomen knew what you liked and they'd pick things out for you. Only in this case it's on the Internet?"

"Actually"—he paused and took a deep breath—"it's really funny you should say that. I got the idea from my grandmother, who worked for years at Saks Fifth Avenue, in Bala Cynwyd." He paused again. "Actually, it was at her funeral that I thought up the idea. And this is the part I've been meaning to get to." He smiled. "See, my grandmother's best friend's daughter was giving a eulogy about how my grandmother was the last of the great salesladies, and how she always knew everyone and what their tastes were. I know that's a bad thing to say, that I thought of my business model at my grandmother's funeral." He looked down and smiled, as if he was thinking of her. Then he looked at me. "I've never told anyone that. But I have to tell you now, the truth is . . ."

And I knew exactly what he was going to say, and I suddenly felt my knees give out.

"The truth is, and I've never even told Lucy this—"

"Then don't tell me," I stopped him. I didn't want to hear what he was about to say next.

"No, I want to. Actually, I have to, because . . . Actually, it was your grandmother who was making the speech."

"Your grandmother was Hester Abromowitz!" I gasped as a shot ran up my spine.

"Yes," he admitted, and then looked at me, concerned. "Are you okay?" he asked me, clearly noticing the blood draining from my face.

My date for the evening was my mother's best friend's grandson. I remembered seeing little Zachary when he was born. I think I remember buying him a blue blanket! And Hester had showed me a million pictures of him through the years.

"I'm sorry, I know this sounds really weird," he said. "I just really liked what your grandmother had to say."

"No, I just . . ." I tried to speak normally and compose myself. "I know my grandmother liked your grandmother very much." My mouth was suddenly dry, so I sipped my Coke and took a deep breath. "She used to tell me how your grandmother knew all the ladies by name, and all the styles her clients enjoyed."

"I don't know why I never said anything. I guess I was embarrassed that I came up with it at her funeral. Your grandmother's words, though—they were so poignant. Your grandmother spoke so beautifully that day about my grandmother and the way she loved her job that I couldn't help but be inspired by it."

"So you're saying that this would never have happened if I— if my grandmother hadn't given that speech that day?"

"That about sums it up."

"My grandmother's words were so strong that it made you come up with this idea?"

He nodded. "Yep, pretty much. Your grandmother is a really

cool lady. Lucy never stops talking about her. Maybe when you come back into town, we can all have dinner one night?"

"I'm sure she'd love that!" I told him.

"Do you think it's too late to tell her how much her words moved me that day?"

"Heck no!" I erupted with a full smile. "You'll make her day! She'll get a huge kick out of it!"

He laughed. "Who says 'She'll get a kick out of it' anymore? Has anyone ever told you that you're an old soul?"

"More times than I can even recall," I told him, smiling and feeling so proud.

After my second cheesesteak, the fries, and two Cokes, I skipped over to the bike.

"I don't even know how you can move with all that food in your belly," he said, walking toward me.

"I feel light as a feather!" I jumped in the air.

"I hope they didn't slip anything into your cheesesteak when I wasn't looking." He laughed.

"Like a drug?" I asked him.

"Yes," he said. "Like a drug."

"I don't care if they did." I threw my hands in the air. "Zachary?" I asked him.

He laughed again.

"What? Did I say something funny?"

"It's just that no one ever calls me Zachary except my mother." He continued laughing.

"Zachary?" I said again.

"What?" he answered, putting his arms around me.

I looked into his eyes. "Lucy tells me I should play coy, but I can't help it. I just want to tell you now that I am having the greatest night of my life."

"I am, too," he said, taking me tighter in his arms.

We looked into each other's eyes and smiled. I wanted to kiss him so bad I didn't care if I'd seen pictures of him as a bare-bottomed toddler in the bathtub. The best way I can describe it was that my lips were magnets and I couldn't keep them back any longer. And then . . . oh, mercy . . . he kissed me.

So I wrapped my arms around him and kissed him right back.

I thought of the people around Pat's, who must have been staring at us and our public display of affection, but I didn't care. All I wanted to do was keep kissing him as we pulled each other in tighter.

I was sweating. I was positively sweating with nervousness and adrenaline. My mind was racing a mile a minute, and all I could think of was one thing: I was falling in love.

I had known Zachary—not Hester's grandson, but this kind gentleman Zachary—for only a short time, but I knew. This man was my soul mate. He was the single solitary reason I had turned twenty-nine that day. This had to be the reason for everything. I was sure of it, positive. I suddenly knew the question I'd been looking for: Who was my soul mate? Zachary was my answer, and I knew it was true.

I wanted to keep on kissing him and kissing him. To experience the perfect kiss, the perfect moment—this was what kissing was meant to be, and I didn't care who saw, and I didn't care what else was going on around us. We continued to kiss and kiss and kiss.

At that point, I could feel only the sensation of his lips touching mine. He was the only person I cared about in this world. He was the reason all of this had happened. This was my wish, my question, my answer. It was Zachary all along—of course it was.

He stopped kissing me for a moment and leaned near my ear.

"I think you are amazing," he whispered. "I think you are beautiful and amazing."

I had never been kissed this way before, not by the few men I'd dated prior to marrying Howard, and certainly not by Howard. How could I have ever kissed Howard in this way? I never loved Howard. I never loved my husband in the way that I was loving this man. And then I realized something: maybe Howard didn't love me in this way, either. Maybe Howard had his secret, too. He didn't love me in the way that I didn't love him. That was why he had affairs. He was trying to find something that I was just incapable of giving him. Surprisingly, I wasn't upset about this newfound revelation of how stupid and pointless our life together had been. This was my chance to experience the one thing I never got to feel in my entire life: true love.

"Just keep kissing me," I whispered back to Zachary.

And he did.

It must have been ten minutes before he took my hands in his and looked into my eyes.

"Is it too soon to ask you to marry me?" he asked with a grin.

I'm not going to tell you what happened next.

I mean, if a lady doesn't have her dignity, what *does* she have?

I can tell you, however, that he was a pure gentleman, a kind, considerate . . .

Oh, I can't keep it in!

We made love! We made mad, passionate, unadulterated, pure love. It was a night of passion for the record books!

You might not want to hear this from someone who could be your grandmother, but you have to understand. Whether we're seventy-five or twenty-five (or seventy-five trapped in the body of a twenty-nine-year-old), women still need to feel that passion. No matter what age we are, we still want to feel the warm body of a man who is there only to unleash the deepest, darkest parts of our most secret sexual desires. Every woman should feel that at least once in her lifetime. If you're married to a man who can give you that on a nightly basis, my hat's off to you.

I'll tell you this: the things that he did to me, Howard never did to me, in all the years we were married. Who taught this boy these things? Seriously, where did he learn to do the things he did to me? Did other women teach him these things (and where did they learn it?) or did he learn it from that Internet? Does *Playboy* magazine still dole out that information?

Well, it could be this: maybe we both felt so free that anything was okay. Maybe it was me. I'll tell you something, I never felt that free with my body. Howard never once asked to see my body. Never once. He never took off my clothes like Zachary might have (or might not have—I mean, I'll tell you as much as I can, but really, a lady doesn't kiss and tell) just to look at my body and feel the parts of my body that I had felt earlier that morning. I'm not talking the private parts here. I'm talking about touching and feeling everything from my smooth elbows to the curve of my shoulders to the tips of my toes. Who knew that someone touching the small of my back could send me to a place of sheer exhilaration, the likes of which I never felt before?

I don't even know how many times we did it (I am blushing still, even as I'm telling you this). I don't know how many times he kissed my lips (and every other part of my body). In those few hours, though, all those gushy things you hear, stuff like how your bodies become one and how you can feel each other's thoughts, I felt all of them. I felt it every time he looked into my eyes and every time he kissed a part of my body. I felt it every time he even touched a part of my body, and I felt it with every word that came out of his mouth. It was a lifetime of love encapsulated into one night. If I summed up all my years with Howard, it would have equaled ten minutes, maybe less. Five.

Afterward Zachary was cuddling me in his arms. We were both hot and sweaty, but I still needed the blanket to keep warm.

I loved feeling his arms around me. I felt so safe, like everything was meant to be. I didn't even know what time it was. I thought it must have been three or four in the morning, but I came to find out later that it was much earlier than that. I had fit a lifetime into just a few hours.

My back was up against his body—spooning, I think they call it. My mind was racing, thinking about the day, about Lucy, about Barbara, about Howard.

Isn't that crazy? I tried to get him out of my head, but I just couldn't. As much as I was feeling for Zachary at that point, my mind was on Howard. I was so damned angry at Howard. I was angry that I'd wasted my life with him. I thought about those times when Barbara was little and I knew he was out cheating on me. I should have left him. I could have found another life. I could have found love. Instead, I wasted everything I could have had for the sake of security.

Back and forth I went, my mind was going a mile a minute about Howard. I was angry, I was sad, I wanted to tell him how I felt. I wanted to have it out with him. I wanted to tell him, *Great, I got all the diamonds in the world, but once, just once, couldn't you have just slipped me a note with a heart on it? Couldn't you just once have told me I looked pretty when I didn't spend hours dolling myself up? Couldn't you have once, just once, come home with some flowers because you were thinking of me? Not because you cheated on me and you felt bad, but because you thought about what a great wife I was, or how well I was bringing up your daughter? Damn you, Howard! Didn't you think I bought your daughter up well? Was I not a great wife to you? Did I ever make any huge demands on you? Did I shut my mouth and let you do what you wanted? How did you pay me back? How did you pay me back, Howard?*

"What are you thinking about?" Zachary asked as he pulled me in closer.

I didn't answer him, though. I just kept thinking of Howard. *Am I right? Was I a terrible wife? Did I get lazy in the way I loved you? Did I not tend to all of your needs? Why couldn't we have ever discussed it? Why, in all the years of our marriage, couldn't we have sat down and discussed the state of the marriage? What were your problems with the marriage? What were my problems? How could we have made it better? Instead, we spent all those years tiptoeing around each other.*

But now I had the chance to change everything.

"Hey," Zachary whispered as he spooned me tighter. "Where are you?"

He was right. My body was right up against him, but my mind had clearly gone someplace else.

"Sorry," I said, taking his hand. "I was thinking."

"Are you upset about something?" he asked as he turned me around to face him. "Is there something you're not telling me?"

"What do you mean?" I asked him.

"All of a sudden you're different. Are you regretting something?"

"About you?" I asked him. "I don't regret anything about you," I said, giving him a peck on the lips.

"Do you regret we slept together the first night we met?" he asked, concerned.

"Oh god, no. Trust me, I don't regret this night for a second. I wanted this more than you could ever imagine."

"So . . ." He paused. "Is it Howard?"

My heart jumped when he said that. Did he know? Did he know the truth? How did he know?

"Why would you . . . How do you know about Howard?"

"Because you mentioned him a bunch of times this evening. Was he a long-term thing?"

"He was." I started to tear up.

"Were you engaged to him?" he asked me.

"Yes, I was. I was very young, though," I told him.

"Is it over now?" he asked me.

I didn't know how to answer that at first. In one sense, there's no way it couldn't have been over. The man dropped dead in his coleslaw from a heart attack. Even if I didn't love him and he didn't love me, would he always have this hold over me?

"Yes," I said, stroking my hand through Zachary's hair. "It's over now."

"So what is it?" he asked.

I turned around again and he resumed spooning me, pulling me in tight. Tears came out of my eyes. Thoughts of my husband and the life that we shared went through my head.

"I . . ." I said, wiping my eyes. "I have a major regret in my life."

"That's it?" he asked.

"That's a lot," I said. "Believe me, it's a lot."

"No," he said, turning me toward him again. "It's not a lot."

"No, you don't understand," I told him. "Believe me, you don't know the half of it."

"What I know," he said, "is that you've got a lot years ahead of you to make up for anything that you've ever regretted."

"No, I don't. That's the point," I said.

"Trust me," he said. "You may not think you do, but you've got a lot of years to change what you think you might have done wrong."

At the time, I thought I knew what he meant. Later, I would take his words and turn them into something very different. I wasn't yet at that point, though. I was still twenty-nine, and I was still in the bed of this young handsome man who only wanted to share the world with me.

What if I *did* have a lot of years ahead of me? Throughout the day, I had thought about the possibility of staying twenty-nine. For all I knew, I would be twenty-nine forever. Sure, I'd wished to be twenty-nine for a day, and I got my wish, but I didn't get it in writing. Maybe I could have a choice. Maybe I could stay twenty-nine forever if I wished hard enough. Lucy would understand. Barbara would get on with her life. Frida already said she would learn to deal. This wasn't about them anymore, though. This was about me. This was about righting the wrongs in my life.

I had been given a gift. I had been given the greatest gift that could be bestowed on anyone. It was a gift better than diamonds or a closet full of clothes or an extravagant trip.

I had been given the gift of starting all over again with someone else.

And this time I was going to do it right.

A smile came over my face. All the baggage I had with Howard, I was now able to drop. I was going to start all over again. Maybe Zachary and I would move far away and I wouldn't have to speak to anyone from my former life. I would miss Lucy, but I'd still speak to her from time to time. I could move on with things.

I wondered if I could even start another family. Men do it all the time. This time I would bring my children up right. I would teach them to think for themselves and to be independent, but at the same time insist when I thought something was right.

"I have something that I think is going to make you feel better," Zachary said, getting out of bed and heading toward the kitchen.

"What is it?" I called to him.

"It's a surprise," he said.

I sat up in bed and propped the pillows and smoothed out the sheets as I waited for him.

This was what it felt like to be taken care of. Whatever he was bringing back, the smallest of things would be more appreciated than anything I could ever want.

He appeared in the doorway.

In his hand was a plate. On the plate was one cupcake with a candle in it.

"Happy birthday," he said.

"When did you get that?" I said, laughing and clapping my hands.

"I actually got it this morning, when I met you," he said, coming toward me as he shielded the candle from going out. "I meant to eat it today, but I never got the chance. It's funny, because I only went in there for a muffin. I've never bought a cupcake in my life, but it just looked too good to pass up. Now I know why I bought it. It was meant for you." He sat down beside me and placed the plate on my lap. "Make a wish," he whispered.

So I did. I closed my eyes tight and said my wish in my head over and over.

I wished that I could start all over again.

I wished that I wouldn't turn back to seventy-five.

I wished that I could be twenty-nine this year and thirty the next, and so on.

I wished that I could be with Zachary and relive my life with him.

And then I opened my eyes and blew out the candle.

I smiled. This could work. This had to work.

"Thank you so much for this," I said as he unwrapped the foil from the cake.

"Take a bite," he told me as I opened my mouth. So I did, and then he did the same.

"Did you make a good wish?" he asked when we were halfway through.

"Yes," I said as we kissed, getting icing on each other's faces.

We finished the cake, and Zachary got under the covers again.

"Blue Eyes?" I asked him as he got on top of me and started kissing me.

"What is it?" he asked. "Anything."

"Let's go away," I said. "Let's go far away and be together."

"I was thinking the same thing." He smiled. "I was thinking that I'd love to take you to my favorite bistro in Paris. I want to take you to Rome and sit at an outdoor café and drink espresso with you. I want to climb the steps to the Parthenon and walk on top of the Great Wall of China with you. How does that sound?" he asked me.

"That's exactly what I was thinking," I told him.

"Do you have to go back to Chicago tomorrow?" he asked me.

"Do I what?" I asked, then I remembered. "No, there's nothing that I have to go back to Chicago for. Nothing is keeping me from going anywhere!" I shouted with excitement. "How about you?"

"I'm free to go, too!" he shouted. Then he said, "You know, I never asked you what you do. What's your job?" he asked.

I tried to think of something to tell him. I almost said "computers," but I knew he'd never believe that in a million years. So I told him the truth.

"I'm qutting my job," I told him. "I was there for a lot of years, but lying here with you I realize that I don't need it anymore. I want to do a lot of other things with my life."

"Good for you," he said.

"Thank you," I said to him, and I meant it. I was proud of myself. I was thrilled. I was over the moon. "And now I get to do what I really want," I told him.

"And what's that?" he asked me.

"I get to be with you." I smiled.

We kissed passionately as he wrapped me in his arms.

And then we made love again.

But I don't kiss and tell.

My eyes shot open.

I had no idea what time it was. Zachary's apartment was pitch-dark.

Memories of a life that hadn't even occurred came pouring through my head.

It was the life Zachary and I would live together.

There would be pet names. He would come to know that I don't like the sheets tucked in at the bottom of the bed. He would hate that I leave little gobs of toothpaste in the sink after I brush. He would like his newly washed socks to be placed starting on the left of the drawer, and he would joke, "This way none of the socks get jealous that I'm wearing one pair more than another." He'd learn that I always like at least a half a tank of gas at all times in the car, because you never know. We would eat at seven-thirty, not eight. We would be in bed by midnight. Zachary would always put an extra blanket on my side of the bed in case I got cold. Sometimes in the middle of the night we would both wake up instinctively at the same time and hold each other until we both fell asleep again. Sometimes we would wake up, and neither of us could get back to sleep, so we'd just talk about the day we had or what was on tap for the next day. Or we would make love.

I could see us making goo-goo eyes at an outdoor café in Paris, or skiing down slopes in Switzerland. All of the dreams we talked about in our one evening together would come to life. We would decorate our home with the treasures we picked up in these places. These trinkets would become stories from our life. We'd make new friends together. Some of the wives would become my closest friends. They would become the women I'd reach out to if I needed some estrogen time. They would call me to grab a cup of coffee, or to take a quick jaunt to a shop.

I would become an integral part of Zachary's business, picking out the clothing for his Web site and becoming familiar with the latest designers all around the world. Zachary would begin to rely on my opinions. He would take them very seriously. I would have a knack for knowing exactly what to buy. I would begin to understand the Web site, and make it even easier for people to shop. The business would go from being his to being ours. It would become even more successful because of my input.

I would be introduced to his family in a way I had never known them before. His mother would be older than me, and I would respect her. I would ask her for advice even though I already knew the answers. We would spend holidays with his family. They would become my family. He would talk of his grandmother, and I would listen and tell him I wish I'd met her.

We would get older. We'd be forty, fifty, sixty . . . seventy-five. Would we have children? I don't know. Maybe we would. We'd have a daughter, and she'd be like Lucy. I would insist she figure out her own life instead of living mine. I'd make sure she had no insecurities about herself. She would be independent and freethinking. My advice would be just that, advice. My children could take it or leave it. There would be celebrations, and there would be times of grief. We would say good-bye to older relatives and welcome new ones.

Then Zachary and I would live out the twilight of our lives. We would look back with joy on a life together. Maybe we made some mistakes, but we did it together. We stuck it out for each other. We always put each other first, before anyone else. The love between us was undeniable. In our last days, we'd ask ourselves as we did so many times before: *How did we get so lucky?*

My eyes widened as fear shot through my body.

I knew I had to go back.

It's not that I wanted to; I didn't want to. The warmth of Zachary's arms around me was more than enough to keep me there forever. The comfort of his bed, the way his legs lightly touched mine, his relaxed breathing, in and out.

My mind was running a mile a minute. Would I get out of that bed? Everything depended on my staying or getting out of bed. If I stayed, my new life would begin. If I got out of bed, my old life would stay intact. I did not want to get out of bed. Everything in my body told me not to get out of bed. My mind, however, was telling me something very different.

Barbara.

Frida.

Lucy.

Howard.

They were my life. A life without them was no life. The other life I was thinking of—that was someone else's life. How did all this happen, anyway? It was just a birthday wish made by an old woman. A wish that doing it all over again would make things right. There was no way I could continue my life without the people I loved. I would learn from my mistakes. I would make the future right.

I had brought Barbara into this world. To abandon her, even at this late stage, would hurt too much. I love my Barbara. I love her more than she will ever know.

To leave Frida at this point in our lives, even if I did see her from time to time . . . it wouldn't be the same. We wouldn't understand each other anymore. Sometime in our lives a pact had been made, and I realized now that I couldn't break it. We began our lives together. We experienced each decade of our lives as they changed and we changed. How could I not see it through to the end?

I took a deep breath.

I could not run away from the life I had built. It wasn't right. This was not the second chance at life I was meant to have. I was not meant to have a second life. I just needed to know that the first life was worth it.

I looked over at the clock to see what time it was, hoping that I still had time to get out of there before . . . It was 11:59! And then the clock turned to midnight.

And right then I changed. Again.

It was odd. It wasn't as if it happened slowly. I felt it in the blink of an eye. One second I was breathing easy; the next second I felt as if a hard shell had suddenly grown on top of my skin.

One day. Twenty-four hours. That was all I wished for on my birthday, and whether I liked it or not, that was what I got. All that thinking that I could stay twenty-nine had been pointless. It was the wish. The wish was being twenty-nine for a day—not a week, and not a lifetime.

One day. And it was all over.

I placed my hand on my neck.

It didn't feel smooth and supple as it had that day.

Now it felt tough and fatigued.

Every single part of my body ached, but I had to get out of there as carefully as I could, without waking Zachary. I felt like I had run a marathon, but I couldn't think about the pain at that point. Could you imagine the look on his face if he opened his eyes and saw a seventy-five-year-old woman lying next to him naked?

I slowly turned to sit up and put my feet on the ground. The hardwood floors started to creak as I put my weight on them. I grabbed my lower back to lessen the pain as Zachary rolled to the other side of the bed and began snoring loudly. Thank goodness for his snoring; he wouldn't hear me. I knew that from my time with Howard. When Howard was in such a deep sleep, I could have banged pots and pans in his ears and he still wouldn't have woken up. I knew I was safe as long as I heard that deep gruff sound coming from him.

I knelt down and felt around the bed until I located the fabric of my black dress. I crept toward the bathroom, feeling the walls and furniture around me like I was blind. I was blind. Everything was completely blurry around me. Why I didn't just throw my glasses into my bag, I'll never know. As I shut the door to the bathroom, I turned on the light and squinted my eyes as I tried to bend down and put on the dress. Oh, my back, my legs, my bunions! I had gone from such an easy pain-free body to feeling like I'd just put on a wetsuit that was three sizes too big.

And then, as if I didn't have enough trouble, I couldn't zip the dress. My potbelly was in the way. There was no way I could zip up the dress and move my breasts into the correct position, no matter how many times I tried. I didn't know whether to be agitated or scared at that point. All I kept thinking was *Please don't let him wake up. Please, please, don't wake up.*

Needless to say, I wasn't even going to attempt to find my heels.

I tried to look at myself in the mirror, but it was just too blurry for me to see anything. (By the way, that was fine with me. There was nothing to see. It was just the same old me. I was the last person I wanted to see when I looked in the mirror.)

I turned off the bathroom light and found my way toward Zachary's closet. I grabbed any old pair of pants and a T-shirt off a shelf. Remember, I was doing all of this blind. I wouldn't know what I grabbed until I got home, just that it had an elastic waist and I wouldn't need a belt. I felt around the bottom of the closet and came across a pair of sneakers; at least I assumed they were sneakers because I felt laces. It was easy for me to just slip my feet into them, as Zachary's feet were quite a few sizes bigger than mine.

Don't even ask me how I found my way toward the door to his apartment and undid the locks. My senses were on their highest alert.

I thought about saying good-bye to Zachary. I wanted to

apologize and tell him I wouldn't be going to Paris with him, or to Italy. He would find someone else to do those things with. I had already done them, anyway. He would find a young woman who respected him and loved him for who he was, that I was sure of. I wondered if he would be hurt when he woke up the next morning and I wasn't there. Would he call Lucy looking for me? It would bother him for a little while, his heart would be a little broken, but he would get over it. After all, he was young. He had his whole life in front of him. I had already lived my life.

I slowly opened the door. The shoes were so big it took more energy to keep my feet in them than to walk toward the elevator. Thank goodness it was late. Could you imagine the look on anyone's face if they saw this old woman leaving Zachary's apartment dressed in his clothes? By the time I got into the elevator, though, I was relieved that I had gotten out of there without being noticed. Now all I wanted to do was get home.

How far was I from home?

I could barely make out the street sign in front of the apartment. If I was seeing correctly, I was only a few blocks away. I couldn't hear anyone on the streets at all. A big metropolis like Philadelphia, and there was no one on the street. At that point, though, I couldn't have cared less who saw me. By that point, home was the only thing on my mind. I just wanted to get to the safety of my home. I just wanted to go to bed and stay there. Block after block I walked, squinting my eyes, hearing the trudging sound of the sneakers against the pavement as I made my way down the street. All around me I could see lights from storefronts glowing in reds and yellows and blues. These lights were my only guide. I knew that the big smear of red light on

Chestnut Street had to be the sign over the Continental Restaurant. I wasn't far. I just kept thinking, *Just a few more blocks and I'll be home. Safe.*

Only a few hours before I had been happy—more than happy, exhilarated and excited. Now I was sadder than I'd ever been in my entire life. But it was the right thing to do. It was right that I turned back to seventy-five. Still, I was mourning what might have been.

I found my way to Rittenhouse Square, my street, and turned toward my building. I could see a figure standing some ways down.

"Mrs. Jerome?" I heard the voice call out.

I stopped. "Ken?" I squinted my eyes to try to get a better look.

I could see the figure of him walking briskly toward me. When he put his hand on my shoulder, I knew that I was finally home.

"Are you okay, Mrs. Jerome?" he asked me.

"I'm fine," I told him as we walked toward the door. "Don't you ever get an hour off from work?" I asked him as he helped me through the door.

"Your family was worried about you, so I gave Carl, the night man, the night off. "I've been watching for you all night."

"Thank you, Ken," I told him as I heard the elevator door open. "Are they up there?"

"They're all up there. Mrs. Sustamorn came down a little while ago, but then she went back up. She waited with me for a little bit, but I told her to go back up and try to get some sleep."

"Thank you for looking out for my family," I told him as he pressed the elevator button.

"Do you need help up?" he asked.

"Thank you," I said, jingling my keys. "I can take it from here. You've been very kind."

"You've always been pretty nice to me, too, Mrs. J. I'm glad you're back," he said kindly as the elevator door shut.

I opened the door to my apartment and saw the fuzzy images of three sleeping bodies spread out on my couches and chairs. I didn't want to speak to any of them. I just needed to think about what this day meant.

"Gram?" I heard Lucy call softly as I saw one figure rise slowly from a chair.

"Yes," I called back. "It's me. I'm going to sleep."

"Ellie?" I heard Frida call to me as I headed to my bedroom. I turned toward her.

"Your back must be hurting as much as mine is right now, Frida. Go upstairs and get into your own bed."

I walked into my bedroom and over to my bedside table, where I knew I had left my glasses. I put them on and the world finally came into view.

"Mom?" I heard and I turned to see Barbara standing in my doorway. She was in one of my robes. The belt barely wrapped around her body. Her hair was loose from its usual tied-back look and was hanging straggly around her face. Oddly, she looked better.

"Barbara," I said and sighed. "Before you start in on me, I'm very tired right now, and I would like to go to sleep."

"I wasn't going to start in." She exhaled and smiled lightly. "I'm just glad you're home."

I paused, not knowing what to say. I was forgetting all that we had discussed earlier that evening. "Well, thank you," I said. "I just need some rest right now."

"Mom?" she asked, coming toward me.

"What is it?" I asked.

She put her arms around me and gave me a big hug, resting her head on my shoulder. I didn't want to hug her back. I didn't want to hug anyone at that moment, but I couldn't just shoo her away, even though I didn't want to be touched. I was still wrapped up in my own thoughts, and I wasn't ready to deal with anything. So I put one arm around her and patted her back for a moment, but she kept hugging me. She wouldn't stop. So I opened my arms around her and hugged her back. I rested my head on her shoulder and relaxed my body until she was almost holding me up. I realized I needed that hug, and not the other way around.

A moment later we stopped hugging and she smiled at me. I smiled back.

"Barbara, I love you so much," I told her as I combed the hair hanging in her face behind her ears with my fingers. "You mean more to me than you will ever know."

"I love you, too, Mom," she answered.

"I want to talk, I do. I want things to be right between us."

"So do I, Mom. I don't know how things got so crazy between us."

"I know, and I'm sorry for that. Right now, though, I need to rest. Once my head is clear we'll talk about everything."

"Are you sure there's nothing I can do for you?" she asked me.

"No, thank you, sweetheart. I just need some time to think."

"You'll call me if you need anything," she said.

"Yes. I'll let you know."

"I'll shut the door so you won't be disturbed," she said, walking out and closing the door lightly behind her.

I walked over to my closet and began to take off Zachary's clothes. Next to me was my full-length mirror. How I got through the streets looking like I did I'll never know. Thank goodness Zachary never woke up. Oh, thank goodness! In front of me was an old woman, old and shriveled. I almost forgot who that woman was. I bent down as easily as I could and slipped off Zachary's shoes, then his sweatpants, then the ratty T-shirt I had thrown on. I felt like I looked, like I had aged almost fifty years. I couldn't look anymore. I stuffed the outfit deep in the back of my closet, where those dude-ranch blue jeans used to be. I would pick those jeans off my bedroom floor later. All I wanted to do now was get into bed.

I threw on one of my old nightgowns and walked out of my closet and over to my bed.

As I rested my head on the pillow, I looked around the room. Only twenty-four hours earlier, I'd loved that room so much. Now it was everything to do with the past I seemed to be stuck with. I was confused.

Why did I wish to be younger? How would it have answered the one question I needed answered? If Zachary wasn't the answer, then what was? Who was my soul mate? Was it Howard? I still didn't know. Did I love him? Did I ever love him?

On my seventy-sixth birthday, should I wish to start my life over at twenty-nine, and not for just one day?

I took off my glasses as I rolled over onto my stomach. I positioned my boobs more comfortably. There was nothing more I needed to see that day.

I leaned over and turned off my light.

And I wished.

I wished that I was content with my life; that even though I didn't know the answer to my question, that even though I might never know the answer, this pain in my heart would leave.

I wished and wished.

And as I lay there in the dark with my eyes wide open, I thought about it rationally. That's what a seventy-five-year-old woman does—she rationalizes. After all, she's used to it after all those years. For the first time in my life, though, I knew that there was no point to wishing or wanting or trying to recapture youth.

It was that simple.

I had to leave Zachary and our life together behind. My second chance at life lay ahead of me, with the family I loved. But a wise and rational woman can also feel sadness and regret.

As much as I tried to rationalize, the sadness kept raging inside of me.

For the rest of my life, I would never be twenty-nine again.

F rida Freedberg slept like a log.

The next morning she opened her eyes and stared at the ceiling of her bedroom. How comforting it was to see her ceiling. She was back in her own warm bed. She bent her legs and pulled her body in as she wrapped the covers tighter around herself.

She glanced over at her clock and saw that it was half past eleven in the morning. Frida always slept late, but this was much later than usual. She had missed her morning programs, but so be it.

She got out of bed and took a shower. She wasn't very hungry that morning, so she just made some toast and ate it as quickly as she could.

She had a lot of things to do that day. Well, there was one thing in particular she wanted to do, but it would take a couple of hours to get up the nerve.

She went into her closet and pulled out the pair of blue jeans she never wore, the ones she got with Ellie that time they went to the dude ranch. Frida had chickened out of getting on the horses, so she'd just stayed in her muumuu and sipped iced tea by the pool. The jeans were a little snug, even with her girdle on underneath, but no bother. They would fit as the months went by. They'd even get too big, and she'd have to buy another pair if she stuck to the diet she was planning.

She matched the jeans with one of her dead husband Sol's old blue oxford shirts. To make the outfit look more feminine, she threw on some long gold chains she hadn't worn in twenty years, and finished the look off with a pair of gold stud earrings. She put on her sneakers from the day before and was ready to leave the house by noon.

She grabbed her keys, as well as an extra set of keys to leave downstairs with Ken. She took her purse, her checkbook, and her wallet with two forms of ID, checking three times to make sure she had everything.

Frida left the apartment with one hand on her purse and one on the door. Then she checked again to make sure she had her keys and shut the door.

She got in the elevator and pressed the number for Ellie's floor.

"Ellie?" she called, knocking on her door.

There was no answer.

Frida used Ellie's keys to open her door. The blankets she and Barbara and Lucy had used were folded and piled on top of one another by the couch, where she remembered putting them before she left the night before. Frida took a look at herself in the Paris mirror in front of the door. It was only for a second, but that was all she needed to notice how attractive she looked that day.

"Ellie?" Frida whispered as she slowly opened the door to El-lie's room. The room was dark. The only light coming in was at the sides of Ellie's blinds. Ellie was lying on her stomach, as she always did when she slept. Her head was facing the opposite di-rection. She flinched when Frida called her name, but she didn't turn her head.

"Ellie, it's past noon. I'm going out to run some errands, and I wanted to see if there was anything you might need," she whispered.

Ellie didn't answer her.

"Ellie, is there anything you need?" she whispered again.

"No, that's okay," Ellie answered with a slumbering voice.

"I'll be back to check on you later, okay?"

Ellie grumbled.

Frida locked the door to Ellie's apartment and took the eleva-tor downstairs.

"Hi, Ken." She smiled as he opened the door for her.

"Have a good day, Mrs. Freedberg," he answered lethargically.

"Ken," she said, stopping before she reached the door. "I just want to thank you for looking out for Mrs. Jerome last night. That was a very kind thing for you to do."

"Oh, it was all right. I kind of felt responsible for letting that girl up the other day."

"Well, I want to thank you just as well." She smiled as she held out her hand.

"I appreciate it." Ken smiled as he shook her hand, feeling her pass him something in between their connected palms.

"I'll be back in a little bit," she said, walking out the door.

Ken watched her leave and then looked into his hand. Frida

had slipped him a folded five-dollar bill and an extra set of keys to her apartment.

"Well," he said, nodding at the bill, "it's a start." He laughed as he placed her keys in the closet and pocketed the money.

The first place she went was to the cell phone store she'd passed on Walnut Street many times before. So many times she'd thought about walking in, but today she actually would.

Two hours later, she had her own cell phone. It was a handsome little thing, black with a flip top. She walked back down Walnut Street, memorizing the phone number they had given her. Frida had signed up for a two-year plan so the phone was free, but she also bargained with them for free insurance in case her phone was lost or stolen. What a terrific deal!

Moments later she found herself in front of a hair salon. She peered in through the window and noticed that some of the chairs were vacant. It was one of those sleek salons where all the kids went. At first she was hesitant about walking in; the place seemed quite intimidating with all the attractive young people milling about. But she took a deep breath and seized the moment.

"Hello," she greeted the woman behind the counter. "I was wondering if any of your hairdressers might be free today for a shampoo and blow-dry."

"I think Szechuan is free right now," the receptionist answered warmly, looking into her book. "Yep, he's free," she said, getting up. "Let's get you into a robe. Fabulous necklaces, by the way," she added.

"Oh, thank you." Frida blushed.

Forty-five minutes later, Frida's hair had been washed and

combed and blown straight. She would think about Szechuan's suggestion of lightening up her grays, but that would be something to do another day. She would definitely be back. The hair salon was much livelier than her normal salon. She liked the way they treated her. She seemed special in their eyes. Evidently they didn't get many seventy-five-year-old women, and that made her feel unique. Szechuan had straightened her normal curled updo into a free-flowing bob. She agreed with Szechuan when he told her she looked five years younger.

She strutted down Chestnut Street with a skip in her step, glancing at her reflection in each storefront window. It hadn't occurred to her at all that day that her heartburn wasn't acting up, that her arthritis seemed to be gone. The sneakers did hurt a bit, but she figured they'd get more comfortable as she broke them in.

As she strolled back to her apartment building, she wondered if she should have had her makeup done, too, but then she thought she'd save that for another day.

She was ready to do the one thing she'd wanted to do for years. If she didn't have the guts to do it today, she'd never do it.

"Nice coif, Mrs. F.," Ken greeted her as she entered the building.

"Oh, it's nothing." Frida giggled. "I just thought it was time for a nice change."

"Change is always good," he said.

"It is, isn't it?"

She pressed the up elevator button. She thought she might check on Ellie once again, show her the new hairdo and phone, but she was on a mission, and there was no stopping her now.

There had been many times before that she had thought about doing it, but her nerves had gotten to her. What if it didn't turn out the way she wanted it? What if she was laughed at? Today, though, she decided there was no time like the present.

She entered the elevator and pressed the correct floor. Maybe she could be an example to Ellie and stir her from the depression that seemed to have taken her over. She was, after all, still worried about her friend. Whatever had happened to Ellie the day before, she would come out of it. Ellie was strong, much stronger than Frida ever was. She knew Ellie. She knew she'd snap out of it eventually. Just thank goodness she was okay. It was hard not to worry about Ellie, but Frida knew she just couldn't anymore. She hoped that Ellie had answered the question that had been bothering her for years. She needed to trust that her friend was fine. And she would be.

Frida walked down the hallway, approached the apartment door, and gave it a knock.

"Just a second," the voice inside called out.

Frida's immediate instinct was to run (or at least walk swiftly because of the pain from the sneakers). Maybe she was making a mistake. What made her think that she could actually go through with this?

"Who is it?" the voice asked.

"It's Frida Freedberg," she answered with a tinge of nervousness in her voice.

"Frida!" the voice answered warmly as Frida heard the locks being turned.

The door opened. There he was, handsome Hershel Neal, in one of his handsome argyle sweaters.

"Well, this is a nice surprise. Frida, you look lovely today."

"Thank you, Hershel," she answered, patting her head. "I had my hair done this morning."

"Well, it's very becoming." He smiled. "Would you like to come in?" He motioned as he opened the door wider. "I was just preparing myself a cup of coffee."

"Actually," she said nervously, clearing her throat. "Actually, I was just going to the coffee shop around the corner. You know, the one with the nice tables and chairs set up outside? I thought it was such a nice day that it would be lovely to sit out there and do some people-watching."

"Oh, I see," he said.

"Well," she said, then paused. "I was wondering if you were free. You might want to come with me. It's a beautiful day, and they have those tables where you can sit outside. Did I say that already?" She realized she had just repeated herself and knew she was red in the face, which made her giggle like a schoolgirl.

Hershel hesitated for a moment. Frida tensed up. How stupid she suddenly felt. Of course he wouldn't want to go with her. He only had the hots for Ellie. What was she thinking? How could she get out of there? Alternative plans went through her head. She'd go back to her apartment. She'd read the full instruction manual to her new cellular phone. She'd make a brisket for Ellie.

"You know what?" he said.

"No, that's fine, if you're already making coffee . . ." she mumbled as she took a step to walk away.

"No, actually, it would be good to get outside instead of being cooped up inside all day. I'd love to go with you." He smiled.

"Oh!" She smiled back at him.

"Let me just get my sportcoat."

"I'll wait here," she said, not knowing what else to do.

"Come on in," he said. "I'll only be a second."

Frida felt absolutely exhilarated.

"Something is different about you, Frida," he said as he shut the door. "I just can't put my finger on it."

"Oh, it's just the hair," she said dismissively. "That's all."

"Well, the new hairstyle is doing wonders for you." He smiled as he closed the door.

barbara's day after

Everything was different that morning.

Barbara had never seen her husband, Larry Sustamorn, as happy as he was cuddling with her in bed.

To think, all it took to excite Larry Sustamorn after all these years was the one thing she had refused to give him since the early days of their marriage. She had seen a magazine article about it a few months back. She had taken only a glance at it at the time, deciding her marriage was fine and didn't need any help.

Now she knew better.

Barbara hadn't gotten home until four in the morning. All she could think about was having a snack and then getting into bed. She threw her purse and keys on the wooden bench by the front door and headed to the kitchen. Once there, she grabbed her secret stash of jalapeño poppers from the back of the freezer and threw them in the microwave. Five minutes later she had a plate full of enough steaming poppers to satiate the appetite of a family of four.

Figuring she'd eat her poppers in front of some late-night television, she picked up her plate and left the kitchen, crossing through the front hallway again on her way to the den. It was then that she saw the figure sitting on the couch that faced the door.

He looked like a pathetically thin old dog—*her* pathetically thin old dog.

"Larry?" she spoke softly, resting her free hand on his shoulder. Larry opened his eyes.

"Oh, hi, Barb." He exhaled groggily. "I was waiting for you to come in, and I guess I fell asleep. Is everything okay?"

"Everything is fine. Well, today was crazy, but I'll tell you all about it in the morning. Were you waiting here all night?"

"Yeah." He yawned as she helped him up from the couch. "I tried calling your cell phone a bunch of times, but I didn't get any answer."

She sighed and set the plate of poppers on the side table and took her husband's hand.

"I'm sorry if I worried you, Larry."

"It's okay," he answered indifferently. "Just as long as you're home safely."

As they walked up the stairs toward their bedroom, it dawned on her. That fateful day, and then coming home to Larry, had taught her something. As she rested her head on her pillow next to her husband, she wondered, had she ever taken a step back and looked at her life?

Barbara Sustamorn never had a job after she married Larry. Money was just this thing she went to the bank for. It never ran out, and it never once occurred to her that it *might* run out. She never saw a credit card bill, or even an electric bill. Her closets were full of whatever she wanted to buy.

There was one person who was responsible for this.

One person who never criticized her weight or told her to exercise more. One person who never asked her to stop agonizing over the most trivial things. One person who always called three times a day to see how her day was going. There was never a question that he might be cheating or doing something else behind her back. He was always home at six-thirty on the dot. He had joined her in bringing up the most perfect daughter. Had she ever thanked him? Had she ever once truly showed her appreciation? And most of all, how had he put up with her all those years?

She looked over at Larry, who had already fallen back to sleep. She caressed his receding hairline. What the heck had she been doing spending her life in a constant state of anger and frustration? It was time to stop worrying about her mother. It was time to stop worrying about Lucy. They had their own lives to live.

The bottom line? It took that one day away from her normal life for her to realize what was truly important. What seemed like a day from hell was really a gift to help her see her life for what it was. What did she realize? Her life was glorious. It was a life that the majority of the world could only dream about living.

Who made it possible for her to have such a carefree life?

One person.

Larry Sustamorn.

Of all the people in her life, Larry Sustamorn was the one person she should have put first, before anyone. By the grace of God he was still there for her. For that, Barbara Sustamorn vowed to herself that she would spend the rest of her days thanking him.

And as a result, the following years would be the happiest of her life.

Hours later, Larry awoke to a new a sensation. It was a sensation so stimulating he thought he was dreaming. He opened his eyes and drew back the covers to find his wife in a position so exciting to him he was positive he had to be dreaming.

As Barbara looked up at Larry, she couldn't remember the last time she'd seen him with a bigger smile.

And by the by, who knew that Larry Sustamorn still remembered how to return such gratifying sexual favors?

Later that afternoon they were still lying in bed.

"It's fun to take the day off, isn't it?" He smiled.

"You bet it is." She smiled back. "Mrs. Rovner can wait to have her cavity filled tomorrow."

"You ready for another round soon?" he inquired, playfully tapping her on the arm.

"Larry, you're crazy!" she cackled as she kissed him back.

"Oh, am I?" He kissed her lips. "And maybe later we'll go to the jewelry store and replace the stolen jewelry. My poor little Barbie, being held up at gunpoint. I think you also deserve an extra little trinket for being so brave."

"*Oh, Larry!*" she shouted with delight in her thick nasal accent. "*Oh, Larry, Larry, Larry!*"

seventy-five years and
one week later

I was tired and I needed to sleep. I slept for a week. I don't think what I was feeling was depression; I was simply tired of thinking about everything. Only I couldn't stop. In between thinking about my question and what the answer could have been, I slept.

Sometimes I dreamed that I was young again. That I was with Zachary and we were living that life I had imagined earlier.

Other times I dreamed of Howard. Howard was here, he didn't have the heart attack that day, and we were in the old house, going about our lives. Then I'd wake up and be back to this reality.

I don't know how many times Barbara has called me already. I just tell her I'm tired, but I'm not ready to talk yet. I know I should, I know she's waiting for me, but I'm tired. She tells me she's coming down, but I insist she doesn't. The odd thing is that she actually listens to me. The talk we all had that night really got to her in some way. That and, I suppose, getting mugged.

I don't know how many times Frida has come down here

with food and more food, but I tell her I'm not hungry. At least she never mentions what happened. She's gone on two dates with Hershel Neal, and if there's anything to be happy about, that's it. I don't know why she never mentioned her feelings for Hershel. She never said a word. Oh, I hope it lasts, I really do. She seems different. She got her hair done in a different style, and she's wearing a little more makeup. Lucy seems to have given her a complete clothing makeover. I guess that's what happens to you when you get locked out of your apartment for a day and you see your oldest friend lose fifty years overnight.

And as for Lucy . . .

Lucy comes in every night and does her laundry or putters around while I'm in my room under my covers. I hear her walking around the apartment, turning on the television set, opening the fridge. She stays for a couple of hours and then comes to my bedroom, cracks open the door, and tells me she'll be back tomorrow.

She's the only person who doesn't tell me to get out of bed already. She's just there, and while I appreciate it, I'm not ready to talk about anything yet.

As a matter of fact, she's here now. I hear her outside the door, walking back and forth. God knows what she's doing.

"Gram?" I hear her whisper as the door to my bedroom opens just slightly, letting the light from the living room flow in.

I spoke too soon.

"I'm resting, sweetie," I tell her.

"Gram?" she says in her normal voice this time.

"Lucy, another time," I mumble to her.

"Gram," she repeats, opening the door wide, letting all the

light in as I bury my eyes in the pillow. She walks over to my bed, and now she's standing in front of me.

"Gram, it's time. It's enough already."

"Lucy, I just need my rest."

She gets on the bed and lies down next to me and puts her arm around me.

"Gram, this can't go on anymore."

"I told you," I say, turning my head away from her, "I just need to be left alone."

"Not you. I know that you're confused right now, but don't forget there's someone else who's hurting, too."

"Lucy, you got what you wanted," I cynically tell her, turning back toward her. "You wanted to spend the day with your grand-mother when she was twenty-nine, and you did. And what did I get out of it?"

"I'll tell you what you got!" she cries out. "You got a guy so distraught and brokenhearted that he's holed himself up in his place just like you have!"

"He is?" I ask her, surprised.

"Jesus, Gram. Zach keeps saying he fell in love with you and going on and on about how he's never felt anything like that so quickly, and why did you run away? He's called all three Ellie Jeromes in the Chicago area. He's thinking about heading there. He's pissed off at me because I won't give him your num-ber . . . or her number . . . I don't even know at this point. You have to talk to him."

I pause, then answer, "No way, Lucy. I can't do it. You must be out of your mind if you think I'm going to talk to him. Do you know what it would be like to talk to him when I look like this?"

I ask her, throwing off the covers and exposing my seventy-five-year-old body.

"Yes, like a grandmother. Like Ellie Michele's grandmother, or whatever we said her name was. I can't get through to the guy."

I think about it for a second as we lie there. There's no way I could see him again. I couldn't look into his blue eyes and know that I could never be with him. To think that I couldn't run my hands through that gorgeous head of hair, to explain to him what I knew. Maybe I *am* depressed.

"Lucy, I . . . I just can't." I lay my head on the pillow and turn away from her again.

"Jesus, Gram, what are you so upset about? What is it that was so bad that it's made you become a recluse? You say I got what I wanted? Well, damn straight. You got what you wanted, too!"

Now I'm angry with her. "What the hell did I get out of this whole thing? I want to know, Lucy—what did I get? You got what you wanted, but you know what I got?" I sit up in bed and stare right into her eyes. "I got nothing but heartache. I got to see what it was like to be young again? Big deal. My daughter learned from her mistakes and moved on. Frida turned a corner with all her anxieties. But me? I never got to know why all this happened. I never got an answer to my question. I was supposed to be selfish. I was supposed to be doing this for myself, and not for anyone else, and I got nothing in the end. And you know what? That pisses me off."

I punch the pillow and lay my head on it again.

Lucy is now fuming at me. I can see she is, but frankly, I don't care.

"Well, Gram, guess what?"

I don't answer her.

"Boo-hoo."

"What the hell is that supposed to mean?"

"I mean boo-hoo that you didn't get the answer to your question. Boo-hoo to all of it."

"You have no idea what you're talking about. You have no idea what it's like to live as many years as I have. When you get to be my age, then we can talk. Until then, Lucy, you have nothing to say on the subject."

"You think you're so old? What do you think? Do you think your life is over before you find that answer?" she asks me.

"Yes, as a matter of fact, I do."

"You know as well as I do that you've got the constitution of someone twenty years younger than you are. Believe me, with the attitude you've got going right now, you're going to waste the next twenty years of your life, and then what?"

"And then that's it," I grumble.

She takes a deep breath and gets off the bed. "Fine, live this way." She heads toward the door. "Live the rest of your life this way. See if I care."

"Thank you, I will," I tell her, burying my face in the pillow.

"I gave Zach your number. He asked if he could call my grandmother to talk about Ellie. He also said he had something else to tell you, but I don't know what. The least that you can do is talk to him about what happened."

"You better not have," I warn her.

She stops and puts her hands on her hips in dramatic fashion. "For once this week, Gram, stop thinking of yourself. Start thinking like someone from your generation!"

I hear her shut the door to the apartment, but now I'm up. I'm so angry with her I could scream.

It's almost eleven at night, but I've got so many feelings going on in my head, everything from anger to sadness. Damn her.

I put on my slippers and walk out of the bedroom. I can't remember the last time I walked around the apartment. It almost feels like these other rooms didn't exist.

I walk into the kitchen to make myself a cup of tea. I put some water in the kettle, turn on the stove, and grab some tea bags. I go into the cabinet and take out a cup and saucer. I use my good bone china every day. You should, too, if you don't have small children. It's a lesson I've learned: enjoy the things you have. Until recently I hadn't used the good china since a few years before Howard died, when I gave my last Thanksgiving dinner. There was so much cooking and cleaning for me to do after the dinner that I said my time was over. I told Barbara I was passing the baton to her. Barbara doesn't make the turkey or the stuffing or anything else. She gets it catered. I think that's wrong. She can't throw a turkey in the oven?

Oh, screw it already with what Barbara does wrong. She's a good girl.

Anyway, it occurred to me one day that all that gorgeous china was boxed up and I wasn't doing anything with it. Even in my current state, it still gives me a thrill when I take out my china for a simple cup of tea.

I bring my cup into the dining room and sit at my table.

It's so quiet in this apartment as I bring the teacup to my lips and then put it back on the table.

There are memories of my life everywhere I look. The walls

of my home are different, but its contents are the contents I've saved my entire life. Even the table I'm sitting at—five generations of women in my family have sat at this table. This gives me a little spark of joy. This was my mother's table that she oiled and salved constantly. How she loved this table. How many holiday dinners were spent around this table? So many generations dined there, my grandmother and mother, my mother and me and Barbara, all the way down to Lucy. I can almost hear the laughter and all the conversations we've had at this table. I can smell my grandmother's brisket and my mother's apple pie. I realize this table will be here for the next generation in my family. Barbara and Lucy will own this table one day, and if Lucy is lucky enough to have a child of her own she'll sit here, too.

I pick up my cup and saucer and walk toward my black baby grand piano. It's the most expensive side table anyone could ever own. I can't remember the last time I had that thing tuned, and I can't remember the last time anyone played it, but I don't care. Barbara didn't think I should bring it with me when I moved, but I insisted on it. I still love that piano. I love it in all its beauty, from the shine coming off the sides to the whites of the keys.

I look at all the pictures I've compiled through the years, framed in silver. The happy, smiling faces of each family member and friends don't tell the whole story, just the good parts, and for right now, it's all I want to see. Barbara at ten blowing out the candles on her birthday cake; Barbara at eighteen, at her high school graduation; Howard and me on one of our many wonderful trips; and so on. Then I see a picture so jarring it makes me drop my good bone china cup and saucer on the floor, shattering them. It's a picture I've never seen before, but it's set in a silver frame like all the others. It's next to the picture of Barbara and Larry on their wedding day, and just beyond Lucy's prom photo.

It's Lucy and me. Me at twenty-nine. It's the picture we took last week, before we went on the big date. We took it with her camera phone. The picture scares the living daylights out of me. Maybe because it's proof that it really did happen. They say that pictures don't lie, don't they? For that one day, I was a seventy-five-year-old in the body of a twenty-nine-year-old. The smiles on our young faces prove that. I got to do something with my granddaughter that no one else has ever gotten to do. For one day I lived the life my granddaughter lives. I got to see what it was like to live in her generation. I've never seen smiles on two happier people. It's such a beautiful photo that I don't even care that I spilled tea all over the floor and it's ruining my hardwood. I can't stop staring at this picture.

It must be over ten minutes before I set the picture back on the piano and head toward the kitchen to get a dishrag and the small wastepaper basket. I bring them back to the living room, where I clean up the floor and throw the broken china pieces into the basket.

As I look around the room, my eyes lead me to the books on the bookshelf just beyond the dining room. A lot of them were mine, but most of them were Howard's. I kept his old law books, which he studied from time to time. I like the way they look, with their leather-bound covers and gold-etched writing, so I kept ten of them. Really, though, they give me comfort. It makes me feel closer to Howard when I miss him from time to time. Even when Howard retired, it gave me such a nice feeling to see him get a new law book in the mail. It told me that being a lawyer wasn't just something he did to earn a lot of money; he truly liked what he did and was interested in keeping up with it long after he didn't have to anymore. He studied the laws and verdicts in these books for cases he sometimes spent years on, cases of the clients he came to know as friends. The books remind me of stories he'd tell me from his life, stories from his work life, which was most of his life. These were his scrapbooks of memories. It's very much like my converted bedroom/closet, the one that holds the clothes and all the beautiful memories attached to them. Howard had his books. I have my closet.

I take one of the books from the shelf. I don't know why I'm doing it. Something in me is causing me to take it in my hands. The damn thing is so heavy; it must be five hundred pages. Did he really read all these books? I have never taken these books from the shelf. The only time I ever touch them is when I dust. I had movers pack them up at the old house, and the movers put them on the shelf here. Boy, they really jammed them in there.

As I continue to pull at one book, another comes out with it and starts to tip over the side of the shelf. I quickly try to grab it while holding the other law book in place, but it falls out of my hands and onto the ground.

I pick the book up off of the floor and take it in my arms. The leather smell from the cover is already making me feel better, more secure in some way, if that's possible. Why? I don't know.

I open up the book to the first page and run my fingers over the ones I've yet to look at. The pages feel lopsided, though; Howard must have written notes in here. So I turn to the middle of the book, and that's when I find them.

Jammed between pages I find papers and cards and notes, all

with my handwriting on them. As I sort through them I realize they're all from me.

To Howard on this special birthday.

Happy 10th Anniversary to My Darling Husband.

Happy 25th Anniversary. Seems like yesterday.

Dear Howard, You don't need my luck! I know you're going to win this case today. I have all the faith in you. Can't wait to celebrate!

And on and on. I grab another book and, sure enough, there are more cards from me. I take another book off the shelf, then another. There's a picture of us standing in front of the Eiffel Tower. I remember asking someone to take that picture. Here's another from Miami Beach, when we were young kids, just married. There are birthday cards, pictures, notes. I take down the rest of the books and leaf through them. I find so many cards and pictures and notes I wrote him through the years, I can hardly hold them all in my hand. He saved every one. But why? Why didn't he tell me? Why didn't he just let me know that he appreciated them?

And then I come to another book, where I find a bunch of canceled checks between the pages. There must be about a hundred of them in there. I pick one up and look at it. They're all made out to my mother, and they go month by month, years' worth, and I know exactly what they are.

Howard gave my mother a check for two hundred dollars every month from the day we were married until she died some twenty-five years later. I forgot about that. Believe me, two hundred dollars was a lot of money in those early years. I know he upped it with inflation, but I had nothing to do with it by then,

and I'm not going to look now. The check went out from his office. When Howard gave my mother that first check, he told her
that it wasn't to be spent on groceries or paying bills. It was for
her to enjoy her life. My mother was able to have an apartment
in Boca Raton, Florida, and play bridge to her heart's content.
The one thing I was never really sure of was if my mother actually said to Howard that he needed to give her the money, as
kind of a dowry, or if he did it by himself. I never asked. A wife
just didn't ask those questions then. Still, handing me that first
check to give her and then knowing she got checks every month
after that—God, I loved him for that.

And suddenly I remember a conversation Howard and I had
a few years back, something I totally forgot.

A few years ago, just before Howard died, in fact, he and I
were sitting in our backyard, out on the veranda. Howard was
reading the paper and I was looking at a magazine. It was so
peaceful out there. I'd had gorgeous cushions made for the deck
chairs, a butterscotch crème color, and Howard and I loved to sit
out there in the summertime. Howard said he always regretted
that we never had a pool, but since I never got my hair wet, I
couldn't have cared less. I remember I looked up for a second and
saw that my hydrangeas were in full bloom, their fabulous pinks
and purples lining the backyard. I could hear the birds singing in
that big maple tree on the far side of the lawn. Howard and I had
just come back from a week in Cabo San Lucas so we were both
relaxed.

"Howard?" I asked him. "Remember how you used to give
my mother that two hundred dollars a month?"

"Yep," he said, turning the page of his newspaper.

"Did my mother make you do that?"

"No," he said matter-of-factly. "She let me marry you. I thought she should be paid in return."

He didn't look up from his paper the whole time. He had no idea that what he was saying meant so much to me. I started to sniffle a little bit.

"What?" he asked. He still didn't look up from his paper.

I wrapped my cashmere shawl around myself and took a deep breath. "Thank you," I said and smiled, looking at him.

He looked up at me for a second. Then he patted my leg.

I close the book I'm holding and put it back on the shelf—those checks are still none of my business. Then I put the cards and photos back in each book and place them all back in the bookcase, carefully, one by one. Maybe I'll look at them again from time to time.

I sit back down on the couch and smile. Of course Howard hid all of these things from me—he was always unable to show his love like that. That's not every man from our generation. Sol, Frida's husband, wasn't like that. You could always see that he and Frida were a team. Men of Lucy's generation, like Zachary, they show their emotions. Their fathers must have taught them something they wanted from their fathers, that kind of comfort. Most men of my generation, though, acted like Howard. They treated us like second-class citizens, but now that I think of it, maybe my mother was right all those years ago when she said, "He works hard and he provides for you."

But the cheating? The cheating.

Maybe if I had really pressed we would have finally hashed out everything. He would have apologized, and I would have accepted his apology. I can't think about it anymore, though. It's too late. I'll never know. And then I realize: I can't carry this bitterness for someone who can't fight back. There's just no point. I can't think of what could have happened because the truth is this: nothing would have happened. We would never have talked it out. That's the downside of the generation we came from, and nothing can change it. Today, people get divorced over it, and then their life together is over. I kept my mouth shut. I'm not saying it was right, but that was what we did. We lived our life together and it wasn't perfect, but what is? Would Lucy's generation have handled it correctly? What *is* correct? We live, we learn, we move on. There's only one thing I can do now. I can stop this thinking and wondering. The only thing I can do now is forgive and look at the positive side of our life together.

And then I walk over to my Paris mirror as I did so many times that day. It is me. Staring back from the mirror is the face I've grown accustomed to looking at all these years. I take my hands and smooth the rippling skin on my neck. I slide my fingers along the lines of my crow's feet, my smile lines. I know I'll never get to the point in my life where I'll enjoy seeing this weathered face. The one thing I can take solace in, however, is that the way my face looks now is proof that I have indeed lived a long and worthy life. It is a face full of years of smiles, tears, and grief, but above all, joy.

It is time to move on.

I walk over to the phone and dial Lucy's number.

"Hi, it's me. I'm still pissed off at you, but I'll get over it. Listen, what's Zachary's number?"

zachary

Why I'm meeting him, I have no idea. Why I'm brushing my hair and putting on makeup, and why on God's green earth I've changed my clothes three times, I don't know. What's he going to do? Is he going to realize the woman he fell for that night was actually me?

I knew that Zachary would be up when I called him last night. I just knew he'd have that same sadness in his voice that I did when he picked up the phone. Even the ring on his phone made me feel closer to him as I listened to it repeat two, three times.

"Yeah?" he answered in a groggy voice. I knew he wasn't sleeping.

I hesitated for a moment when I heard his voice. I didn't want to hang up, though. I just liked hearing the sound of his voice.

"Hello?" he asked again.

"Zachary?" I asked, clearing my throat.

"Yes?" he asked in his normal tone.

"It's Mrs. Jerome, Ellie's grandmother."

"Oh, hi," he said with a question in his voice. Who could

blame the poor boy? "Hello, Mrs. Jerome, how are you?" he said with a melancholy undertone.

"I've been under the weather the last few days, but from what Lucy tells me, you have been, too. Am I right?"

He took a deep breath and gave an audible sigh. "Mrs. Jerome, I just don't understand it, and Lucy won't give me any clues. I'm sorry you had to call me so late. I don't know what Lucy has told you. I just want to know what happened with your other granddaughter."

I could hear the pain in his voice. It was just like mine—Lucy was right on that front. Unlike me, however, he had someone who could help him through it. He just needed some grandmotherly advice.

"Zachary, are you free tomorrow, possibly for breakfast?"

He paused again, then said, "Yeah, yes, I'm free."

"Fine. There's a little café just on the other side of Rittenhouse Square from where I live. Are you familiar with that café?"

"Sure, I go there a lot."

"Fine. I'll see you there at eight. Is that all right?"

"Eight is fine. Thanks for seeing me."

"It's the least I can do for you. I'm sorry if this has added any grief to your life."

"Thank you, Mrs. Jerome, I appreciate it."

"Please, call me Ellie."

So now I've been up since six. Actually, I didn't sleep much last night; every hour I just kept looking at the clock. Truthfully, I think my sleeplessness could be blamed more on all the sleep

I've gotten in the past week than on feeling nervous about seeing Zachary again.

When I awoke this morning I took Zachary's clothing, the sweatpants and the shirt and the sneakers that I'd thrown in the back of my closet, and washed everything (except the sneakers). I folded it all up and put it in a bag to take with me. I didn't want to take the clothes. What I really wanted to do was keep them here with me. But in the end, I felt it was better that I give them back.

I decide to wear a pair of beige slacks this morning, and a lilac silk top. I put on my favorite earrings, a pair of diamond studs Howard gave to me years ago. As I take a look at myself in my Paris mirror before I leave, I think I look well put together. At five minutes to eight, I am on my way.

Zachary is already seated with a cup of coffee when I arrive. He looks as terrible as I've felt. God knows the last time this poor boy shaved. Or bathed.

He stands up the second he sees me. Always the gentleman, even in the state he's in. He is dressed in a T-shirt and track pants, much like the ones I carry in the bag I have to give him.

"Hi, Mrs. Jerome, good to see you. Thank you for meeting me."

I look into his blue eyes and see nothing of the feelings he showed when he looked at me the last time I saw him. I can only steal glances at those blue eyes. *Blue Eyes*, I want to call him. I know, though, that I never can again.

"Zachary, I'm glad you agreed to meet me this morning," I say, sitting across from him. "First, I wanted to give you back the things my granddaughter borrowed from you. She asked that I give them back."

"Oh, well, thanks," he says unhappily as he takes the bag.

"I know you might not understand this now, but maybe someday you will. My granddaughter, Ellie, I know she had a wonderful time being with you. She told me herself."

"She did?" He perks up slightly.

"She did. It was very difficult to do what she did, to leave you in the middle of the night like that."

"I just couldn't understand it." He slumps in his chair. "I know everything was sudden. I know from your point of view, you're wondering how two people only knowing each other for a day could feel so strongly about each other." He pauses. "But I did."

I stop him. "You don't have to explain it to me. I know exactly what you're talking about. The two of you had a profound connection. It has nothing to do with how long you knew each other."

"I thought you might think it was childish to feel that way."

"Naivete is one thing. Knowing what's right is completely different," I tell him.

"So then what happened?" he asks, grasping for words. "Why did she leave like that?"

I have gone over the answer to this question a million times through the night. In the end, the answer is simple: "Zachary, in Ellie's case . . . Ellie had responsibilities. She thought she could run away from them. We all think we can, don't we? In the end, she just couldn't. She knew she had to learn to accept them."

"I don't understand. Did she have a family?"

"Yes." I exhale. "She has a family."

"And Howard?" he asks.

"She loves Howard very much. Whether she could admit

it or not, she loves Howard, and will always love Howard. But what she really needed was just one day off from life to think about everything. So she came here to Philadelphia, she enlisted Lucy as her accomplice, and she set out to live one day in her life free of responsibility. It was supposed to be a fun day, doing things she hadn't done in a long time. All of it was supposed to have nothing to do with real life. Instead, something happened. She met you."

"Is that what she told you?" he asks.

"She didn't have to tell me anything."

"So then why did she leave?" he asks again.

"She wasn't going to. She was all set to do just that, change her life and start all over again. The problem is—and, thankfully, you don't have to know this yet—but . . . sometimes you can't change what's already set in stone. She had her doubts, but the truth is, Howard is her one and only. Her family is what matters to her most, and Howard is the one she built it with. Taking that one day off from life, that's what made her realize it. You have to know, though, for as much as she needed to leave, she also wanted to stay. Sometimes you have no choice in life but to stay where you are and work it out."

"You know, I did have the feeling she was still with Howard." He nods.

"Oh, she is," I reiterate. "For better or worse, she'll always be with Howard." And then I say something that even makes me stop for a second: "Howard is her soul mate." And as the words come out of my mouth, I know they are the truth.

My question has been answered. Who is my soul mate? For better or for worse, it will always be Howard Jerome.

"Actually, I knew it because of something she said to me."

"And what was that?" I ask, wondering what it was I could have said.

"She told me she had regrets about her life."

My hand starts to shake so I put it under the table, hoping he won't notice.

"And I told her," he continues, "that she's young, she's got a lot of years to make up for something she might have regretted."

It is the third time in a week I've heard this said to me. And for the first time, I really heard it. For the first time in a week, I smile.

"Thank you for giving Ellie such a gift," I tell him.

"What do you mean?" he asks with a perplexed look on his face.

"Zachary, I want you to hear me when I say this, and I don't want you to ever forget it."

"Okay."

I take a deep breath. "The night she spent with you is something she will never forget. You gave her a second chance at her life. I know that it's something she will always take with her," I tell him, tears in my eyes. "Sure, she's with Howard, but you will always be in her heart."

"Well, I appreciate that," he tells me, tears coming to his eyes as well.

I go into my bag and pull out the travel-size package of tissues I always carry around. I hand him one and then use one myself.

"Thank you." He sighs as he wipes his eyes.

"No, thank *you*," I tell him.

"For what?"

"For Ellie's night."

"You're welcome," he says softly.

We sit for a moment dabbing our eyes. I know that what I have said has helped him. I know now that everything will be all right.

"So?" I say, dabbing my eyes one last time and exhaling deeply. "You think they've got pancakes here? I'm suddenly very hungry."

"You know, I don't think they do, but that sounds good to me. I haven't eaten a lot in the last few days, and I'm suddenly hungry, too. I know a place that makes great pancakes a couple blocks from here, if you've got the time," he says.

"As it happens, I do have the time." I smile. "Does the place you're thinking of happen to have an outdoor café? It's such a beautiful day to sit out in the sun. It would do you good to get some sun. You look like you've been cramped up in your apartment for days."

"Actually, I have. That's a good idea," he says, getting up from his chair and helping me up from mine.

"You know, Mrs. Jerome . . . Ellie," he says as he places his elbow out for me to take hold. "Thank you for your wisdom. I really needed it."

I lock my arm in his as we begin to leave.

"Zachary," I say, looking at this young man. "When you get to be my age, that's the best compliment a person could receive."

"Mrs. Jerome, you're also a very cool lady."

"Lucy says that, too," I say emphatically, beaming.

"By the way, there's something I've been meaning to mention," he says, holding the door for me.

"What's that?"

"How weird is it that you and your granddaughter have the same name and you both fell in love with guys named Howard?"

"I know," I say, adding, "crazy coincidence, isn't it?"

seventy-six

I'm seventy-six today.

And that's fine with me.

I didn't do much in terms of my birthday today. I had other things to do.

Tonight was the engagement party, and it was more than my pleasure to throw it. As usual, The Prime Rib did a fabulous job. The coffee was just right, and the crab cakes were sublime. My salmon was cooked to perfection. Barbara ate every last bit of her steak.

Frida didn't want much in the way of a grand party, but I begged to differ. How many times do you get to throw your best girlfriend an engagement party?

Well, I got to do it twice. The first time with Sol, all those years ago, and the second time tonight, for Frida and Hershel.

"Mom, make sure The Prime Rib has enough candles," Barbara called me this morning to tell me. "Frida wants the whole thing by candlelight, and you know your friends will complain they can't see their food."

"Barbara," I told her, "I've got the situation under control."

Some things never change, do they?

Or do they?

"That's all I wanted to remind you," she said. "It's going to be a gorgeous night," she added.

I honestly didn't think anyone would even remember my birthday. Lucy has Frida coming in for so many fittings for her wedding dress I don't know how she doesn't get lost in remembering what gets taken in here and what gets let out there. I work in Lucy's office a few days a week, helping her with buyer's meetings. When Frida came in the other day I told her to stop losing so much weight, but she says she can't help it now, with all the exercise she and Hershel do. Believe me, you don't want to know what kind of exercise they're doing. She's like a schoolgirl, though, when she gives me the dirty details, so I listen to what she wants to tell me. Trust me, it will be good when Hershel finally makes an honest woman out of her.

"Ellie," she said to me one day, "I want you to find happiness with as nice a man as I have."

Don't think I won't. There's even someone I've had my eye on. I see him in the park when I'm sitting out in the sun. Don't worry, he's my age. I actually knew his wife, Leona Price. Such a shame she died—Alzheimer's. I would hear from my girlfriends about the way he took care of her until she passed on. I used to see the two of them at cocktail parties and other events through the years. He always seemed like a very nice man, and when he approached me in the park that first day I was more than happy to talk to him. Who knows? Maybe I'll ask him to be my date for the wedding.

I have to say that I loved how all of us looked tonight. We

all wore outfits from Lucy's summer collections. You know, she now also does a line for the over-fifty set. If you had told me one year ago that my Lucy would have two successful clothing lines . . . Well, I would have believed you. And best of all, she gets 75 percent of everything the stores sell!

Did I mention the name of Lucy's other line?

Ellie. Just, simply, *Ellie.*

I'm so proud of Lucy. She never fails to make my heart sing.

Every now and then Lucy and I will be sitting in my apartment, eating our secret meal—though these days we're off the cookie-dough ice cream and on to rocky road—and one of us will bring up something from that fateful day. It always ends with one of us regretting not buying the one thing I wanted.

We never got the underwear.

So what happened to Zachary? He went on, like I said he would. He's dating a very nice girl now, and I'm proud to say that I'm the one who set them up. She's Elaine Shipley's granddaughter. I happened to run into Elaine at the pedicurist one day and she was mentioning how good-natured and attractive her granddaughter Claire was, but all these men seemed to just take advantage. I hadn't seen a picture of Claire; I didn't need to. I just saw in Elaine's eyes what I had in my eyes for Lucy. A lot of younger folks think their grandparents just hear that two people are single so we set them up. Hey, kids, the joke's on you. We've got more wisdom than that.

The other week I had Lucy and Johnny and Zachary and Claire over for dinner—I like to give them all a home-cooked meal sometimes. Zachary walked over to the piano, where he saw the picture of Lucy and Ellie Michele. There was a lot of talking going on around the table. Johnny and Claire were in a heated discussion over something; I don't know, I wasn't really listening. My attention had turned to Zachary as he took the picture in his hand and looked at it for a moment. It was just few moments that he had that picture in his hand. He gave a little smile, and then he put it back and looked at the other pictures.

I know he still thinks of her. I think of her, too.

Sometimes he'll ask me, "By the way, how is Ellie doing?"

"She's very happy," I tell him.

You know, life is funny.

The truth is this: in my life, I did the best I could. Are there regrets? Sure, there're always regrets, but there're a lot of truly wonderful things that outweigh the regrets.

Those are the things I like to think about now.

If you don't believe me, look back to when you first met me. Look at all the things I regretted not doing. If you look back at that one day I got to have, you'll see what I did. I did everything I always wanted to do.

I made a difference in Lucy's work.

I got to experience Lucy's world.

I got to learn new things, to see the world in a way I hadn't seen it in a very long time.

I got to remember what it's like to feel physically beautiful again.

I got to fall in love one more time, and experience the bliss and heartbreak that come with it.

And if there's anything I learned from that day it's that I can still do all of those things, even at seventy-six.

Am I still jealous of Lucy?

In some ways I'll always be a little envious, but only because of the era in which Lucy gets to experience her age. That's the one thing I'll never be able to experience, no matter what age my body looks. My mind is a product of my generation. In my entire day of being twenty-nine, that's the one thing that never changed. My body was twenty-nine, but other than that, I was still the same person. Lucy's mind belongs to her generation. That will never change. So really, if I think about it, I'm not jealous. I'm just a proud grandmother.

But through it all, I still had one question in my mind, something I needed to find out. And I did.

I loved Howard Jerome.

I loved him with all my heart.

It's a nice thing to finally be able to say this without a doubt in the world.

No marriage is perfect, just like no vacation is perfect. Sometimes it rains, sometimes your hotel room faces the parking lot. When you look back on it, though, when you really start to think about it, those are the things that don't amount to much in the big picture.

So tonight, after the dinner, and after the speeches, Frida and Lucy and Barbara suddenly appeared with a cake for me. It was such a nice surprise, and so unexpected. The cake was from The Swiss Pastry Shop, of course. This time, though, there was only one candle on the cake, which was provided by the restaurant. It wasn't that Barbara didn't want to get seventy-six candles. She did, she actually bought them and intended to put all seventy-six on my cake. There was just so much going on what with the engagement party and getting herself and Larry dressed and out of the house that she simply forgot the candles and left them at home. All of my girlfriends and I had a big laugh about it as we welcomed Barbara to the menopause club.

"I'd let you know where the meetings take place," I joked as we all broke into hysterics, "but I can't remember where they are."

"I hope they're in the freezer section at Whole Foods!" Barbara joked back as she fanned away yet another hot flash.

As they placed the cake in front of me and everyone sang "Happy Birthday," I closed my eyes.

"Make a wish!" Frida called out.

"NO!" Lucy shouted. No one understood why, of course, except the two of us. I glanced at her and gave her a sign that she shouldn't worry. As if a wish on a candle could turn a person's life back forty-six years.

And as I closed my eyes again, I wished. I wished that the rest of my days will be lived in serenity. I wished the same for those I love.

And that is exactly what I wish for you.

My dear. May you have everything you want in your life. If you should get it all, however, and you still don't like the outcome, don't take it as failure. Take it as something to learn from and move on. Believe me, no matter how old you may be, whether you're twenty-nine or seventy-six, no matter how many years you've got left, trust someone who had to learn it the hard way: you've still got time to change.

And that, my friend, is my lesson for today.

acknowledgments

First and foremost, I want to thank the amazing seventy-something women I interviewed for this book. Your generosity, honesty, and frankness were more than I could ever have asked for. I hope I've done you proud in creating a character that captures the best of who you are.

To Trish Todd, whose spot-on edits made me see the light. Thank you so much for all you've done, and to everyone at Touchstone/Fireside for all your hard work, for which I am forever grateful. I also want to send my heartfelt thanks to Trish Grader, for bringing me into the fold.

An eternal thank-you to Brian DeFiore, who through the years has gone beyond just being my agent to become my shrink, a shoulder to lean on, chief movie critic, and all-around partner in crime. And thanks of course to Kate Garrick, Melissa Moy, and Adam Schear, who are always so kind and never seem exasperated with all my queries.

To one of my closest friends and my lawyer, Eric Brooks, for threatening to beat up the other kids if they tried to steal my lunch money. Metaphorically, of course.

To my Hollywood agent, Brian Lipson, whom I enjoy chitchatting with more than many of my girlfriends. And when it comes to business, you do your job so fabulously well.

As always, I bear a debt of gratitude to Susan Swimmer, Lesley Jane Seymour, Erin Moore, and Allison Dickens. Without you, oh, heavens, I don't know where I'd be.

I send lots of love to the Berg-Goldsteins, who from the start have treated me like one of their own, and only cringed slightly when I reminded you I might one day be your matriarch.

To my big brothers, David and Michael, and my sister-in-law, Samantha, because when I'm seventy-five, you'll still be referring to me as "Baby Deans." To my cousin Michele, who, like me, knows the importance of taking a day. And to my niece Noa, because I am already so proud of who you are.

And finally and most especially to my father, Barry Halpern, and my husband, Jonathan Goldstein, who share the most valuable trait of all. As long as I live, I will never know two men with more love in their hearts for the women in their lives.

29

Haunted by the death of her husband and the unresolved problems of their marriage, Ellie Jerome makes a wish on her seventy-fifth birthday to be twenty-nine again, just for one day. When she wakes up the next morning and finds that her wish has come true, it turns her whole world upside down. She sets out to have a day without responsibilities or worries in the company of her twenty-five-year-old granddaughter Lucy, never imagining the consequences of her wish.

When Ellie's daughter, Barbara, and best friend, Frida, find that she has disappeared without explanation, they form an unlikely team determined to find out what is going on. Over the course of one unusual day, the women each come to terms with what it means to be family, and discover that it is never too late to start your life over.

QUESTIONS & TOPICS FOR DISCUSSION

1. Inspired by the number of candles on her birthday cake, Ellie wishes to be twenty-nine again for a day. What age would you choose to return to and why?

2. Ellie believes that if she can have just one day of her youth back, she can erase her regrets. Do you think it's possible to make up for such regrets in a day? Do you think Ellie really believes this?

3. Barbara and Frida spend a disastrous day wandering around Philadelphia, trying to find the missing Ellie. When they are reunited with Ellie and Lucy, Lucy tells them that they need to get their own lives. Is it as simple as that? In what ways has Ellie encouraged their dependency on her?

4. Which of the three women do you believe has the biggest changes to make: Barbara, giving up her quest for Ellie's approval; Ellie, learning to treat Barbara like an adult and not a child; or Frida, learning to assert herself?

5. Lucy is thrilled at the chance to spend a day with her newly young grandmother. Think about your own grandmother—can you imagine doing the same with her? What do you think she would have on her "to do" list?

6. Ellie writes off many of her regrets by saying that was just what you did in her day. Is this an accurate portrayal of her generation, or is she dodging responsibility for her actions?

7. Frida and Ellie have very different outlooks on life and aging. Ellie wants to go back and redo her youth, while Frida believes that "what's done is done" (p. 186). Have their different marriages influenced their outlooks, or is it a difference in personality? Which do you agree with?

8. Thinking about her marriage to Howard, Ellie ponders which is better: to marry for love or to marry for security. Is this question a product of her upbringing in the 1950s, or is it still relevant for women today?

9. Ellie cares greatly about presentation and image, and has had some cosmetic surgery done. What are your feelings on plastic/cosmetic surgery? Do you plan to take advantage of such procedures as you age?

10. As Ellie's day comes to a close, she fantasizes about staying young and running away with Zachary, but in the end she chooses her old life.

Did she make the right decision? What would you have done in her place?

11. After finding the cards and notes that Howard saved over the years, Ellie comes to the conclusion that he was her soulmate, despite all his flaws. Is she just resigning herself to the reality of the past, or is the proof of his love for her really enough to make up for his affairs?

12. Ellie notes that being seventy-five gets her special treatment, and that this makes her feel old. Is this truly a bad thing? How does our society treat the elderly, and what needs to change?

A Conversation with Adena Halpern

What inspired you to write 29?

I am fascinated by Ellie's generation of women. They are the women of my mother's generation who came of age in the 1950s. If they weren't married by 22, they were considered old maids and they had three choices for an occupation: teacher, nurse, or secretary. As they tell me, "We listened to our mothers and we respected their choices for us." To me, these women led such glamorous lives. Most of them (those who I knew) didn't work, they drove fancy cars, and they got their hair done—a lot. This was who I wanted to be when I grew up. It took growing up, however, to realize that what seemed so idyllic on the outside was not always so rosy. Sure, some of them enjoyed their lives, but as I found out, many of them have unfulfilled dreams that leave them with regrets. These are the women who missed out by one generation on all the fruits of the women's lib movement. It was their story I wanted to tell. What would you do if you could live for one day and were able to live those dreams? Would you do it?

The idea of going back (or forward) in our lives is a popular Hollywood theme (*Big*, *13 Going on 30*, *Freaky Friday*, and *Vice Versa*, for example). Did any of these films influence the development of the novel?

Funny enough, no. *Roman Holiday* was the movie that influenced me most. Much like Audrey Hepburn's character, Ellie gets this chance to take a day out of life that's unlike any other. She falls in love. She does things she could never do in her situation, but in the end she knows that she must go back to her life. Like Hepburn's character, Ellie needs that day to realize it. Using the ability to be young for one day was the best device I could think of for Ellie to truly be able to have a day that would be unlike any other.

One more movie that influenced me was Neil Simon's *The Out-of-Towners*. Barbara and Frida are like Jack Lemmon and Sandy Dennis in that movie. They can't catch a break. They can't get anything to eat. Everything that could go wrong for them goes wrong. You feel as exhausted and relieved as they look at the end of the movie when Lemmon and Dennis finally get into their hotel room. That's what I wanted it to feel like when Barbara and Frida finally got into Ellie's apartment.

How long did 29 take to write? Do you schedule time for writing, or work when inspiration strikes? Tell us a little bit about your writing process.

Counting the time it took to interview various women and get the story straight, the book took me about a year to write. Before I start writing a book there are two things I always do. First, I write the first 50–75 pages. That's how I develop the voice of the character. Within these 50–75 pages, I might include characters or lines or themes that I didn't think of when I conceived of the idea. This leads me to the next step: writing the outline. I hate writing outlines, but they really are the most important step in writing a book. The outline is my blueprint. I look at it constantly to see where I am in the overall story. The thing I love most about writing a book, as compared with, say, writing a screenplay, is that screenplays are very structured. Books are structured of course, but to a point. You're able to go off the beaten track and expand on an idea. This can take days and then you forget what happens next in the story. That's why you really need the outline to see where you're going.

As for the actual writing of the book, that's the best part. When I'm writing a book, that's pretty much all I think about. I work five days a week as with a normal job, but I also work when the inspiration strikes. When this happens, I'll jot little notes, a line, or sometimes a paragraph on scrap paper when inspiration hits. Funny story: I was at the market and I was thinking about the chapter "I Don't Kiss and Tell." I wrote the sentence where Ellie says to Zachary, "I regret my life," on the top of the shopping list so I would remember it. Later that day, my husband came to me looking concerned. He said to me, "Is everything okay?" "Why?" I asked. He pulled out the shopping list and pointed to that sentence I had written and said, "Because I found *this* in the kitchen." We had a laugh about it. Also, I came up with the last paragraph of *29* while I was at the gas station filling up my tank. I wrote the whole thing on the back of a bunch of old receipts. It was kind of hard to decipher what I wrote once I got home, but I got the gist of it.

In the acknowledgments, you thank all the women you interviewed. What was the most surprising thing you learned from them?

The most surprising thing I learned about the women I interviewed was just how honest they were. All I did was ask them this one question, "What would you do if you could be 29 for a day?" These women answered me so truthfully that it was almost uncomfortable. They got this look in their eyes when I asked them this question, like somehow I could grant them this wish. I thought I'd get jokey answers. I thought I'd really have to pry and sometimes I did, but for the most part, they just told me what they would have done.

29 hinges on Ellie's regrets about the way she lived her life. Have regrets been a force in your own life?

I regret 90 percent of anything I say in a given day. I regret that I just admitted that. I know it's the main reason I'm a writer. It's why I love what I do for a living. If I could type out everything I ever said, I'd never stop pressing the delete button. This is the neurotic in me speaking of course. The other part of me knows that I should only regret maybe 20 percent of what I say on a given day. Who cares what people think? I'm like Barbara in that way. I'll wake up in the middle of the night regretting something I've said. A part of me knows that the person probably wasn't offended by it, but still. The late actress Kitty Carlisle used to look at herself in the mirror each morning and say, "I forgive you for whatever you did yesterday." I do this a lot. It always seems to make me feel a little better.

Another thing I regret, or wonder about, is if I'm having enough fun in my life. Have I experienced everything I wanted to experience at my age? Have I seen everything I should have seen? You know that question, "If heaven exists, what would you like to hear God say to you when you arrive at the pearly gates?" I want him to say, "*Now, that was living!*" I don't think he'll say that though. I think he'll say, "*You didn't go out enough.*" I don't attend enough parties. I often wish I were a Washington socialite. They seem to go to a lot of balls. I'm never in a situation where I'm required to wear a ball gown. This is a huge regret in my life.

Throughout the book, you alternate viewpoints between Ellie, Barbara, and Frida. Which of these women was the most difficult to write? Which was the most fun? Who are you most like?

Ellie, Barbara, and Frida were a total blast to write, but I would have to say that Ellie was the most fun and the most difficult. Ellie is every one of my mother's friends' voices. I know that voice very, very well. I've been hearing it my entire life. That voice is very direct. When they tell a story, it always goes off the beaten track. There's always some advice for you in the end.

The part that was difficult was making sure that Ellie was the seventy-five-year-old woman of today. People still think of a seventy-five-year-old woman as someone sitting in a rocking chair on the front porch. I'm sure that person still exists; it's just not any seventy-five-year-old woman that I know. Sophia Loren is seventy-five. Julie Andrews is seventy-four. Carol Burnett is seventy-six. You wouldn't find any of these women wearing galoshes and granny glasses, would you? It was very important to me that I got this right and it was difficult not to stereotype that seventy-five-year-old "granny." I wanted to create a character who seventy-five-year-old women, or their daughters and granddaughters could look at and say, "*She's just like my* (fill in the blank)."

That's where Frida came in. Frida is that stereotypical seventy-five-year-old woman. She couldn't stay that way though and I had to figure out why she was that way. I realized it was because she thought that was the only way a woman of her age could live. It took that day for her to realize that wasn't the case.

29 is narrated mostly by Ellie, but also offers Barbara and Frida's point of view. The only character whose perspective isn't shown is granddaughter Lucy. What made you decide to structure the novel this way?

This is Ellie's story. Ellie needed to figure out her problems in her own voice. To hear Ellie speak to the reader from the heart is to know exactly who this woman is. Also, it was Ellie's day and I wanted to experience that day through Ellie's voice.

Barbara and Frida are secondary. To let them speak in their own voices would have made it their stories too. I didn't want to do that. I wanted this book to be about a woman who has spent her life wondering what could have been. When Ellie finds her answer, it directly addresses the problems Barbara and Frida have in their own lives.

The city of Philadelphia becomes a character in its own right. What about Philly drew you to choose it as the setting?

I've lived in Los Angeles for the past eighteen years, but Philadelphia is my home. (I sound like an advertisement.) Sometimes it's easier to stand back (like 3,000 miles away) to see where you really came from. It took moving away all those years ago to be able to see how beautiful my city really is, both for its physical attributes and its people. Even though Philadelphia is a large city, it still feels like a small town. I could come back to Philly and run into an old friend walking down the street and the conversation could pick up where we left off years before. Philadelphia is like the bar in *Cheers*. Everyone knows your name or your brother's name or your cousin. That's a club I'm proud to be a part of. Ellie is a part of that environment. Ellie's roots are there. Like me, the generations of Ellie's family are what make Philadelphia the city that it is. To me, that's its history. I couldn't place her anywhere else because Ellie was exactly the type of woman I knew and admired when I was growing up.

The difficult dynamics of Ellie's family life are key to the development of the novel, and are arguably universal issues for women—the mother-daughter relationship is notoriously difficult. Are the characters informed by your own personal experiences, or are they inspired by a more general view of this dynamic in our society?

As a daughter, when you're writing about a mother/daughter relationship, I think it's next to impossible not to bring some of your own baggage into it. I really tried not to. Honestly, this is the first book I've written where you couldn't pick a character and say it was me or someone in my family. You would never look at me and say that I was the model for Barbara. I'm not fifty-five, I'm not overweight, I live 3,000 miles away from my mom and I didn't marry Larry the dentist. Ellie is definitely not my mother. She has never relied on my father like Ellie did with Howard. My mother has always been much more independent than that. In terms of our relationship, my mother and I don't bicker like Ellie and Barbara.

Having said that, like Barbara, there's a part of me that always wants to make my mother proud. I want to win the award for best daughter in the world. This is not something that takes over my life the way that it does for Barbara. It's just an itch that's always in the back of my head.

So when I was writing the passage where I describe why Barbara is the way she is and that need she has to make her mother proud, I didn't set out to bring this aspect of my personality into it. It was only when I read it over that I realized, oh crap, that's me.

I think that feeling is pretty much universal though. I can't imagine I'm the only daughter who wants to make her mother proud. Therefore, I'm going to chalk that up to a universal theme . . . and maybe ask some girlfriends of mine if they have that same issue.

Who are your influences as a writer?

I'm a voracious reader, but truthfully, I'm influenced more by movies than I am by books. My style of writing is less descriptive and more expressive. I'm not one to go on about what a room looks like. I find that boring. I like to hear what the character says, their tone, their voice, and I like to see what's going on in their head, what's behind their words.

I got my bachelor's degree, as well as my master's degree, in screen-writing so a lot of what I write seems more cinematic. I get that a lot and I know it's because of my training. When I'm writing a book, for me, it's like watching a movie play out in my head. Writing a screen-play, however, and watching a movie are two very different things. Writing a screenplay has to be very structured. It has to have three acts on three particular page numbers. The major dramatic question of the movie has to carry you from scene to scene, even though it doesn't seem that way when you're watching it. That's why I prefer writing books to movies. I hear the conversations between the characters and I write them down. I don't have to worry specifically about what page I'm on. That is so freeing, especially when you've been trained to write screenplays. The best thing I ever did was learn how to write screen-plays so I could write books. Don't get me wrong; writing a book is really, really hard. I like the way the comic Lewis Black once put it: "Writing a book is like having homework that never stops." Once I was able to free myself from the structure of the screenplay, I felt like a chef who had learned how to make a soufflé with one arm tied behind his back. It's not any better, but it can definitely feel more liberating.

Woody Allen, Billy Wilder, Neil Simon, Larry Gelbart, and Carrie Fisher have all influenced my work in one way or another. The film *It's a Wonderful Life* influenced my previous book, *The Ten Best Days of My Life*. Preston Sturges, however, is probably the biggest influence on my work. Consider movies like *Miracle at Morgan's Creek* or *Christmas in July*. Those movies are more than fifty years old, but they still stand up. The movies flow so easily because the dialogue is quick and precise. You really listen to the dialogue for fear you might miss something. Actually, I just remembered this. Barbara's last name, Sustamorn, was influenced by the names of Sturges's characters. His characters have such amazing names, like Trudy Kockenlocker, for example. There are three characters in *Christmas in July* whose names are Tom, Dick and Harry. That's genius. Barbara and her husband, Larry, seem like such pathetic characters on the outside that I thought it would be great to make them even more pathetic by giving them a name that sounded like "such a moron."

What books were on your bedside table when you were writing?

I'm pretty sure I was reading Curtis Sittenfeld's book, *American Wife*, but I don't know that it influenced me when I was writing the book. It should have, because not only was I reading about a first lady, but the presidential election was going on. I don't think any of that shows up in 29 though. Does it? Let me know.

Are you working on any new projects that you can tell us about?

It's always tough to describe what I'm writing. The most difficult question anyone can ask me is, "What's your book about?" I always tend to give them a one sentence log line, but then I always end that sentence with, "but it's about more than that."

So what am I writing now?

The book I'm writing now is a love story . . . but it's about more than that.

Tips to Enhance Your Book Club

1. *29* is set in Philadelphia and features many of the city's major attractions, from cheesesteaks to the Liberty Bell. Ask one or two members of the group to do a little research and present what they find most interesting about Philadelphia to the rest of the group. Other members could bring in food, drinks, or snacks inspired by the city.

2. The photo of Lucy and Ellie at twenty-five and twenty-nine becomes very important to Ellie, once she returns to her seventy-five-year-old self. Have each member of the book club bring in a picture of themselves at their favorite age, and discuss what they liked best about that time in their lives.

3. Ellie is thrilled to be able to wear the dress that Lucy designed in her honor. Ask members to design/describe/find a picture of their own "perfect" dress!

4. Many movies have been made exploring the theme of going back (or forward) in age—*Big, 13 Going on 30, Freaky Friday, Vice Versa*, etc. Have a movie marathon of your favorites after discussing the book.